Outside the Shadows

David Costa

THE ENEMY HIDES IN PLAIN SIGHT. WHEN WE FIND THEM, WE KILL THEM

DEDICATION

To my wife Helena with love, for always being there.
To the Head and Neck Cancer team at the Royal Liverpool Clatterbridge Hospital who helped me get through a tough time in the middle.

Outside the Shadows

This edition published in 2023 by Wire Books.

Outside the Shadows

Chapter 1 1
Chapter 2 8
Chapter 3 10
Chapter 4 28
Chapter 5 36
Chapter 6 40
Chapter 7 51
Chapter 8 79
Chapter 9 86
Chapter 10 89
Chapter 11 92
Chapter 12 97
Chapter 13 104
Chapter 14 127
Chapter 15 134
Chapter 16 140
Chapter 17 147
Chapter 18 161
Chapter 19 166
Chapter 20 174
Chapter 21 177
Chapter 22 192
Chapter 23 197
Chapter 24 199
Chapter 25 208
Chapter 26 212
Chapter 27 218
Chapter 28 222
Chapter 29 228

Chapter 30 232
Chapter 31 242
Chapter 32 251
Chapter 33 258
Chapter 34 267
Chapter 35 271
Chapter 36 286
Chapter 37 290
Chapter 38 307
Chapter 39 321
Chapter 40 325
Chapter 41 333
Chapter 42 337
Chapter 43 342
Chapter 44 346
About the Author 348
Acknowledgements 350
Keep in Touch 351

DON'T ENVY EVIL PEOPLE OR DESIRE THEIR COMPANY

FOR THEIR HEARTS PLOT VIOLENCE, AND THEIR WORDS ALWAYS STIR UP TROUBLE

Proverbs: 24

CHAPTER 1

LONDON HOSPITAL

He felt the noise of the gun rather than heard it, feeling the recoil in his hands as he pulled the trigger twice in quick succession. Double tap, as he'd been taught. Twice in the torso to put the target down, then once in the head to make sure. He held the gun double handed to ensure steady-aimed accuracy. The man in front of him had been pulling a gun from his coat pocket. He wasn't sure if the look in the man's eyes was surprise, fear, or pain as the first two bullets hit home, exactly where he'd aimed. The man on the floor didn't move. His eyes were open, staring, not seeing anymore.

Taking aim once more he shot the staring man squarely between the eyes, the hole smashing through skin and bone. The exit hole left a halo spray of blood on the ground that surrounded the man's head. 'They're not dead until they're dead. They're not dead until they're dead.' The words of his instructors reverberated inside his head, breaking through the image of the man now changed to the face of a woman lying on the ground. Dead. Bleeding. Then Mary's voice came through the flashing images.

'Joseph. Wake up. Joseph, it's me, wake up.'

He opened his eyes. Mary McAuley was the only person who still used his code name that he'd left behind years before, when she'd stopped being his agent and became the woman he loved. David Reece looked into her brown eyes and her smiling face as she leant close and kissed him on the temple. He could smell her familiar perfume and felt her long, dark hair against his head. He looked around the room of the private hospital ward. His vision slowly cleared, and he could make out the outline of a man standing near the door. His eyes, still blurry, slowly cleared, and he could see it was his boss Jim Broad, Director of Operations at SG9, the Black Ops unit of MI6, the British Secret Service. If he hadn't felt Mary's kiss or smelt her perfume or felt the touch of her hair, he would have thought he was still dreaming, still in the nightmare.

Mary was wiping his forehead with a cool, damp cloth, her smile reassuring.

'What's happening?' asked Reece.

'You have been having bad dreams, my darling. We nearly had to hold you down in the bed as you were swinging your arms about,' said Mary.

'You had a fever, old boy. Mary's been here every step of the way, and I've popped in a few times. Do you remember much?' asked Broad.

Reece managed to push himself up on the pillows supporting his back.

'What happened? Everything's sketchy,' he said.

Mary stood up from the bed.

'You were doing OK. The wound in your leg is healing well. But, for the last three days you've had a fever. You were asleep most of the time and sweated quite a bit. You cried out and moved about in the bed a lot, but this morning the fever broke. The doctors said your temperature has come down, nearer normal. I think you're back with us, Joseph. I was afraid I was going to lose you.'

'You sound like a nurse. You're not going to lose me that easily. Thanks for being here, boss.' Reece smiled.

'No problem, David,' Broad replied. 'You're my best agent, and your health is a top priority for me.'

'To answer your question, no, I don't remember much, just some of the usual dreams, the not so good ones.'

Mary poured Reece a glass of water and, holding the cup to his lips, helped him swallow a few sips.

Reece could still feel the dampness in the hospital gown he was wearing, which made the material uncomfortable against his skin.

'I'll need to get out of this,' he said, tugging at the collar of the gown.

Mary put her arms around his neck and untied the strings at the back.

'Yes, let's get that off you. I can get a fresh one from the nurse after you shower.'

Reece stopped her, pulling it all the way off. Stepping out of the bed slowly, he could feel that his legs were weak, but he could stand without help. The en suite shower room was only a few steps from the bed, and he found his strength was better than he thought.

'I think I'll be OK to shower on my own. Knock on the door when you have that fresh gown.'

'OK, but don't lock the door and shout if you need me. I'll give you ten minutes, then I'm coming in, ready or not.' Mary smiled.

'I'll wait, David, if you don't mind. I just need a quick chat on our own. If that's OK with you, Mary?' said Broad.

'I do mind. But if it means he'll get some peace, then you can have ten minutes, but no more,' she said firmly.

Twenty minutes later Reece was back in the bed, sitting up in a fresh gown, and Mary had left to get some coffee. Jim Broad pulled a visitor's chair close to the bed and in the secretive whispering style that he used when not in secure locations, he began bringing Reece up to date with what had happened while he'd been in hospital.

'You know we were lucky to stop that dirty bomb going off in Canary Wharf. Thanks to you and the team we were able to avoid a disaster. It's sad that we lost Anna, and the fact that you're here speaks about how close we came.'

'Tell me about it,' replied Reece, closing his eyes to help blot out the memory.

Broad continued. 'The prime minister would have liked to have come here himself to thank you, but as we don't exist, he felt the attention would bring too many questions. However, when you get out of here, he would like to see you at number ten.'

'No thanks. When I get out of here, I'm heading straight to the airport and a flight back home to my villa in Malta.'

Broad smiled. 'I totally understand, but I had to let you know, anyway. That brings me to the second point I want to bring up. David, you've been involved in two very dangerous operations in a short space of time. During those operations, you've killed three top terrorists. That's bound to have an impact on any man, especially as when you took them out it was up close and personal. I've spoken to the prime minister and Sir Ian, and we've decided you should take at least three months leave, to get yourself fully recovered from your wounds, both physical, and psychological. We even considered making available a Trauma Councillor if you think you need to speak to someone. Of course, such a person would have to be cleared at the highest level and there's not too many of those around.'

Reece lifted his hand to stop his boss. The fact that Broad was here and mentioning the top man, Sir Ian Fraser the Chief of MI6, the British Secret Intelligence Service and the boss of both Jim Broad and Reece. He understood the importance of what Broad was saying. You don't use Sir Ian's name unless you're trying to get your point across and Broad was letting Reece know he had the backing of C in everything he was saying.

'No head people. In my experience, they can make things worse, asking you to relive your experiences. No thanks.'

'Understood. As I said, the fact that you personally have put down three of the world's top bad guys, you know they'll be looking for you. So, for you, and Mary's sake, I want you to take those three months to recuperate. I promise we won't be in touch. We have enough people to get on with things, maybe not as good as you, but good enough for now.'

Reece raised himself up further on the bed.

'When I do leave here, it will be straight to the airport. As for coming back after three months, or anytime, I don't think so. There's only so much a man can do or take in this business, and I think this man has reached his limits. I thank you for your kindness to me and Mary, but I won't be coming back. So consider this my resignation as of now.'

Jim Broad was what people in the espionage business call 'old school'. He was thinking about the words he'd just heard. He also understood David Reece. He felt he had no other option than to agree.

'I hear you, David. I'll be sorry to lose you, but I totally understand. You have given more, much more, than any man should have to give. I'll always be here for you if you should need me. Mary is a wonderful girl. You should marry her and settle down to write your memoirs in the sun. But just remember you've signed three levels of the Official Secrets Act and you'll have to clear any book through the Whitehall D Notice Committee first. We don't want what's in your head out there.'

Reece laughed. 'Write a book? No, the only thing I'll be lifting is a large glass of Bushmills, then a good book to read by the sea. A fictional one that tells nice stories, not scary ones like the ones in real life.'

Mary came into the room carrying two takeaway mugs of coffee. Giving one to Reece, she turned to face Jim Broad.

'I'm sorry, Mister Broad, but as I thought you would be leaving, I only got the two.'

'That's fine, Mary. I need to be on my way.' Broad stepped forward to the bed and shook Reece's hand.

'Goodbye, David. Take care and remember what I said. I'm here if you ever need me. Same to you, Mary. Take care of this man. He's done more for this country than most people will ever know.' He kissed Mary on the cheek and left.

'What was all that about?' asked Mary.

'I resigned. I told him we'll be retiring to the sun and sea of Malta. What do you think? Are you up for that?'

She could feel the tears wet on her face. Setting down her coffee, she sat on the bed before putting her arms around his neck and kissing him.

'Up for it? Just watch me. I want to spend the rest of my life with you. Malta here we come.'

Reece was smiling. 'Yes, Mary, back to Malta, but via Israel first.'

CHAPTER 2

ISRAEL

FUNERAL ONE

There were two funerals that week. The first took place amid the olive trees and sunshine on a hillside above Jerusalem. Rachel Cohen, an agent of Mossad, the Israeli Secret Service, had died while on a mission in England. She was brought home to the land of her birth, to be buried among the other heroes of her country in the cemetery at Mount Herzl.

The cemetery, dedicated to the leaders and people who sacrificed their lives for the state of Israel, was located on the southern slope of the mountain.

The Star of David flag-draped coffin had been transported from England on a special El Al flight to Tel Aviv. Present at the graveside of Rachel Cohen was the prime minister of Israel who, like Rachel had served in the Kidon unit of Mossad many years before she was born. Others saying their goodbyes were senior members of the IDF, the Israel Defence Forces, Mossad, and Rachel's own family, and friends. Her mother, still sobbing at her daughter's loss, stood beside Kurt

Shimon, Rachel's boss. Her mother felt an immense sense of pride at seeing the dignitaries who were there with her today. Shimon, who had been in London with Rachel when she'd been killed, had accompanied her coffin on the flight back to her homeland, organising everything for the funeral through the government department that dealt with such matters. Rachel's father heard the Rabbi's voice but not the words. The thought of his daughter's smiling face, and the birds that were wheeling in the clear blue sky, distracted his gaze from her last resting place.

Kurt Shimon heard the Rabbi's words, the ones he'd heard at similar funerals in the past, *And the enemy shall know I am the Lord when I can lay down my vengeance on them.*

The Director of the Kidon Unit was distracted by his own thoughts, going back to the recent and last mission of the agent he knew by the code name 'Anna Stressor'. Working with MI6 and their Covert Black Ops team SG9, Anna had helped track down the Islamic Jihad terrorists intent on bombing the London financial district, using a plutonium based dirty bomb supplied by Iran. The SG9 team leader, David Reece, had worked alongside Anna from the streets of Malta to the streets of London, until they'd successfully removed the plutonium from the explosives that would have initiated the device, but not before a booby trap set off the explosives. Anna had been caught in the blast and killed instantly. Her final mission had been a success, and David Reece was also injured in the blast, but not before he'd shot and killed the terrorist leader known as 'the Arab'.

CHAPTER 3

CROSSMAGLEN, NORTHERN IRELAND

FUNERAL TWO

Later in the same day that Israel was burying one of its heroes, Irish Republicans were attending the funeral of a hero of their own. It was raining in the graveyard in Crossmaglen South Armagh, Northern Ireland. Not hard, but soft as the Irish called gentle rainfall. The graveyard was crowded. The coffin, draped in the green, white, and gold flag of the Irish Republic, contained the body of Sean Costello. Costello had been killed by a British Security agent on the streets of Manchester while attempting to assassinate the British prime minister.

The British had delayed returning his body by holding it until they'd finished all their investigations into the terrorist operation. For the mourners, the delay, taking many weeks, was not necessary, just one more reason to hate the Brits, not that any more reason was needed. The coffin had been brought from Dublin airport to the family home for an overnight stay. From there it was escorted to the graveyard by an eight-man guard of honour, dressed in black military style, wearing berets, and glasses to match, responding to commands in the Irish language. After a short service in the chapel, the coffin was carried by family and friends before being laid down on a stand beside the open grave. The local priest spoke more words of committal before a man stepped forward to deliver his words from a sheet of paper that he tried to control in his hand as it flapped in the wind and rain.

The speech was along the same lines that many there had heard before. The words describing the ongoing struggle against British occupation of the island of Ireland. The speaker repeated the famous words spoken by Patrick Pearse at the graveside of Jeremiah O'Donovan Rossa in August 1915, 'Ireland unfree shall never be at peace.'

Paul Costello, the brother of the deceased, smiled when he heard these words and thought, *nothing new there then.*

He knew the speaker well, and he knew his connections to his brother who was being laid to rest. Yet another martyr to an ancient cause. Brendan McDevitt, the Chief of Staff, and head of the Army Council of the Real IRA, the offshoot of the Provisional IRA, the organisation formed by republicans who did not accept the Good Friday Agreement, finished his speech.

'Sean Costello died at the hands of the British tyrant. He was a true son and soldier of Ireland. We will never forget him. We will make his killers pay. Our day will come.'

The mourners cheered as three men in full military camouflage clothing, wearing black balaclavas, stepped up beside the coffin and pointing automatic rifles towards the sky, fired off a volley of shots. Again, the crowd cheered as the men turned and were quickly swallowed up by the mourners. This was South Armagh, known during the war as Bandit Country because the security forces couldn't travel by road for fear of the well-placed landmines blowing up their vehicles, and the men inside them, apart. Any surveillance by the security forces would produce little other than a video or photo taken from long range. The security forces had suspected such a scene, but any idea of trying to interrupt or try to arrest at the funeral would only have led to unnecessary violence and bloodshed. Better to stay at a distance using undercover surveillance teams, to try to identify the main players and the movement of any weapons such as those involved in the firing of a salute over the coffin. Then, follow up with arrests and searches later. Anyway, the new Police Service of Northern Ireland, the PSNI, did not have the will, the resources, or the political backing, to enforce the law in South Armagh and the people attending the funeral knew this to be true.

Both sides knew the rules and the risks. Paul Costello was an MLA, an elected member of the Northern Ireland Assembly at Stormont in Belfast. During the war that was known as 'the Troubles' to the British, he'd fought them as a member of the South Armagh Brigade of the Provisional Irish Republican Army. In those days, along with his brother Sean, they'd helped to make the hills, fields, roads, towns, and villages of the South Armagh and border with the Irish Republic, a no-go area for the British Security forces, the army, and police. The only way they could operate was from behind their security base walls and by helicopter. But Costello had seen the end coming long before his younger brother.

The thirty-year war had become a war of attrition, and although the South Armagh Brigade had lost few men, mainly down to premature explosions, the rest of the PIRA units throughout the country had been decimated by the security-force's infiltration through their intelligence agencies. Many of the organisation's top people had been killed or imprisoned. The leaders of the Republican movement could see the way the wind was blowing. They knew to continue with the campaign would mean losing people needlessly and they'd decided that it was time to change tactics and go down a political road of calling for a ceasefire and negotiating a form of peace that would ensure the progress of their aim of a United Ireland.

Thinking back, he could still hear the anger in the voices of the South Armagh members opposing what they saw as treason to the cause and surrender to the British occupier of the island of Ireland. His brother Sean had been one of the loudest, his anger even stronger when Paul had told him he agreed with the leadership that they should stand down, and the stockpiles of hidden weapons be handed over for destruction before any peace talks could be formalised. He remembered at one meeting Sean had stood to his full height, his fists clenched, his face red with anger. Angry words led to bad feelings, to a falling out, and a parting of the ways. Paul helped bring the South Armagh Brigade round to agree with the leadership.

A specially held Provisional IRA General Army Convention backed the pro-ceasefire line. Sean Costello along with others, who opposed the peace process formed a new organisation styling itself Oglaigh na hEireann, which was to become the Real IRA. The fall out between the two Republican groups was severe. Real IRA members pilfered weapons from PIRA weapons dumps before they were handed over for destruction. The South Armagh contingent of PIRA had no intention of handing over all its weapons to what they saw as a British instigated so-called peace process. They would never fully trust the British. The weapons they retained were put into cold storage for the day when they expected the collapse of the whole process. The Real IRA had stolen weapons from PIRA and used them in attacks opposing the peace. A car bomb in Omagh in August 1998, killing twenty-nine innocent civilians being one of the worst attacks in the history of the Troubles. Despite this atrocity, the peace held. The Real IRA became the enemy not just to the security forces and the political world including the United States, but also the Provisional Republican Movement and the Irish Government. Their members were told to leave the weapons hidden in the PIRA hides alone on threat of death and an all-out war with PIRA. The death of Sean Costello, a onetime member of both Republican terrorist groups, had on this occasion, brought both groups together in peace to the room at the rear of Sherry's public house. Those remembering the dead Republican filled the main lounge, many drinking pints of the black stuff, Guinness as it's known to the world. The voices of the men and women, many of whom had fought in the recent war with the Brits and a few who had been fighting even longer, became louder as the black stuff was poured freely and downed quickly in the style of a typical Irish wake.

Paul Costello sat in a corner of the room with some of his local family and friends. Looking round, he couldn't help smiling as he remembered the old quotation.

'God invented alcohol so the Irish couldn't rule the world.'

It was then that Paul Costello noticed a shadow across the table blocking out the light from the ceiling's fanlight. When he looked up, he recognised the tall, broad-built man looking down at him.

'Hi, John Jo.'

'Hello, Paul. I was truly sorry when I heard about Sean. Please accept my condolences for you and your family. You're all in my prayers.'

'Thank you. Thanks for coming.'

The other people at the table continued in their own conversations, appreciating that the conversation between Paul Costello and John Jo Murphy was one they didn't want to get involved in.

'I know you're with your family, but Brendan has something important he'd like to discuss with you. If you're all right with that…can you come with me to the back room?'

The MLA man knew that anything Brendan McDevitt wanted to discuss with him wouldn't be something he'd want to hear. As a member of the Provisional Movement, he did not trust the Real IRA faction or its leader. Crossmaglen was PIRA territory, so Costello knew McDevitt wouldn't step out of line while in the village. Whatever he wanted to say must be important or he wouldn't have taken the risk of asking for a meeting with such a prominent local Republican.

Without any further discussion, Costello followed John Jo to the back room of the pub, which was normally used for small private parties. As he passed through the bar, he was aware of eyes following his every move. Everyone would have their own thoughts on what was happening, but all who knew a little of these things also knew to keep their thoughts to themselves and to keep their mouths shut.

John Jo Murphy came from a South Armagh farming family just outside Forkhill. The family had originally moved to the area from Dundalk across the border in the Irish Republic. His accent when speaking was more southern than northern, softer less guttural. He was around six-foot-tall, broad build, and his dark beard, hair, and eyes gave him a Middle Eastern appearance.

It had been some time since Paul Costello had been in the back room of the bar. It hadn't changed much. The small square tables each with four straight-backed chairs, he remembered would give you a sore back if you sat on them too long. The room was cold. Everyone said the owner, Peter Sherry, was tight with money, so that would explain the radiators being switched off.

Brendan McDevitt was sitting at a table and a young, dark-haired man stood and left the room without speaking, before Costello sat down. He recognised the young man who came from the same estate Costello had grown up in. He also knew that Kevin Kelly had once been a member of the same PIRA unit in Crossmaglen as the two Costello brothers. Now, it would appear he too had crossed over to the Real IRA. Costello knew that young Kevin would now be taking up position outside the door to prevent anyone from disturbing the meeting inside. John Jo sat down at the table, a pint glass in his hand.

'Thank you for agreeing to see me, Paul. I ordered you a Guinness,' said McDevitt as he placed the full pint glass across the table, setting it on the coaster in front of Costello.

'To Sean,' said McDevitt, raising his own glass at the same time.

'To Sean,' Paul replied. 'What do you want, Brendan?'

McDevitt smiled. 'Straight to the point. I thought you politicians were more subtle, playing your cards close to your chest.'

'Thank you for your words at the graveside, but today I must be with my family and friends and you, I'm sorry to say, are neither.'

'Straight to the point once more. Then let me return the favour as I don't want to waste anymore of your precious time today.'

Paul Costello took a long drink from his glass, then looked at McDevitt and John Jo.

'I'm listening.'

'I'm here not only as Chief of Staff of the Real IRA, but also on behalf of the Army Council.'

'I recognise neither. I recognise only one Republican movement, the Provisional one,' replied Costello.

'I don't want to go over old ground. That's not what I want to talk about,' said McDevitt, cutting across Costello's comments.

'As I said, I'm listening,' said Costello quietly.

'Sean died fighting for a cause we both might agree has still to be won,' said McDevitt.

Costello took another sip from his glass before replying.

'You will know that Sean and I went our different ways some years ago. I'm here today because he was my brother and my mother's son. Not because he died on an English street wasting his life in fighting when the people of this country want change. They want us to fight for that cause in a different way.'

'Again, you're going over the very reasons why we stand on different sides of the fence. That's why Sean decided to do what he did.

To die for that cause, the one I believe, despite what you say, will still need to be taken up. But leaving those arguments aside, the reason I wanted to speak with you in person today, away from long ears, and prying eyes, is to tell you what happened in Manchester and why we buried your brother today,' said McDevitt.

'I know what happened in Manchester. Sean was there to kill the British prime minister. As usual, he was acting on his own. He even acted without your permission. A lone wolf willing to destroy the peace process and start another bloody war that would lead nowhere and only slaughter more of our fellow Irishmen,' answered Costello.

McDevitt downed another large portion of his glass before continuing.

'I think we can both agree on one thing. Despite what Sean did, he was doing it because he believed this country is still divided, despite what we both think about the so-called peace process. I think his plan, although he operated as a lone wolf as you call him, would have the backing of many republicans on this island, and if he'd been successful, he would have been regarded as a hero by many.'

Paul Costello looked at both men before speaking.

'No matter what would have happened, I still believe he was wrong, and most of the people on this island would agree. We can go back and forward with this argument till the cows come home and that won't change. You knew that before I came in here. Stop wasting my time. What's this all about?'

'Don't speak to the chief like that,' growled Murphy, starting to stand before McDevitt took hold of his arm.

'Sit down, John Jo. We must remember where we are and whose funeral we're at.'

John Jo sat back down, his eyes never leaving Costello, who was now smiling back at him.

'Yes, John Jo, as Brendan says, remember where you are.'

McDevitt took a drink from his own glass, then leant across the table to ensure Paul Costello heard every word.

'I don't want a fight with you or anyone here, Paul. I wanted to meet with you to tell you the things I don't think you know about Manchester, and what we intend to do about it.'

'I'm all ears,' replied Costello.

'Despite the whys of what happened in Manchester, and the fact Sean was operating without sanction from the Army Council, how he was killed, who killed him, and what went wrong has been clarified to us,' McDevitt continued.

Paul Costello remained silent, his eyes watching McDevitt for every expressive detail. He didn't trust these men, but Sean was his brother, and he was at least willing to hear what they had to say.

'As I' said, we've been getting more and more information about what Sean was doing and what went wrong. Yes, he'd linked up with some Islamic people, one of them originally from the North here.'

Costello cut into the conversation once more.

'I know Samantha Lyndsey. 'She's an old friend of Sean's. He trained with her in Lebanon. I guess they met up again, and that's how he lost his mind and went on that crazy mission. He got killed, and she escaped.'

'You're partially right. But your brother didn't lose his mind. It was a well-planned operation which would have been successful if not for two things.'

'And what would they be?' asked Costello.

'First, Sean was betrayed by an informer and second the informer's handler was an ex-RUC Special Branch man now working with the British security services.'

Costello sat up straight in the chair. What McDevitt was saying was news to him.

'I thought it was down to good luck by the British and their technical capabilities through bugs in buildings and phones.'

'You can be sure the British used all that sort of stuff, but not before they were given a heads up by their tout. To be on the safe side today, I've had this room swept for those very same bugs and it's clean.'

'How can I be sure you're telling me the truth? How do you know about this tout? Who told you?'

'It is true, Paul. But in case you didn't know, we believe Samantha Lyndsey was tracked down by the same people, then murdered in Egypt not long after, probably by the same Special Branch man. As for how we know these things, I'll let John Jo here tell you his part of the story.'

Costello could see John Jo Murphy was smiling.

I hope he's smiling because he knows something no one else does and not because Sean was dead, he thought.

'I want to say how sorry I am about Sean. I was with him on a few jobs, and I drove the van at Bessbrook when he took out the Brit with the fifty calibre. I heard the rumours that he was on a job in England, but like the rest of the army, I had no idea what. It was only afterwards that I found out it wasn't sanctioned, but as I'm sure you know, Sean wasn't one to worry about taking orders.'

'No, he was always one to do things his own way, go his own way and cause nothing but deep shit for everyone else,' said Costello.

Again, John Jo smiled and nodded before continuing.

'Well, the first I knew Sean was up to something was when he called me. I think he was already in Manchester where he'd seen a face from the past. A woman he knew from his days in PIRA. He told me he wanted to know where Mary McAuley was. You might remember her from the old days?'

Paul Costello tried to hide his surprise. Of course, he remembered Mary McAuley. He'd met her at high-ranking meetings of the Provisional Movement during the war and the subsequent peace talks. She'd disappeared off his radar during the talks, and he thought that she'd just stood down from involvement like many others when the peace process brought about the ceasefire, the Good Friday Agreement, and the dominance of the political wing of the organisation. She was privy to many of the movement's secrets, and if what he was now hearing was true, she was not only a spy for the British deep inside the movement, but she'd betrayed its secrets, which he had no doubt had ensured the arrest or death of many of his friends and now maybe even his own brother.

'Yes, I remember her. But why did Sean want to know where she was?'

'As I said, he thought he'd seen her in Manchester, but not only had he seen her he'd seen her with a face from his past, a man from the war days. I made enquiries in Belfast about where Mary had gone to live. She was nowhere to be found. Even her own mother didn't know where she was. I told Sean this and passed on her mobile number to him, which I'd received from her mother. I'm sure, knowing Sean, he would have called her, and with the Brits' technical ability at their GCHQ this helped track him down. We have made more enquiries since Sean was killed. She was back in London recently and according to our contacts at Belfast airport she flew here when her mother fell and broke her hip. She flew back to London the day after that Islamic Jihad team was taken out at Canary Wharf. Some people took photos of the gunman who shot dead the Jihad leader. Even though they seized the cameras, we managed to get one photo from our Islamic Jihad friends.'

John Jo reached into his jacket pocket and placed a photo on the table for Paul to pick up. The picture showed the side profile of a man kneeling beside a body on the ground. He could also see the man had a handgun in his right hand and he appeared to be checking that the man on the ground was dead. John Jo then placed another photo on the table.

'If you place both photos side by side, I'm sure you'll agree they're the same man.'

Doing exactly that, Costello could see the likeness, even though the second photo appeared to be older. Taken from a distance, it gave a full-frontal view of the man's face.

'OK. John Jo, they do look like the same man. Who is he and what's his connection to all this?'

Costello could see John Jo was enjoying this when he smiled and winked back at him.

'Another little part of the story which I'm sure you're not aware of is that the man in the photos is David Reece, an ex-RUC Special Branch man. He's the one that Sean phoned me about. I think Sean recognised him from the old days when Reece would have interrogated him in Gough Barracks in Armagh City. During the war, the PIRA unit in Dundalk circulated that second photo to ask units in the north to try to tie him down for assassination. One of the people who had one of those photos was Mary McAuley.'

Paul Costello could see where this was going, but he waited for John Jo to lay out the whole story before commenting.

'We don't think it was a coincidence that both Reece and McAuley were in Manchester together at the same time when Sean spotted them. We also believe that when the photo of Reece was circulated, she tipped him off, and that was one of the reasons he seemed to disappear from the South Armagh and Newry area. Then again, we find her flying in from London, and then returning there the day after the Islamic Jihad operation was intercepted and their leader killed by the man in the first photo, David Reece, who we now believe works for the British security services.'

'A lot of circumstantial evidence, John Jo. Why have you not lifted Mary and questioned her?'

This time it was McDevitt who replied.

'For the simple reason that she was so high up in the organisation she was beyond suspicion. To lift someone in her position for interrogation would need a lot more than circumstantial evidence, no matter how strong. I think if Sean had been successful in Manchester, and bearing in mind what he saw, he would have been on good ground to have her brought in for questioning by the Internal Security Team. I believe the evidence we have is strong enough to do just that.'

Paul Costello realised what was being asked of him. He knew about the Internal Security Team also known as the Knutting Squad for the way they would torture their victims before shooting them in the head, then dumping them somewhere along the border between the north and south.

'So, you're looking for my support as an MLA and ranking member of the Provisional Movement in letting you interrogate her to confirm your theory? Because she'd still be considered a ranking member.'

Taking another sip from his glass, McDevitt stood, and walked round the table and sat down next to Paul Costello.

'Paul, I think you misunderstand us. We know all about the risks and your high rankings, but as we said at the very start, the difference in the directions we took after the Good Friday Agreement mean we don't have to respect each other's rank anymore because of those differences.'

McDevitt was leaning closer to emphasize his point and Costello could smell the cigarettes and booze on his breath. Just a couple of more reasons for not liking this man. He knew of McDevitt's reputation for wanting to pull the trigger himself after they'd tortured someone into confessing their work for the security forces as an informer, a traitor. Paul Costello knew that a few of them were innocent of the charge, only confessing because they couldn't stand the torture, for that's what McDevitt liked to dish out. Costello knew his reputation and his nickname: Doctor Death. McDevitt was smiling as he continued and looking into his eyes, Costello thought the room had just got colder.

'We are not asking your permission. We know your stance and that of the Provisional IRA. Peace at all costs, even if that means letting someone who was a member of your movement and at the same time a spy for the British walk freely around rather than jeopardise that agreement you made with the Brits. We made no such agreement. But now this spy has caused the death of one of our people by her friendship with the British agent David Reece. We cannot let that stand, and we intend to make her answer for her crime and if at the same time we can make Reece pay, that would be a bonus. I'm telling you this because Sean was your brother and I want you to reassure your leaders that we are not looking for a fight with them.'

'You don't need my permission,' replied Costello. 'I know you only too well, and that you and your people will do what you must do, despite my feelings or thoughts on the matter. If what you say is true, and you succeed in speaking to Mary McAuley, before you do anything to her, or for that matter David Reece, we'll want to hear the genuine evidence from their own lips before you do anything to them. The Agreement, as you call it, is stronger than you think. Both sides will take action to protect it. If people see that you're acting without evidence, that will only make things worse for everyone. We know the

Brits will act. They won't want you having them because of the information they have in their heads. The one thing I do know is that my leadership won't be happy if you carry out a killing on the soil north of the border. For myself, I can only say that I won't stand in your way if what you say is true. Whether my brother was wrong or not in trying to do what he did, he was still my brother, another Irishman killed by the British. But I won't support a death in the North that threatens the peace process. If that happens, it won't only be the Brits you'll have to worry about.'

McDevitt sat back in his chair.

'I think we understand what you're saying. Leave this to us. If I need to speak with you again, someone will be in touch. Now, go back to your family. You need to be with them today. But before you go.' He took a small business card from his jacket pocket and passed it over the table where Costello lifted it. The white card only had a mobile number nothing else. 'That's my private number, and only a few people have it. Call me if you need to.'

Costello put the card in his pocket. Then, without speaking, he finished what was left of the black stuff in his glass and returned to the main bar to sit with his own people. He'd left behind the kind of violence McDevitt loved. The kind he'd been working to stop, and now it was back knocking on his door.

CHAPTER 4

TEL AVIV, ISRAEL

As soon as the doctors had cleared Reece to travel, he and Mary had taken a direct flight from London to Israel. From the travel information Reece read on the plane, Ben-Gurion airport is about twelve miles from Tel Aviv and was originally named Lod Airport but was renamed after David Ben-Gurion, the first prime minister of Israel. Jim Broad had arranged everything, making it easy for Reece and Mary to be escorted quickly through the normal high security at the airport. Outside the main entrance, they were met by the Mossad agent, Ari Rosenberg, better known to Reece under his cover name of Palo Stressor. Reece had worked with Palo and his Mossad partner, Anna, before she was killed. After her death, Jim Broad was able to tell Reece that her real name was Rachel Cohen, the name she'd been born with and the name she'd been buried with, back in her Israeli homeland. The men greeted each other as brothers with a strong hug.

'Shalom, David, welcome to Israel. You are looking much better than the last time I saw you. Did you have a good flight?'

'Good to see you again, Palo. The flight was great, thank you. Mary, this is Palo, a good friend,' said Reece, stepping back to introduce the woman behind him.

'Pleased to meet you, Palo.'

'And so very pleased to meet you, Mary. David has told me so much about you, but he didn't say how beautiful you were,' said Palo, smiling before kissing Mary on both cheeks.

'That's enough of your chatting up my woman.' Reece laughed.

Taking their bags, Palo placed them in the boot of the limo, then held the door open for them to get into the back of the car. Driving out of the airport, Palo kept up a tour guide type conversation.

'I promised your colleague Matthew a tour of Israel if ever he came here,' said Palo.

Matthew Simons was the MI6 Middle East expert who had worked on the last mission with them in Malta and London.

'He told me, and I believe he promised to show you a bit more of England if you're ever there, and don't forget to come and see us in Malta anytime,' replied Reece.

'I would love to. That's a date then. I know you might be tired from your flight, but Kurt Shimon has instructed me to escort you to your hotel to drop off Mary. Then he'd like to see you in his office. If that's OK with you, of course?'

Reece looked at Mary, who raised her eyebrows knowingly. She'd seen too much of his secret life to expect to be fully included. She'd heard him say the words 'Need to know' too many times to think she'd be fully a part of that life.

'I would rather freshen up anyway than sit in a stuffy office,' said Mary.

'We changed your reservation and upgraded you to a nicer hotel, all expenses on us.'

'We're always happy with an upgrade, thank you,' said Mary.

'Yes, it's the Brown Seaside Hotel, one of the famous Brown Hotels group. It is in a great location right on the beach.'

'Then you're forgiven for taking Joseph away to a meeting.'

The hotel was everything Palo had promised and more. After dropping a happier Mary there, Palo drove the short journey to the headquarters of Mossad, the Israeli Secret Service. Like the MI6 and MI5 offices in London and the CIA building in Langley, Virginia, everyone knew where they were, but because of security, and the underground car parking, the people who worked in these buildings could enter and leave anonymously. Taking the lift to the top floor, Palo and Reece were seated in the office of Kurt Shimon five minutes later. Shimon, the director in charge of the Mossad Kidon Units, or Bayonet as it was known, was at his desk. The office wasn't as plush as Sir Ian Fraser's at MI6, the furniture more modern and functional. Reece noticed similarities: the same style of computer and telephone console, but apart from a small camp bed at the far end of the office, everything else showed operational functionality.

Shimon came around the desk and shook Reece's hand vigorously.

'David, David, it's good to see you again my friend. You are well, I hope?'

'Yes, I'm good. Thank you for sending Palo to pick us up and looking after us with the hotel upgrade. It's very kind.'

Shimon invited both men to sit in the chairs in front of his desk before returning to his own position opposite them.

'Nonsense, David. After what you've done, not only for your own country but for the state of Israel, it was the least we could do. When I heard you were on your way, I told my friend Jim Broad we'd look after you. Anyway, there's another reason I wanted to see you here. Excuse me for just a moment.'

Shimon pressed one of the buttons on the phone console and a female voice answered.

'Martha, can you make that call we spoke about, please?'

'Right away, sir,' answered Martha.

Because they'd arrived on the early flight, it had been cool at the airport, but Reece noticed that now it was getting closer to midday. The sun was heating the room through the large windows that looked out over the rooftops of Tel Aviv. Reece had never liked too much heat, that being the reason he always left Malta for cooler climes during the summer months. He thought it was something to do with his growing up and living in the land of his birth that was Northern Ireland. The summers there were always comfortable, even at the hottest times.

He still loved that land and would return there for family occasions: weddings, birthdays, and deaths. The visits for deaths were becoming more frequent as they involved family and close friends from his Special Branch days.

'There is someone here who wants to meet you, David,' said Kurt Shimon.

As he finished speaking, the door of the office opened and a tall, lean man, dressed in slacks and an open-necked white short-sleeved shirt, walked into the office.

The two men sitting with Reece stood.

'David, let me introduce you to Danny Malkah, the Director General of Mossad,' said Shimon.

As Reece stood, he took the hand offered.

'I'm really pleased to meet you, Mr Reece.' The words were spoken with a soft middle European accent.

'Pleased to meet you also,' replied Reece.

The director general pulled a chair across the room to sit down, inviting everyone else to do the same.

'How was your flight? I hope your hotel is all right. Have you recovered from your wounds?' asked Malkah.

Reece was still coming to terms with the fact that he was sitting in a room with the highest member of the Israeli Secret Service.

'Flight good, hotel good, and health almost back to normal, whatever that is. Thank you.'

Malkah took a pack of cigarettes and a silver lighter from his pocket and lit one. He offered one to Reece, who, not being a smoker, refused with a 'no thank you'.

'Bad habit, I know, but we all have at least one. I know Kurt and Palo don't like them either. I know one day they'll probably kill me, but then no one gets out of this world alive – we all die of something.'

He blew a long line of smoke across the room and continued to speak.

'David. I've been fully briefed on everything that happened in Malta and London. I've spoken on the telephone with your boss Sir Ian Fraser, and with Jim Broad. Like Kurt here, they all speak very highly of you and what you've done not just for your own country, but for Israel and the rest of the world.'

'Just did my job,' Reece replied.

The director general took another long drag on the cigarette, blowing more smoke across the room. Reece noticed that he didn't seem to inhale that much and thought what he said about it just being a bad habit was just that.

'Danny, one thing you'll notice about David is his modesty. He is a unique individual who, even though works well with a team, 'is quite capable of doing things alone,' said Shimon.

Reece could feel his face getting warm. He wasn't sure if it was the sun heating up the room through the office window, or the fact he hated being praised in this way.

'You're right on one point, Kurt. I work as part of a team, always have, and the better the team the better the results. When I've worked alone, it was because I had no option.'

'I see what Kurt says about your modesty is true, but that's not the only reason I wanted to meet you. I know you're here to pay your own respects to our agent Rachel who you know as Anna. I've told Kurt that you're to be assisted in this, and Palo here will be with you. Tomorrow he'll escort you to her grave. I've spoken to Jim Broad this morning, and he tells me that you wish to stand down from operations. I must tell you I totally understand your reasons, but you should also appreciate that your dedication and skills will be missed, as I'm sure Jim

Broad has told you. Despite this, I want you to enjoy your stay here. Be assured that if you need anything, either now, or in the future, you have only to contact Kurt and we'll help you no matter what you need.'

Reece was surprised that Jim Broad had told the head of Mossad about the future of his agent, but then again, Jim Broad would do, or say anything to have control of the situation that Reece had left him with. Reece understood that the offer of help at any time appeared to be genuine. He hoped he'd never need it. But it was a good card to have in his back pocket should he need to do so. Reece knew of the background to the close working relationship and history between the British security services and Mossad and his own recent experience.

Malkah stood to leave. The other three men also stood. Once again, he shook hands with Reece. 'Tomorrow, Palo will pick you up, so tonight relax, and enjoy your hotel. I've eaten there before, and the food is excellent. Do you remember Jacob Lavyan?'

Reece was surprised to hear the name again.

'Yes, we met once a few years ago in Belfast.'

'Well, my friend, he'd like to join you tomorrow on your visit to our country if that's OK with you?'

'Yes, of course,' answered Reece. The idea of meeting this man in his own country was something he'd never thought of or expected.

'Good, then have a good day tomorrow. If visiting someone's last resting place can be a good day.'

After the Mossad Chief left, Martha, who had been sitting in the outer office, brought in a tray of tea and fruit, leaving the men to serve themselves.

After pouring the three men black tea and offering a slice of apple to Reece, Kurt Shimon sat once more. Smiling, he leant back in his chair.

'You look a bit shocked, David,' said Shimon.

'It's not every day you meet the head of Mossad in person, and then for him to tell you someone like Jacob Lavyan would like to travel to a graveyard with you. You're right I suppose. I'm a bit shocked.'

'I'm sorry about that, but we wanted to surprise you, and at the same time show you in what esteem we hold you. Anyway, when you've finished your tea, Palo will drive you back to your hotel and plan with you the rest of your stay in Israel. Anything you need to let him know, and I'm always at your disposal if you need me.'

Reece took one more mouthful of the tea and standing, he shook Kurt Shimon's hand.

'Thank you for your kindness. For now, I'd like to have a swim and a shower and relax with Mary tonight. Until we meet again. Shalom.'

'Indeed, Shalom David, enjoy the rest of your stay.'

□

Chapter 5

Tel Aviv

The hotel was just as Palo had said, a definite upgrade. When Palo had dropped him off, Reece found Mary sitting in the spacious lobby with a pot of coffee in front of her. Despite the fact he'd been absent with a Mossad agent for a couple of hours, she was smiling.

'Oh, Joseph, you should see our suite. It's fantastic. We've picture windows looking out at the sea. I think your friends want us to feel good about being here.'

She was talking quickly like an excited child opening Christmas presents.

'It has beautiful marble floors, and the hotel has an indoor swimming pool.'

'Good. I'd like a swim,' Reece replied. 'But I would prefer the sea.'

'The sea it is, then. Let's go.'

The sea had been just what he needed; the waves refreshing not only his body, but his mind. Two hours later, he lay on the queen-size bed. Staring at the ceiling, he could hear the hair dryer in the bathroom as Mary dried her hair, and the low hum of the air con that kept the room cool despite the heat outside the window.

When he told Mary about his visit to Mossad Headquarters and his meeting, he could see her worried frown. He reassured her that they were going home to Malta after their visit and that he was retired. When he told her about the plans for the next day, she'd asked about Jacob Lavyan, he told her just an old friend from the past.

His thoughts went back to the meeting in Kurt Shimon's office, the genuine offers of help and the mention of Lavyan. He considered Jacob Lavyan a friend, in the same way fellow secret intelligence people consider someone in the same business, maybe not a friend as such, but respect for a fellow professional in the same line of business. He'd met Lavyan many years before when he'd visited Northern Ireland. Mossad had a close interest in the links between the IRA and Arab groups who, at the time were the enemies of Israel. Reece had been detailed to take him on a fact-finding tour of the border area of Newry and South Armagh. Lavyan was renowned in the world of espionage. Reece later found out that as a young man he'd been one of the Mossad team who had in 1960 kidnapped Adolf Eichmann. Eichmann had created a new identity and was living under an assumed name in Argentina when the Mossad team lifted him off a street close to his home and spirited him back to Israel where he was tried for his crimes, convicted, and hanged. He told Reece that his job was to help the British understand how Israel tracked down and dealt with their enemies throughout the world making sure the terrorists knew, that as far as Mossad and Israel was concerned, there was no hiding place. Lavyan had spoken of the similarities of the border, and how his own country found itself surrounded by countries, who, if not openly supporting the terrorists who attacked his country, at least gave them a safe living area from which they could attack Israel then return to safety. He also pointed out the army watchtowers on the hills along the border, which made it slightly more difficult for the terrorists to get through. He said they reminded him of the Golan Heights that looked down on Lebanon and from then on Reece had always used the same name for the hills of South Armagh. Reece had remembered the helicopter flights over the hills and looking down he'd think of the dangerous enemy who lived and operated below.

Afterwards, he'd taken Lavyan to one of his favourite bars in Belfast and introduced him to Bushmills Whiskey.

A few years later, he'd heard that Jacob had been part of a Mossad surveillance team that had been watching Mairead Farrell, Sean Savage and Danny McCann: three Provisional IRA terrorists who were planning to set off a bomb in Gibraltar. The Mossad involvement came about because they'd been watching a known Arab weapons smuggler near Marbella in Spain. At the same time, they were tipped off by British Intelligence that the three Irish terrorists were up to something in that area of Spain. The Mossad had followed the three but withdrew when they'd crossed the border into Gibraltar, where they knew the British also had an operation running. The SAS had then shot the three terrorists dead. The Gibraltar operation had resulted in loud condemnation in many political quarters and subsequently in more deaths directly impacted from the killings. At one of the funerals of the three dead PIRA at Milltown Cemetery in Belfast, a Loyalist gunman had attacked the mourners with a handgun and grenades, resulting in more death when three of the mourners had died. A few days later, as the cortege for one of the dead mourners was travelling to the same cemetery, two plain clothes British soldiers who had taken a wrong turn in their unmarked car, accidentally drove into the funeral path. The crowd surrounded the car and dragged the two men from their vehicle before handing them over to a PIRA kill unit. They were beaten, stripped, and shot dead. Reece could still see in his mind the video pictures taken from the Army Heli-Telly camera on the helicopter above the cortege showing the full impact of what happened frame by frame. The hardest part to watch had been when the video showed the two soldiers trying to make a break for it when the black cab had stopped on waste ground. Both men tried to fight their way to freedom before a gunman dressed in black shot both each in turn before running back down to the main Andersonstown Road and disappearing into the crowd. A lesson had been learnt by everyone who had watched the scenes of that day. If cornered, shoot your way out, even if your attackers are unarmed. As one of Reece's SB friends had put it, it's better to be tried by a jury of twelve than be carried by a team of six.

'Penny for them?'

Mary was standing beside the bed, the large white bath towel tightly wrapped showing the curves of her body, her long hair falling loosely around her neck.

'Bad, all bad, and they all involve you and what is under that towel.'

CHAPTER 6

BELFAST

John Jo Murphy had taken the bus from Newry to Belfast. He arrived at the main bus station behind the Europa Hotel and walked through the city, using the time to watch his back and try to spot any surveillance following him, which was why he'd travelled by bus. He had plenty of time to check out the other passengers and make a note of any he suspected as security forces. He knew such teams would easily be able to follow the bus in cars, but when he walked through the city, he used pedestrian walkways where cars weren't allowed. So far, he'd seen nothing to worry him. Two men on the bus had raised his suspicion, but one had got off at Banbridge. The other had been met at the final stop at the Europa by what looked like a girlfriend or mistress by the way she kissed him.

Making his way through the main city centre, he walked through the Castle Court shopping centre, going in, and out of various shops, then stopping to sit, and take some time over a cup of coffee, to pay attention to the surrounding people. Looking at his watch, he saw he had an hour before his meeting at eleven thirty. He always liked to be at his destination at least twenty minutes early, allowing for one final check that he was on his own. He knew that despite all his checks for followers, a good surveillance team could cover him, but he wasn't going to make it easy for them if they were there. Apart from the two photographs he was carrying, it was a piece of paper in his pocket that might cause problems if he was stopped. But most of what he needed was in his head. So far, he'd seen nothing that bothered him. Finishing his coffee, he walked through the centre and out to the rear of the complex where there was a line of black cabs. These cabs mainly serviced the West Belfast Republican areas of the city, and the drivers were mostly sympathisers of that cause. If a Brit or security-force agent tried to use one of the cabs they would soon be spotted, and the word passed on to the IRA. The cab drivers would always engage in conversation with the passengers, and they would need to provide the right answers to the questions to confirm they had a genuine reason to travel anywhere in the West side of the city. Getting into the cab at the front of the line, John Jo asked the driver to take him to Beechmount Parade.

'Are you up from the country, then?' asked the driver, noting his passenger's accent right away.

'Yes, just for the day, just visiting friends,' he replied.

John Jo knew that even though the driver would take him to the Beechmount area in West Belfast, he would still pass on that there was a stranger in town. The local IRA would then send a couple of their young watchers to the Beechmount area to try to identify this stranger and note where he was going. The driver then tried a different tack with another question.

'My uncle Paddy McIlwaine lives on Beechmount Avenue. Do you know him?'

John Jo knew there probably was no uncle, and he wasn't going to play the game.

'No, I'm not familiar with the area. I just know where my friends live.'

The driver seemed to take the hint and drove away from the centre taking the main route up the lower Falls Road, passing the old site of Divis Flats on the left, then the main Sinn Fein offices on the right, just before the main junction with Springfield Road. John Jo could see the familiar mural of the hunger striker, Bobby Sands, on the wall of the offices. The phrase 'Sinn Fein' is Irish for 'Ourselves or We Ourselves' but known by many republicans as 'Ourselves Alone'. A phrase that many supported when it came to the many factions within the Republican movements. As the taxi continued up the road with the Royal Victoria hospital on the left and a Convent on the right, the streets, and houses around him were well-known to John Jo. When the Troubles had started in 1968, as a young man, he'd travelled to the city to support and fight for the local people who were being terrorised by Loyalists gangs from the nearby Shankill Road. The gangs were also supported by the police and the 'B' specials. He had fought these gangs at first with rocks and petrol bombs before the local IRA had brought in more guns, allowing them to fight back. When he'd travelled to the city in those days, it was from a true belief in the Republican cause for a United Ireland. and as a young man he'd believed the violence was only the start that would bring in the southern government in support of likeminded people in the north. That never happened. The rescue from the Republican Government in Ireland never came. When he'd been sworn into the PIRA in a house in Crossmaglen, the person swearing him in was Sean Costello. Like Sean and others, he not only mistrusted the Brits, but he hated them as well, and he now found himself as the Operations Officer on the GHQ Staff of the Real IRA. Sean had gone off the books with his plan to kill the British prime minister, but John Jo and the other GHQ and Army Council members would have welcomed him back if he'd been successful. Because he hadn't succeeded, Sean Costello had to be spoken of publicly as a rogue agent operating without permission of the Real IRA Command. And to prevent an internal war with the PIRA, they had to step back from supporting his actions. John Jo recognised the small terraced semi-detached houses as the taxi turned right off the Upper Falls Road into the Beechmount area along Beechmount Avenue, before turning into Beechmount Parade.

'What number?' asked the driver.

'Just drop me here please,' John Jo replied.

The cab pulled up at the kerb.

'That's four fifty please,' said the driver.

John Jo gave him a fiver. 'Keep the change.' He got out of the cab and waited to watch the vehicle drive up the Parade before turning right at the top and back towards the city. He started walking the same direction as the one taken by the cab. He walked slowly, paying attention to any movement in the street. There was no one, and no traffic. Everything was quiet. He walked on the left-hand side of the street, which was about two hundred yards long. When he arrived at the junction where the cab had turned towards the city, he saw a young lad sitting on a wall watching him. He had seen this lad before when visiting the city and he knew he was one of the scouts and lookouts for the local Real IRA unit. He nodded towards John Jo, who nodded back. He was telling John Jo everything was OK for his meeting. John Jo crossed to the other side of Beechmount Parade and started walking down it in the opposite direction to the one he'd come. The house he wanted was number 43, halfway down the street. The front downstairs curtains would be closed even though it was the middle of the day, another sign everything was ready, and he was expected. Looking at his watch as he walked up the short path to the front door, he smiled as the hands showed eleven thirty exactly. He liked things to be well-planned and that would be important if this operation was to succeed.

The door was opened by a small balding man, who with age, had gone overweight. Despite his appearance, John Jo knew that Brian McNally had a reputation for being a vicious hard man in West Belfast. Previously the Officer Commanding the PIRA Unit for the Beechmount and Lower Falls area, he'd left PIRA in protest at the Good Friday Agreement and had crossed over to the Real IRA with half the men under his command. It was well-known he'd personally looked the senior Republican leaders in the eye when he'd told them there was nothing good about any agreement with the Brits.

'Come in John Jo, and welcome,' said McNally.

The houses in the Beechmount area had changed little. They had mostly been built as semi-detached two up two down terraced houses in the 1930s before the Second World War. It wasn't until the sixties and seventies that grants were available for extensions being built at the rear to take in another bedroom and indoor bathroom. Prior to that, the toilet was in the backyard, and having a bath in a large steel basin in front of the living-room fire once a week was the highlight of the day. John Jo often thought the conditions people had to put up with then were justification enough to rebel against the Unionist and British Governments. A small three-piece suite almost filled the front room where McNally invited John Jo to sit in one of the armchairs opposite him. The fire was well alight with yellow and red flames, giving off a comfortable, warm heat. To John Jo, the furniture and the room looked like it hadn't been changed much since the house was built, with old, flowered wallpaper and family pictures in black frames.

'Glad you could see me at such short notice, Brian. I need your help with a project we are working on. Is it OK to talk here?' John Jo was only too aware that the Real IRA units had suffered badly because of the bugging and surveillance capabilities of the British Security and Police services.

'Yes, no problem. I had it swept for bugs this morning by one of our technical people. And as I'm sure you noticed, some of our boys are outside keeping an eye out for any of our friends. Your phone call said you'll need a couple of our guys who are reliable. I have two boys in the kitchen having a cup of tea. Now what can we do for you? How can I help?'

John Jo settled back in the chair before replying. He had been on the road since early morning, and it had been a long time since he'd had breakfast.

'A cup of tea and a biscuit, if you have one, would be good. Then we can get down to our chat.'

'Ah, no problem. How do you take it?'

'Black, one sugar.'

McNally went into the kitchen. John Jo could hear a muffled conversation before McNally returned with a mug and a small plate of plain biscuits, setting them on the coffee table.

'Help yourself. But watch out, that tea's hot.'

John Jo took his time, blowing into the mug before taking a small sip, then dipping one of the biscuits into the tea and eating it before it was too soft or dropped into the mug. He looked across at Brian McNally. He knew this man had been through much for the cause. He had been arrested while carrying out an attempted bomb attack on a shopping centre near Belfast city centre. A passing police patrol had spotted the false number plates on the car he was travelling in while transporting the bomb. He had been sent to the maximum-security maze prison where, in 1983, he'd been one of the 38 PIRA prisoners involved in the great escape.

Along with a few of the other escapees, he managed to get to the safety of the town of Dundalk in the Republic of Ireland. He stayed there as one of the OTRs or On The Run, and evaded capture by the British until the OTRs were given a 'get out of jail free' letter from the British government after the Good Friday Agreement was signed. While in Dundalk he continued to carry out operations with the border units, and on a few occasions delivered weapons and explosives to the Belfast and Tyrone Brigades, to carry on the war. John Jo knew that Brian McNally had made sure that much of those munitions was still under his control and now available to his comrades in the Real IRA to continue with the war effort against the Brits.

'The job I want you to do, Brian, is very simple, but there are two parts to it. The first is to knock down and either injure or kill an old lady.'

'Fuck me, John Jo. Are we killing old ladies now? I don't think that'll go down well with the boys or with me for that matter,' said McNally, taking a sharp breath before John Jo raised his hand.

'Hear me out first, Brian. When I tell you the reason why, and the second part of the operation, you might understand better why it must be this way. As for the boys. I'll leave that down to you, who you use, and how much you need to tell them. But the whole thing is top secret, only a small few need to be told or used.'

For the next hour John Jo told McNally everything he knew about Mary McAuley. How she was a tout working for the Brits, how Sean Costello had found out, and the evidence that she was working with her ex-SB man, who was now an agent for the British Security Service. He described how Sean Costello and the Arab Jihadist had been killed by the same man, and why they thought McAuley was now working with the Brits.

He could see from the expression of anger on McNally's face that this had all come as a total shock to him. He knew McNally had been at many high-grade PIRA meetings where McAuley had also been present discussing both military and political issues. He knew, like him, McNally would be thinking about the many volunteers killed on active service. Like the eight at Loughgall and the three in Gibraltar. They were some of the best people they had, and such deaths had helped bring the organisation to the talks table. You can only lose so many of your best people before you're crushed completely. This was the argument used by Gerry Adams and Martin McGuinness when they led the Provisional Movement into the talks with the Brits, and the breakup of the organisation, leading to the breakaway formation of the Real IRA.

'Fuck, John Jo, Mary McAuley? Are you telling me the truth? Are you telling me that bitch sat there in meetings then went to her SB bastard and told him everything?'

'I'm as shocked as you, Brian. But it's the truth, the bitch was, and still is a tout working for the Brits.'

'Bloody hell. So, what are we going to do?'

'This is where you and your boys come in, and why they need to knock down this elderly woman. The lady in question is Mary McAuley's mother. We know she recently fell and broke her hip and that's what brought McAuley back from London to visit her in hospital, before she returned to London to be with her SB man when the Arab was killed. Her mother has since been released from hospital, but she attends the City Hospital for Physio once a week. She currently lives in a small house on the Lisburn Road, which we think belongs to her daughter.'

McNally stood and threw a large log onto the fire, which had almost gone out. As he sat down, he stared at the ceiling in thought before speaking once more.

'So, what do you need?'

Taking a piece of A4 paper from his inside coat pocket, John Jo handed it to McNally.

'That is all the information you'll need about the tout's mother. I've had a couple of our own intelligence people watching her for the last few weeks. It details her movements. She uses a taxi when she goes and returns to her hospital appointments, but now she can walk a bit more. With the aid of a walking stick, she can walk the short distance to the shops on the Lisburn Road. On Tuesday mornings, she seems to meet up with two friends in the café in Sandy Row beside the shops. I would think the time to hit her would be then. Whether she ends up in the hospital or the undertakers, we believe that will bring her daughter out of the woodwork. Once your boys have done their part, I'll contact you to plan the second part, which will be to lift the tout and deal with her. You know the rule that has never changed, Brian, even with this agreement with the Brits. Once a Volunteer is Green Booked no matter what happens. To give information to the enemy is treason, and that means a sentence of death.'

McNally knew what the Green Book said about informing. The book was in effect the book of rules that volunteers agreed to.

'You can tell the boys in the kitchen the first part of the operation for now. I'll be in touch to brief them for the second part, but make sure they're aware of the secrecy needed.'

John Jo reached into his pocket once more, then handed a photo to McNally.

'That's a photo of the old woman. She should be easy to recognise and the fact she'll have a walking stick should help. Tell your boys not to fuck this up. You can tell them that this operation is on the instructions of the Army Council if you need to impress upon them how important it is.'

'Don't worry, John Jo. The lads are the best I have. They have done a few jobs, and they know how to keep their mouths shut.'

John Jo stood to leave, and McNally showed him to the door, shaking his hand before he walked away from the house. He turned left to walk slowly back towards the Falls Road where he would get one of the many black cabs. As he walked away from the house, he spotted the same youth still sitting on the wall, ever watching.

□

CHAPTER 7

ISRAEL

The hotel lobby was bright, yet cool. Reece and Mary had gone for a swim in the early morning light, then walked hand in hand along the seafront promenade, watching the waves crash against the shore. It reminded Reece of his early morning walks in Malta. The water at that time of day was cool rather than cold, refreshing, clearing the mind of sleep and the extra alcohol they had in their system after staying up late in the hotel bar. The pain in his leg had been easing. *It must be the swimming, which was a form of physiotherapy*, thought Reece. Although, now and then, he could also feel a stab of the shrapnel in his right shoulder, an old wound that would never leave him.

Palo had sent him a text to say that they would be picked up at 11 a.m. This gave them enough time to return to the hotel and enjoy the superb continental breakfast, before taking a pot of tea to the lobby where they would wait. At five minutes to eleven Palo walked in, followed by an elderly white-haired man who, although slightly stooped, walked with determination. They stood to greet the two men. Reece had told Mary as much as he knew about Jacob Lavyan, a hero of the country he'd served all his life. Palo introduced Mary and Reece to the man standing by his side. The man, who wore large, black-framed glasses, put out his hand for Reece to shake. He carried a plastic shopping bag which he set on the floor beside the table.

'Shalom, David. It has been a long time, too long for friends,' Lavyan said, smiling.

'And Shalom to you, Miss Mary. I'm pleased to meet you also.'

Lavyan's grip was firm, showing there was still strength there if he needed it.

Jacob Lavyan had aged well, thought Reece. He had more hair than Reece and despite his age his brown eyes were clear and alert, his body looked strong, and he carried very little excess weight. Reece could see the muscles in his arms that filled the linen grey jacket he was wearing. He could imagine those arms around the neck of his enemies.

'Would you like some tea?' asked Mary, inviting the two men to sit down.

'That would be lovely, Miss Mary,' replied Lavyan his face beaming.

Mary waved for the waiter to bring two more cups and some more tea.

'You have come a long way, David. When I was told you were coming and the reason you would be here, I knew I should meet you once again,' said Lavyan.

'It's good to see you again, Jacob, although under the circumstances they're not the ones I would wish for.'

The tea came and Mary poured for everyone.

'Have you always lived in Israel?' she asked.

Reece noticed how Jacob smiled when Mary spoke to him.

'Yes. I was born in Israel on a Kibbutz. My parents were Russian immigrants who came to Palestine in 1928. My life has been Israel and everything I've done is for the land of my birth. My parents instilled in me a passion for what is right in life, and I've always tried to live up to that passion.'

He had given more in his answer than Mary had expected.

'Anyway, we should be going soon. It will take just over an hour to get to Jerusalem. But before we leave, I have something for you both,' said Lavyan before reaching into the shopping bag at his feet. He removed a boxed bottle of twelve-year-old Bushmills whisky, which he handed to Reece.

'I remember the headache I had the next day when you introduced me to this in Belfast, David. Still your favourite I'm told. I can tell you. It was difficult to find in Tel Aviv.'

'Your sources and memory are correct, Jacob. When we open it later, I'll toast your good health.' Reece smiled.

'Ah, you'll have to drink with Palo and Mary as I'm under doctor's orders.' Jacob winked.

Reaching into the bag once more, he pulled out two polished white pebbles and sat them on the table. Mary looked at them a slightly confused look on her face.

'Let me explain. These are very important stones. In Israel, it's a tradition that we don't leave flowers on a grave, so everything that's left is of equal value. It is our way of paying our respect that we leave a pebble, thereby letting the family know in what high esteem the person in the grave is thought of, and to let them know that we've been there.'

Mary lifted one of the pebbles and, holding it up to the light, she could see the sun shining off it and felt its smoothness.

'A wonderful way to pay respect. I feel honoured that you've brought these for us. I was wondering about stopping somewhere for flowers, but I think this is a much better idea.'

Reece lifted the other pebble and put it in his pocket. He took the now empty bag and placing the whisky back inside, walked over to reception, leaving it there until they returned.

Palo drove the air-conditioned car with Lavyan beside him and Mary and Reece in the back. During the drive, Mary seemed very excited, like a little child at seeing more of the country than just the sand and sea. Speaking like a true tourist she was asking the standard questions. 'What's the weather like all year round?' 'What's the history?' 'What's the local food like?' Lavyan and Palo answered every question both knowing that the questions were her way of distracting them from why they were here. Ever since the day Reece had first approached Mary to recruit her as his agent inside the IRA, he knew they'd both lived with danger and death in their lives. Reece knew that the death of the woman whose grave they were now going to visit had been felt a lot harder by Mary than she was letting on. That was one of the reasons he'd made the decision to retire now. They both had seen enough of death and had been too close to it for some time. The drive out of Tel Aviv and onto the motorway to Jerusalem had taken them through built-up suburbs to the valleys and hills surrounding the city then into the green countryside. This surprised Reece, as he'd expected the land to be like Malta, with little vegetation and brown dusty ground. Instead, olive, cypress, and eucalyptus trees filled the scenery with lush green grass. Now and then, Lavyan would point out a house or a hill. 'The prime minister has a summer house there. My family would picnic in those trees occasionally.' Reece could see Mary was hanging on to Jacob's every word. Like Reece, she was soaking in everything, and he knew they would talk about this experience many times in the future, over bottles of wine back home in Malta.

Now and then Palo would chip in with memories of his own, indicating where he had grown up and where his family lived. Where the best seafood restaurants were, and the best place to drink coffee. The time passed quickly, and now Palo took the scenic route through the hills. As they came round a bend, a few miles ahead, they could see on a plateau the outline of the city of Jerusalem. The dome of the Temple Mount shining in the sun like a giant upside-down orange. The city, half modern, half ancient, with its famous walls, and places of importance to Judaism, Christianity, and Islam did not disappoint from its description in the brochures. It took the breath away when seen for the first time.

'It's beautiful,' said Mary.

'It is,' replied Palo.

'It's a World Heritage site,' said Jacob. 'There's a mixture of Jews, Muslims, and Christians living there. And despite all its wars and troubles, is still sacred to all. We will take you there later. The old city has the most important sites to visit. Temple Mount, the Western Wall, the Church of the Holy Sepulchre, the Dome of the Rock, and the al-Aqsa Mosque to name the most important ones. The city has something for everyone old and new.'

As the city came closer into view, Reece could understand why it was held in such high esteem by so many religions and peoples. The whole view expanded across the horizon, seeming to rise above them into the blue sky.

'First, we pay our respects,' said Palo, as he took a side road to the left that ran parallel with the city.

The road now twisted around the mountain, winding higher, and higher. Reece could see many cars parked on one side of the road, narrowing the space to drive. The grey tarmac seemed to reflect the sun's light, and he noticed that Palo and Jacob had put on their sunglasses. Eventually they came to gates in the middle of a large wall with the words Mount Herzl National Cemetery written in large gold letters. Two soldiers with automatic rifles checked Palo's documents before they waved them through to park up near a large modern building.

'This is Mount Herzl, our national cemetery, named after Theodor Herzl, who we consider to be the father of Israel. It is also known as the Mountain of Memory. He is buried here on the top of the mountain. That building ahead is the Herzl Museum, which you can visit later if you wish, but first let us go to find Rachel. We will find her grave in the Military Cemetery,' said Jacob.

The heat outside the car was cooled by the breeze that seemed to surround the mountain. It was just after midday, and the sun was almost above them. They followed Palo who led them through another set of gates. In front of them was a large black marble stone raised on a mound with gold letters in Hebrew.

'That is where Herzl is buried. The letters just say Herzl, and they're engraved on all four sides of the stone,' said Jacob.

Palo led them down a path. Reece could see that the graveyard was on separate levels. As they walked down each level with similar headstones, on each level, the shapes changed.

As they reached the first level, Palo said, 'The leaders and prime ministers of Israel are buried here,' he said, pointing to the gravestones.

Looking across the ground, Reece could see how the spot had been chosen for its significance of looking down on the city of Jerusalem below them. They walked a short distance down to the next level. Again, Palo stopped, and pointing at the headstones, he spoke once more.

'Here are the graves of the heroes and military personnel who gave their lives to the state of Israel. Along this front row is where Rachel is buried among the heroes. Please follow me.'

The headstones were all the same and as they passed them, Reece and Mary could see the pebbles and small stones that had been left by those who knew them in life.

Then they reached the marble headstone carved with the name in black letters that stood out against the white: Rachel Cohen in Hebrew and English, with the Star of David above her name. They stood facing the grave and Reece had a sudden flash of the memory of seeing the woman he knew as Anna for the first time as she'd walked out of the hotel lift in Malta. He remembered the dress that showed the outline of her body as she moved, the smile, and the laughter she could bring to any situation. In one word, she'd been beautiful.

'If you would like to place your pebbles now? Place them here on the top,' said Lavyan.

Reece took the pebble from his pocket and, standing beside Mary, they both placed them on the top of the headstone. As they did, the cool breeze seemed to blow slightly harder. Reece felt it was Anna passing by saying 'hello,' saying 'thank you.'

'Would you like to say a few words of remembrance or anything? The prayer to the dead, which is a Jewish right, has been said, but if you like I could repeat it now on your behalf,' said Palo.

'Yes, that would be good. Thank you. Please do. Then I would like to say something and maybe you would too, Mary?'

'I have a short quote I know if that's all right?' answered Mary.

Palo nodded and, stepping closer to the headstone, he turned to face them, the city of Jerusalem in the background behind them.

'I shall speak in English, which I hope is acceptable to you as I'm sure it will be to Rachel and to our God,' said Palo.

'God, full of mercy, who dwells in the heights, provide a sure rest upon the wings of the Divine Presence, within the range of the holy, pure, and glorious, whose shining resemble the sky's, to the soul of Rachel, daughter of Israel, for a charity was given to the memory of her soul. Therefore, the Master of Mercy will protect her forever, from behind the hiding of his wings, and will tie her soul with the rope of life. The Everlasting is her heritage, and she shall rest peacefully upon her lying place, and let us say: Amen.'

They all replied Amen. Reece stepped forward, taking the same position that Palo had now vacated, and faced the way Palo had. Now, for the first time, he could see the city and looking at it, he thought, *this was a peaceful place to be if you were dead.*

'Thank you both for allowing Mary and me to be here today and thank you for those words, Palo. When I was in Special Branch in Northern Ireland during an operational break, I took a walk through a graveyard in the area I was working. I memorised the wording that I saw on a gravestone, and I think the words mean the same to everyone no matter where you are or what God you worship, and I hope you, and Rachel will understand them.'

'Think of me as you walk by, for where you stand so once did I, where I am now so you will be. Prepare yourself to follow me.'

Reece stood to the side to let Mary take up the same spot he'd spoken from. He could see the tears on her cheek, which she didn't try to hide or wipe away.

'Like David, I'm proud to be here, and proud to have known Rachel, or Anna as I knew her, even if it was only for a short time, but I thought of this quote while we were driving here, and I think it says exactly what we all want to say.'

'To live in hearts we leave behind is not to die.'

Mary touched the top of the headstone, then turning, took Reece's hand, and with her other hand wiped the tears from her cheek.

'Thank you for being here with us. It's made the whole experience more bearable. It's a beautiful place, so peaceful and quiet, even though the city isn't far away. I know Rachel is where she would have wanted to be. Back home among her people in the soil she worked so hard to protect,' said Reece as he shook both men's hands.

The breeze seemed to pass by them stronger again. Reece looked around, trying to take in the whole picture to lock it in his memory. The clear blue sky, the olive, and citrus trees, the green grass, the white headstones in rows standing strong against the world. Like the graveyard he'd walked through all those years ago, each one telling a story of a person's life in a few words, but in each, everyone was the same, everyone was dead, everyone was with their god or none. Their stories told their journey for now, finished.

Reece knew Mary well enough to know she'd want to go to the city and find a good cup of coffee and maybe something to eat. As they left the mountain, the road rose gently towards the city of Jerusalem, and it seemed to be bright white in the sunlight with the buildings rising above. It was obvious Palo had driven here many times using the streets off the main central road. The buildings were modern to begin with, then changed to those of older brick, most painted limestone white with closed shutters against the heat.

Entering the old city, Reece could see heavily armed soldiers patrolling in pairs, ensuring the safety of the citizens, *Jew, Muslim, Christian, or no particular faith,* thought Reece. It reminded him of his own days of service in Northern Ireland. keeping the two communities apart while trying to protect the innocent.

In a small square, Palo found the parking space he was looking for. Leaving the car, they walked the short distance to sit at a table outside one of the cafés that surrounded the square.

'This café is run by a friend and serves the best Arabic coffee in Israel,' said Palo.

The square was small and the buildings, at least three storeys high, had closed shuttered windows blocking the fierceness of the afternoon sun. It felt cool with a gentle breeze, and Reece could smell bread and coffee in the air. The coffee and pastries were as good as Palo had said.

'It's beautiful,' said Mary, looking around the square. 'It reminds me of some of the places in Valletta.'

'I don't know much about Malta other than what I saw when I was there, but I'll go there again when I'm not working,' said Palo.

'I've been there a few times. As you say, Miss Mary, it does remind me of this city. Especially the old part,' said Lavyan.

'You both should come and visit us, and stay for a while,' said Reece.

'It's a deal, but now let us show you around the old city, then we'll drop you back at your hotel,' replied Lavyan.

For the next few hours, that was exactly what they did. They visited all the holy sites and because of the identities of their companions they were allowed to go right to the heart of some, passing the guards who would normally stop the everyday visitors. Jacob and Palo were better than any tour guide, not only telling the history, but the secrets only they knew.

'The Temple Mount with its golden dome is one of the holiest sites,' explained Jacob. 'It has been fought over for centuries by many religions.'

The site that struck Mary the most, was when they came to the Church of the Holy Sepulchre with its two blue domes. Again, Jacob explained:

'The church was built over what your Christian faith believes is the site of the crucifixion of Jesus and then the tomb where he was buried.'

Again, because of whom they were with, they were able to go down into the area of the tomb which, having no natural light, was lit by many candles.

'It's so quiet and still,' said Mary, and tears rolled down her cheeks once more. Reece put his arm around her. Mary was one of the bravest and strongest women he knew, but she had a sentimental side to her he'd seen a few times before.

'Would you like to light a candle?' asked Jacob.

'Yes please,' said Mary.

Mary and Reece both lit candles, placing them in the holders against the wall, lighting up the small corner where they stood.

'I'm sorry about the tears. I felt so many memories here. They just seemed to come,' said Mary.

'The tomb affects many people, Miss Mary. I'm sure you won't be the first or last person to feel this way,' said Lavyan.

They left the church and the old city and drove down the coast. The city sat on a plateau in the Judaean Mountains between the Mediterranean and the Dead Sea. Reece tried to imagine what it was like to travel to from the days of Jesus, the Crusades, and right up to modern times when it was still being fought over.

This time, the journey seemed to take a little longer, because Palo had taken a route away from the motorways. At times they had to stop on the narrow roads to let other vehicles pass, and on two occasions having to let shepherds guide their sheep across the road in front of them.

Yet again, the land reminded Reece so much of Malta, and he started to feel a need to get back there, to what was now his home of peace and rest. The next few days, Reece, and Mary were left to explore on their own. Reece hired a car to drive wherever the mood took them and on two occasions had to turn back into Israel when they came to the border crossing with Jordan. They visited the main cities on the coast and in the evenings walked hand in hand through the streets and along the seafront of Tel Aviv. The night before they were due to leave, they dined at one of the many seafood restaurants near the hotel. The wound on Reece's leg had almost healed. The swimming and walking acted like the hands of a physiotherapist. He was taking fewer pain killers, even for the pain in his shoulder. Reece had noticed that Mary seemed more relaxed as well. She was laughing more. Her eyes had some of the old sparkle back. The sparkle he'd only seen when they walked and swam in Malta. He believed this was down to the combination of the trip and the fact that she now knew he wouldn't be going back to the old ways. They were halfway through their second bottle of Chablis, the dry cold wine that had, over the years, become a favourite of both when dining at a special place with special meaning. Reece felt the time was right and even though he didn't have a ring, he knew this was the woman he wanted to spend the rest of his life with.

'Mary?' he said, as he took her hand across the table.

'Yes?'

'I know this is maybe not the right time and place, and maybe I should wait until we are back in Malta, but somehow, I feel it should be now. You know I love you, and I know we've been through our fair share of things together, but I want to spend the rest of my life with you.'

'I want that too, darling.'

Reece smiled before he continued.

'What I'm saying is, I want you to marry me. I want to commit my life to you if you'll have me. Will you marry me?'

For a second, he could see those sparkling eyes start to well up with emotion. Mary stood and rushing round the table she just about gave him time to stand before she was in his arms, kissing him. When their lips separated, Reece held her at arm's length.

'I take that is a 'yes' then?'

'Yes, oh yes, yes,' she answered before kissing him once more.

'Where's my ring? And why didn't you get down on one knee?' She teased with a smile.

'What? With these knees? You would have to help me up, and as for the ring. I know a little jeweller in Valletta that we can visit when we get back.'

They didn't wait for dessert, instead walking along the promenade.

They could hear the sea as the waves crashed onto the shore. Above the sound, Reece could feel the buzz from the phone in his pocket.

Checking the text, it was from Jacob Lavyan. Before you leave tomorrow, can we've a quick coffee in the morning, just the two of us?

He replied yes that he'd see him in the hotel lobby at eleven. Once again, he felt his past interfering in his future, but he wasn't going to let it interfere tonight. This was his night, and he was going to spend it with the woman he loved.

'Who was that?' asked Mary.

'Just Jacob. He wants me to have coffee with him in the morning.'

'Why?'

Reece could see the concern in her face.

'Maybe to say goodbye and hopefully with another bottle of Bush? But don't worry, I'm not going back on my word. Those days are over for good. I just want to get back to our room and work off some of that food.'

Her smile was there again, but not as strong as the one when she'd said yes.

'But what about your knee?'

'As I said, you'll have to help me.'

Their flight wasn't until 8 p.m. so they had a full day to do a little more sightseeing and shopping. Reece had left Mary doing just that when he returned to the hotel lobby for eleven and his coffee with Jacob Lavyan.

He had ordered a pot for two. It had just been placed on the table when the old agent came through the doors, alone this time.

'Shalom, good morning, David. I hope you're well and ready for your journey home?'

'Shalom Jacob. Yes, thank you and you. Are you well?'

Both men shook hands. 'Yes David. For an old man, I'm very well on this beautiful day. I see you have coffee. Excellent, this will be my third of the day already. When I worked in operations, I became a coffee addict, having to keep awake for long hours.'

'I'm the same, Jacob, and for the same reason.'

Both men sat and Reece poured the two cups, leaving it black for each to decide on milk and sugar.

'So, Jacob, what are we here for?'

'Ah, the policeman is still there in you, the question right up front.' Lavyan poured a little milk into his cup and took a sip before continuing.

'First. Thank you for seeing me. I know it's your last day and I'm sure you and Mary are busy with your last-minute shopping and packing.'

'I'll always make time for an old friend,' said Reece.

'That is why I'm here, David, because we are friends. We both live in a world where they are few and our enemies many. It is about one such enemy that I wish to talk to you and my story goes back to the time we met all those years ago.'

Reece poured a little milk into his own cup. The coffee was strong and from what he'd heard so far, he thought he was going to need it.

'You remember when I came to Belfast? Well, I had many meetings with your senior officers and MI5 at your headquarters. We discussed many things, mainly about how your terrorists were suspected of linking up with the ones from my part of the world here in the Middle East. We knew the IRA was getting weapons and training from the various Arab terrorist groups and countries. Indeed, you must remember the shiploads of weapons from Gaddafi in Libya? Your security people even captured one.'

Reece nodded as he remembered the capture. The Eksund ship was loaded with everything a terrorist army would need. He also remembered Sean Costello the man he'd shot dead in Manchester. His file showed that he'd trained as a sniper in the Bekaa Valley in Lebanon with other terrorist groups, mainly Arab.

'Before I arrived in Belfast for those meetings. I received a full briefing of my own from our analysts here in Tel Aviv and then from our staff at our embassy in Dublin. These briefings were mostly in general terms regarding the situation at the time. However, there was one piece of information I couldn't talk about at that time, because it would have put one of our own agents in danger and made the close relationship we had with the British government difficult.'

Reece sat forward in his chair. 'Can I stop you there, Jacob? As you know, I'm no longer an agent of the British government as you put it, and I don't want to be pulled back into anything. Last night I asked Mary to marry me, and she accepted. We both want to live out the rest of our days in peace. Having been through such a life, I'm sure you understand.'

Lavyan poured himself more coffee and without adding any more milk took a sip. Smiling, his eyes were full of laughter.

'Congratulations, she seems a wonderful lady. Do not worry my friend. I totally understand what you mean, and I would never interfere with your plans. What I'm telling you hopefully might never bother you again, but I believe you should know, if only to protect yourself and Mary, in what I hope will be those peaceful years to come that you talk about. So, please hear what I have to say. It may be to your advantage.'

Hearing the word protect, Reece could feel his pulse quicken. The word usually meant trouble, and he wanted to avoid anything to do with protect or trouble.

'What do you mean?'

'As I said, I received briefings about the situation in Northern Ireland at that time. You may not know this but we, the Mossad, had agents who were members of the IRA especially in the border area of South Armagh where we had a particularly good one. The IRA man was part of a unit operating in South Armagh and he originally came from Crossmaglen but was living in Dundalk with others on the run from the North's security forces. For security reasons and to protect the source, I never knew his name.'

Lavyan stopped to take another sip of his coffee. Reece was not surprised that Mossad had agents within the IRA. If the terrorist organisation was working with the enemies of Israel, then it would be common sense to recruit agents within those organisations.

'Why should this affect me now?' asked Reece.

'Maybe it doesn't, but just in case, I think you should know what some of the reports mentioned, from that one agent. As I said the agent originally came from Crossmaglen and I need not tell you how we recruited him. You yourself, having done the same job at one time, would know only too well the how's and whys of the recruitment process along with the running of the agents once they're recruited.'

Reece merely nodded in response.

'The information this agent passed on alleged that a senior officer in the RUC Special Branch was working with the Provisional IRA. He was passing them information and protecting their people from capture by disrupting the British operations against them, especially in the border area.'

Reece continued to listen without interruption as he'd been taught many years before, to let the person across the table tell all before asking any questions. His stomach was turning. He could feel the anger inside him start to rise.

'We were only allowed to operate inside the Republic of Ireland. Our country had an agreement to operate jointly with the UK against the same enemies where there's a danger to both our peoples, but to operate only within the boundaries of each other's country with their permission. Our embassy in Dublin, like your embassies around the world, retains an intelligence-gathering remit. In that remit, especially during the terrorist war you were involved in, we targeted those people we were able to identify as being involved. Of course, our interest was, as you know, of any connection between the Irish terrorists and our Arab enemies.'

Reece was pleased to hear Lavyan call it a war and not the Troubles as the politicians labelled it. It was a war, not a simple case of trouble, with thousands being killed, and maimed.

Lavyan continued, 'So it was that our people in Dublin were able to target and in some cases recruit as agent members of the IRA living in the South of Ireland. This man was part of a vicious unit based in Dundalk. I won't say how we recruited him or why he agreed to work with us, but the information he provided we passed on to your security people. But, like all intelligence agencies, to protect our agent we kept back any information that would have exposed him to the other terrorists he was working with. Anyway, he gave us some information which helped with the interception of IRA operations, mostly those involving the movement of explosives across the border for use in the north and the British mainland. To our knowledge, he never took part in any murders or directed attacks on the security forces, but as you know, you can never trust an agent fully. Then later, he was able to provide briefings on the progress of the peace process negotiations and the thinking at the top of the terrorist organisation which we did pass on to London.'

'Trust an agent, tell me about it.' Reece smiled.

Jacob waved to the waiter walking through the lobby.

'Can I have a pot of tea with some fruit please?' he asked the waiter. 'What about you, David? Would you like some tea?'

'No thanks. I'll stick to the coffee.'

'Please bring some fresh coffee for my friend.'

When the waiter left, Jacob continued with his story.

'I cannot be specific on most of the intelligence this man brought to the table as I wasn't working in Dublin, but my briefing before I went to Belfast included the information that this Special Branch Officer was working with the IRA in the border area. The only thing our agent could tell us was that he held the rank of Detective Chief Inspector and was based for some time at Gough Barracks in Armagh City and his area of operation was the Southern Region of the province of Northern Ireland.'

'Can you tell me when this was? It might help me identify who he was,' asked Reece.

'My visit was in 1984, so it would have been around that time. The agent had been working for two years before then.'

It was a long time ago, and even though Reece tried to remember names and faces, the one thing he did know was that there was a frequent turnover of SB personnel to protect them from discovery by the terrorists they were working against. He knew that at any one time there were four or five DCIs working in Gough Barracks, the old army base in the centre of Armagh City. Reece had worked there himself for six years when he was attached to the Tasking and Coordination Group South, TCG(S), with responsibility of working with other agencies in the covert operations in the south of the country.

The tea and coffee arrived, and Reece watched Lavyan cut an apple into wedges and take a bite of one, then sip his black tea. The light of the sun coming through the large windows at the front of the hotel was now casting shadows where they sat.

'So, what you're telling me is that this man was working with the IRA against us, and your people never told our people?'

'Exactly. We thought it was too dangerous for our agent who might be discovered and tortured and murdered by the IRA. You must think of the kind of damage that could have done to our relationship with many countries not just in Ireland but Britain and the USA. The Americans at that time were supporters of the Republican movement in your country, mainly because of the Irish vote which a few presidents relied upon to get elected.'

'So why tell me this now?'

Jacob took another bite of the apple wedge and chewed for a few seconds before he replied.

'A few reasons, David. We know because of your background, and because of what you've done for your country and ours, you'll understand the secrecy in having to protect this information. The agent, although still alive, is no longer active, so he cannot give us any more information. The main reason I'm telling you this is that if you're ever in your own country again, you need to be aware of the danger that this Special Branch man, if he's still alive, could bring to you. Our people in this country believe you've done us a great service when you killed the Arab in London, and the respect we know you have for Israel. Therefore, we should let you have this information for your own protection in the future. So, what I'm telling you is, for now, for your ears only. Your people in London and Belfast have not been told, but if they're as good as we think they are, they must know about this man, and for their own reasons they choose not to do anything for now.'

'I'm finished with all that now. As you know, I've retired from SG9 and MI6 and I intend to go back to Malta tonight, to marry Mary, and relax with a book by the sea.'

Lavyan leant forward and smiled.

'I'm eighty-three David. I retired twenty years ago from the Mossad. Since then, I've run my own business still working with the various Israeli Intelligence organisations in a consultancy capacity. My work advises business groups around the world on their internal and personal security. Have you ever heard of the External Relations Department, the ERD?'

Reece shook his head.

'It was formed by Yitzhak Rabin in 1974 after several failed operations by our intelligence agencies with a remit to oversee future operations as a sort of watchdog and report back to him. The ERM has several departments, one of which is the Foreign Liaison, which works with Israeli military attaches and other IDF personnel working overseas. I'm the current head of that department within the ERM. I find I'm still contacted by Mossad and Amman when they need advice, or the use of my many contacts throughout the world when it's needed for the benefit or protection of Israel. What I'm saying David is this. Now that you're outside the shadows, as we say about someone like yourself with a past in the undercover intelligence world, you may find that your own country in the future may contact you when they have need of you. I think of you as a friend, but also someone I could contact if I needed your help or advice. You would be just one more of the large number of people in the world I could approach if I need help. The same goes for you, if you ever need my help or that of my organisation, we'd be here for you.'

Reece took his time before answering and filled his cup with more of the Arabic coffee. After taking a sip, he sat back, and tried to relax, taking in what Jacob had just told him?

'I appreciate your trust in me, and all you've told me. It goes without saying, that what you've said will remain confidential between us. As I've said, I really do want to retire from it all, but of course I would be foolish not to accept your offer of help if ever I should need it. So, in that context, you can come to me should you ever need my help. After all, what are true friends for?'

Lavyan's eyes lit up with a smile as he reached across the table to touch Reece's hand.

'Good, good. We are like the film Godfather, when they say I might need you to do something for me one day and that day might never come.' He laughed.

'Just don't ever let Mary know. I've made her a promise and I intend to try to keep it.'

As if on cue, Reece saw Mary come through the hotel doors into the lobby and looking around she smiled when she saw Reece. Both men stood to greet her.

Taking her hand, Jacob bowed, and kissed it.

'Shalom, Miss Mary, and congratulations. It's wonderful news.'

'Thank you. You are the first to know.' She smiled. 'So, what else have you two been talking about?'

'Would you like some tea or coffee?' asked Reece as Mary put down two shopping bags and sat beside them.

'No, thank you. And don't try to change the subject, Joseph.'

Both men laughed. 'We've been mostly catching up on old times,' said Reece as he looked across at Lavyan. Knowing that wouldn't be enough to satisfy her, he continued,

'Jacob has been telling me that, like me, he's retired from the spy business. He now works in his own right as a consultant to big business around the world.'

'Consulting on what?' asked Mary.

'Mostly on how organisations can beef up their security systems. From protecting their buildings and assets to the people who work for them,' answered Lavyan.

'And he's offered you a job, I suppose?' said Mary, looking Reece in the eye.

'No, not as such. I would just be his contact in Malta,' answered Reece.

'I totally understand your worry, Miss Mary, but I'll never ask David to go back to his old ways. I know only too well what it means to leave all that behind. Like myself, David would only help me in a consultant capacity. I'm getting too old to be running around and I've built up a network of people I can trust around the world. Each one is first and foremost a friend, and I insist they're not connected to any government agency. I run a respectable business, and some of the people who ask my advice would insist that I'm not connected to any such government. David and I'll always be friends, and we'll always be there for each other as friends, and that goes for you too, Miss Mary. I hope we'll be friends. For now, I would hope I get an invitation to your wedding, but at my age, please don't wait too long.'

Mary relaxed. Sitting back in the chair, she smiled at both men.

'Of course, you're invited, and don't worry, when we get back to Malta, the first thing on the agenda is setting a date. I've already got a few things for the day, or should I say, the evening.' She winked at Reece as she lifted one of the bags but didn't open it, leaving it to both men's imaginations.

'I think you've made him blush, Miss Mary. I look forward to your invitation, then. But now, I must go.' He stood to leave.

'Can you not stay for lunch with us?' asked Reece.

'Yes, stay please,' said Mary.

'I would love to, but I have an engagement of my own. You have a lot to do before your flight, and I would fear that when we get talking, it would be a long lunch.' Lavyan laughed. 'But I promise I'll see you again. Maybe in Malta and we'll have that lunch together as old friends do? You take care of this lovely lady, David. She's very special.' He kissed Mary on both cheeks, then shook hands with Reece.

'Shalom, my friend. Until we meet again.'

'Don't worry, Jacob. I'll take care of her and enjoy doing it. Shalom, until we meet again.'

The old man left without looking back or waving, and Reece thought he had a lot more on his mind than what he'd discussed with him.

After lunch, the rest of the day was spent relaxing and packing the two cases, which, with Mary's shopping, were now a little heavier. Palo picked them up at seven for the short ride to the airport. He made little conversation. At the airport, he escorted them through security and into a private first-class lounge where they were treated like celebrities by the staff before they were escorted to their seats on the flight to Rome, which took off on schedule at 20.00hrs. They booked into the airport hotel and after a late dinner returned to their room before catching the early morning flight to Malta. By lunchtime the next day they were at the Villa Joseph in Quara and having unpacked took the short walk along the seafront to the little café on the hill, where they sat, and looked at the waves crashing on the rocks below.

It was a cold day, so Mary squeezed up close to Reece, putting her hand in his jacket pocket for warmth.

'You'll have to meet my mum. I'll give her a call later,' said Mary.

'How is she since her fall?'

'She's recovered well. She walks with a stick and now she's living at my house on the Lisburn Road. It's a lot easier to get into the city or to see her physio at the City Hospital.'

'Why don't we get her a flight out here for a few days and she can meet me in nicer weather and circumstances?'

'That's a great idea. I'll ask her.'

'How do you think she'll take to me, an ex-RUC Special Branch man? If she's as good a Catholic as you say, she won't be happy that I'm a divorced heathen with kids.'

'Oh, Joseph. Don't worry, she won't bite you. She hated my ex as she knew he beat me, so anything is better than that. Anyway, it's me you're marrying, not her.' She laughed.

'That's good news. I'm not into fighting with old ladies.'

'Even though it's cold, Joseph, I'd rather be here than anywhere else in the world.'

'Me too,' replied Reece. 'But we can't stay long. There's somewhere else we need to be.'

Mary sat up and turning looked into his eyes, slightly worried at what he was going to say, not sure what to expect. 'Where, Joseph?'

'This afternoon we've to go to a little jeweller's shop I know in Valetta.' He smiled.

'My ring, I almost forgot.' She kissed him. 'Let's go.'

CHAPTER 8

BELFAST

They had been watching her for an hour. In fact, they'd been watching her at the same time every day for a week. They had changed vehicles three times during that week to avoid being noticed. It was easy to follow the old woman, but boring for the two men watching her. Now, as Rosie Smith crossed the road at the end of Hugh Street and turned left onto the Lisburn Road, the two men in the white transit van watched once more. The old woman walked with the aid of a walking stick.

'What the fuck is all this about, Jimmy?' asked Frank.

'Don't ask me, I just do as I'm told. But it must be important, or Brian wouldn't have ordered us to do it. I thought we were two of his best. A couple of the kids could have done this. But ours is not to reason why.'

'Aye, I know, ours is but to do our die.' Frank laughed, which started off Jimmy, whose fat belly shook when he laughed.

Frank would be considered by some to be the better looking of the two. With his muscular body that showed time spent in the gym, and with the beginnings of a beard on his long face, he had his fair share of the opposite sex to play with. He started the engine as they watched a bus pass them, pulling into the stop where Rosie Smith always got on. They followed the bus, but both knew by now the routine, as it travelled down the Lisburn Road towards the city before turning into Sandy Row where the old woman always got off before entering the Food for the Day café, where she'd sit for an hour with two women friends, having a late breakfast before travelling back on the bus following the same route home. It always amazed Frank Walsh that these three old women could have so much to talk about and they each could eat a full Ulster Fry breakfast each day. Maybe it was their only meal of the day, but by the look of all three women and how they walked slowly, each with a large waistline, he could only believe that they also ate more when they got home. Having the walking stick, the old woman walked slower than the other two, who would walk in the opposite direction. Frank had always been careful with his weight and fitness. The way he looked at it, if he had to run, he could do, and he smiled to himself as he looked at Jimmy Bailey thinking if we must run Jimmy you're fucked. Rosie Smith had to cross the busy road to get to the bus stop on the other side and her return journey to Hugh Street. It was now 11 a.m. and her routine never varied. The traffic now was not as busy as the rush-hour two hours before. Once more Walsh started the engine, but this time, instead of following the old woman, he drove in the opposite direction to join the Grosvenor Road to its junction with the Falls Road. Turning left, he drove the final mile to Beechmount, where they parked around the corner before walking to the house and knocking the door of the home of the Belfast Officer Commanding the Real IRA, Brian McNally. Both men had been in the kitchen of the house when McNally had met with the man from South Armagh. They had heard a little of the conversation and after being briefed by McNally on the importance of doing a good job, they both felt they had. McNally answered the door and brought them through to the small kitchen at the back of the house.

'Everything OK, I hope?' he asked.

'Aye, boss, no problems,' replied Walsh.

McNally went to the cooker and, opening the oven, he put on oven gloves and took out a tray with a hot pizza on it and set it on a board on the kitchen table. Taking a circular pizza slicer, he cut the pizza up into triangles before placing two of the larger slices on a plate and setting it down in front of the two men.

'Help yourselves. I'm sure you're peckish.'

Both men sat at the table and took a slice.

McNally then filled two mugs of tea and set them in front of the men before joining them.

'Help yourselves to the milk and sugar. Now, fill me in on where we are?'

Both men were chewing the pizza, and it was Frank who spoke first, talking with his mouth half full, something his mother had told him not to do.

'Her routine is the same every day. Leaves home at the same time, then takes the bus to the café in Sandy Row. Meets up with two women friends, chats over a full Ulster then around eleven returns home by the same route she came.'

'Does she still use the walking stick?'

'Yes, she walks with a slight limp on her right side,' replied Walsh.

'What's this all about? Why all the interest in an old woman?' asked Jimmy.

'I know I've kept you in the dark, but that was for reasons of security. If you had been pulled in and questioned, the less you knew the better. You both have done a great job. Now, the time has come to move this operation to the next stage.'

Both men had finished eating, and in the quiet of the kitchen paid attention as their leader spoke. McNally told them the story of Mary McAuley and her betrayal of the Republican Movement with her Special Branch friend.

He elaborated how from her access to the senior people in the Provisional IRA during the war, then after the peace, she'd told her SB man the organisation's secrets.

'Fuck's sake, the bitch,' said Jimmy, interrupting.

'There's more, Jimmy. After the whole peace process thing and the Good Friday Agreement, she still gave information to the Brits. She might have gotten away with it if she'd not set up Sean Costello to be killed.'

Both men knew the story of Costello, who had been shot dead by the Brits in Manchester. They'd heard the rumour that he'd intended to kill the British prime minister, but he'd been shot down like a dog in the street.

His funeral had only taken place a few weeks ago, and he was buried as one of them, a member of the Real IRA.

'Are we sure she set Sean up?' asked Frank.

'Yes. he'd recognised her in Manchester, and she was with her SB friend. He was going to deal with her himself, but they got to him first.

But all that's in the past. The time has come for us to deal with her. This has been given to us by the Army Council. You two will play an important part in the operation. It's Wednesday now, tomorrow you'll nick a car and store it overnight, then on Friday you'll knock the old woman down with the car and burn it afterwards. After you get rid of the car, I'll see you in the Wolf Tone Club and brief you on what happens next. Everything will depend on how well you do the job in the next few days.'

Frank thought of the words once more, *Ours is not to reason why, ours is but to do and die.* Still, he had to ask why. 'Who is this old woman and why do we have to do this to her?'

McNally knew one of the men might ask, and he didn't want to use his position in the organisation to threaten them into doing something they were not happy with, but he'd picked these two men for a reason.

'I thought one of you might ask. I picked you two because you're a team and because of the jobs you've done together before. You always do the job well, you know how to keep your mouth shut, and the fact that this is being sanctioned by the Army Council, I had to use my best people. We've looked at this woman who, I can now tell you, is the mother of Mary McAuley.'

Both men sat up at this information, keeping silent to let their leader talk further.

'We have an agent in the City Hospital where the old woman goes for her physio. The house she lives in on the Lisburn Road belongs to her daughter. We have looked at finding McAuley but with no luck. We think she might be in England. So, to get her back, the plan is to knock down her mother with a stolen car which will look like it's been driven by joy riders who have nicked it. Whether you kill her or seriously injure her in the process, when you do hit her, it will be enough to bring McAuley back here. When she does come back, we'll lift her to answer for her crimes. Are you both OK with that?'

Both men looked at each other before nodding in return.

'Will there be any kickback from the Provos?' asked Jimmy.

'No. They have already been told we intend to make McAuley pay for her treachery. Don't forget Sean Costello's brother Paul is an MLA at Stormont. They won't want anything done that might jeopardise their cosy relationship with the Brits. That's why it must look like a genuine accident. How we deal with the daughter is another matter. For now, you just need to work to my plan a bit at a time. The final part of dealing with her will be in the Republic, not in the north, so therefore not interfering with their fucking peace process.'

Again, both men nodded their understanding.

'Good. Now go home, get some rest. Nick the car and store it for Friday morning. Stay away from the bars and clubs until this is over. The part you're playing is most important. There will be further things for you to do down the road. Keep the van, we'll need it again.'

When both men had gone, McNally left the house, and walked to the main Falls Road. He used a phone box to call a number in the Republic of Ireland and briefed the man with a South Armagh accent to expect his package soon.

CHAPTER 9

MALTA

Valletta, when you drive along the coast and the sun shines on the city from the sea, is like a pink cloud rising. Sparkling across the harbour from Sliema, the city shone in the midday sun. Reece enjoyed driving at this time of day with the air con on, when they were in the hot summer season, but now they were in what some would call winter. Although it was still warm, it wasn't needed. The fact that the traffic drove on the same side of the road as he drove in England and Northern Ireland made it even more enjoyable, not having to worry what way to go when roundabouts came. Mary was, as usual, quiet while he drove, just wanting to be lost in her own thoughts and watching the beautiful world go by. The radio was on the local station. Radio Malta played music they both enjoyed. Reece drove around the inner harbour and entered the one-way system of the city, before finding a parking space in one of the car parks outside the city walls.

'When we get the ring, can we find somewhere overlooking the harbour? I would like to celebrate with a glass of champagne,' suggested Mary.

'No problem. I think I know one or two places that would hit the spot.'

They walked hand in hand up one of the streets that led to the city centre and the long main street of the inner city. The street through the centre of the city went from the main entrance gate across to the city walls to the World War Two Military Museum. Where they were going was almost in the middle: a small jeweller's shop, just off the main central Victoria square. Mary took her time. The small, tanned man behind the counter smiled while he showed her trays of rings, none showing a price. Mary almost picked up one from the first tray but looked at three more before returning to the first tray and lifting the ring she'd seen before. She tried it on. It fitted perfectly, which to her was another sign it was the right one.

'Oh Joseph. I love this one. What do you think?'

Reece didn't care if she liked it. He was happy if she was happy.

'It looks great on your finger.'

The ring had a round sapphire with a diamond on either side.

'It might be expensive,' she said.

'If you feel it's the one for you, then you should have it. You like it, I like it, and I would rather you had something you'd seen and picked, than something I picked that was wrong for you. Let's get this one and go celebrate.'

The small man smiled as Mary handed him the ring.

'I'll take this one.'

'Does madam want to wear it now?' asked the small man.

'No. Can you put it in a nice box, please?' she replied.

'Are you sure you don't want it now?' asked Reece.

'No, Joseph. I want you to do it right.' She smiled.

Reece understood and paying for the ring they walked back down the street they'd come up to the walls of the harbour looking towards Sliema and the harbour mouth looking out to the sea. At the wall, Reece turned towards Mary.

'I guess this is right. You know I love you, and I want to make this commitment to you to spend the rest of my life with you.' Getting down on one knee and taking her left hand he slipped the ring onto her finger. He could see the tears start to stream down her cheeks.

'Oh yes, Joseph. I do. I love you.'

They kissed and hugged and stopped a passing tourist to ask her to take a photo of them on Reece's mobile.

'We have this photo, our moment in time. I'm so happy Joseph.'

'Now that we are committed to each other, and you have the ring to prove it. I want you to call me David. It is my real name, after all, Joseph is in the past and David is our future.'

'OK, agreed. Now, David, where are we going for that glass of champagne? Then I really must call my mother.'

'And I suppose we should bring her out here to help us celebrate.'

'Oh, David, I really do love you.'

□

CHAPTER 10

BELFAST

The theft of the car was easy. As he always did, Frank Walsh just went for a walk around the Ballymurphy estate, to choose the car he'd take later. Then that night he'd return and using his two-foot-long thin metal ruler, he would put pressure on the side window, slide down the ruler, and press the release button to open the door. Before he reached that stage, however, he'd use the electronic device he bought on the Internet, which would deactivate the car alarm. He would then use a different switch on the same device, which, with a car such as the Vauxhall Vectra would overrule the electric key card, allowing him to start the engine and drive away.

During the terrorist war, the Provisional IRA had made it a kneecapping offence to steal cars in West Belfast without their permission. He had taken a bad beating, years before, for just doing a lookout for a friend who stole an old banger, so they could scream around the estates and do handbrake turns. His friend had not been so lucky. The Provos had shot him in both knees, leaving him to die in the alleyway after one of the bullets had ricocheted and nicked his femoral artery. Since the Good Friday Agreement, kneecappings were out, but steal the wrong car, one that belonged to a connected member of the Republican movement, and a beating from a couple of its hoods could do just as much damage as a handgun. Now Frank always made sure of the people he stole from, making sure they would do him no more harm than make a claim on their insurance. From his connections in the estate, he was able to establish that the red Vectra outside 94 Ballymurphy Road was just what he was looking for. He left it until 2 a.m. on Thursday morning before he was dropped off by Jimmy Bailey, who drove the transit van slowly past number 94, then turned at the top of the road before parking to take up the job of lookout. He flashed the lights twice to let Walsh know it was good to go.

Frank listened. It was quiet, no traffic or people. A couple of houses had their bedroom lights on, with curtains pulled, none overlooking his approach to the drive with the car he was going to steal. He had checked that number 94 had no outside lights or CCTV during his walk earlier in the day. Now working in the dark, he was in the car and driving it down the Ballymurphy Road with Jimmy in the transit covering his back within five minutes. They drove out of the estate and, taking the main roads, parked the car safely in a lock-up garage on the Andersonstown Estate. Both men were home safely in their own beds before 3 a.m.

The next day, Thursday afternoon, Walsh, and Bailey returned to the garage. They had picked up a set of number plates which would refer to another red Vauxhall Vectra – one that hadn't been stolen. They switched the plates on the car they'd taken from 94 Ballymurphy Road. Anyone checking out the registration would find that the car was clean. Both men cleaned the Vectra, making sure they'd left nothing that would identify them. Everything was set for Friday morning when an old lady might have a last day on earth. They locked up the garage and took the transit for a drive round the estate checking for any security forces surveillance teams; they saw nothing.

'Well, that's that sorted for tomorrow, Jimmy. Let's call it a day and get a bite of lunch.'

'Sounds good to me. I'm starving. You are paying?'

'You can fuck off. I paid last time.'

'Worth a try.' Jimmy laughed.

CHAPTER 11

SANDY ROW, BELFAST

Frank Walsh had driven round twice before he could find a space facing the right direction from the café. It was 10:50 and if everything went according to plan, the old woman would be coming out of the café soon. Walsh still didn't feel comfortable about having to knock down the old woman. Shooting at soldiers or police or blowing them up with booby traps was a totally different story, but trying to kill an old woman just didn't seem right. But an order was an order, and the order had come from the top man in Belfast. He just had to keep thinking to himself that it was justified. Bringing a traitor to justice was enough to satisfy his worry. He had been careful to look for any traffic wardens. Belfast City Hall loved the money that they brought in with their tickets. He knew the way they operated, checking the parking spaces over the lunchtime period when people were desperate to find somewhere to park while nipping in for sandwiches or lunch. And of course, it was one of those bloody wet Belfast days. The rain couldn't make up its mind whether to come down hard and fast or slow and steady. At least this might keep the traffic wardens away. He had seen none and now that he was parked up; he had a good view of the doorway of the café. The traffic was light, but he had to be sure of the distance he'd have to cover. He knew where she'd cross the road would be slippery. It would be difficult to keep control of the car when he hit her, he didn't want to end up crashing into another car and stuck in the road, with police, and emergency services coming down on him. It had to be quick and clean to get away safely. He had left Jimmy, who was parked up with the transit van, on the waste ground where he'd go afterwards. When he last spoke with Jimmy, he'd told him he'd hit the old woman at leg level so that she'd bounce off the bonnet and roll onto the road. *This way*, he thought, *there was a chance that she'd only end up seriously injured in hospital.* He still didn't feel good about knocking her down.

'Two. Can you hear me OK? This is one?' Frank spoke into the walkie-talkie.

'Loud and clear,' replied Jimmy.

'She'll be coming out any minute now. How's things your end?'

'All quiet. All good here.'

Both men knew that despite the walkie-talkies being end-to-end, there was still a possibility that they could be picked up, either by radio scanners, or by the security forces, so the less said the better.

'Good, see you soon,' said Frank.

Because of the rain, he had to keep using the wipers now and then, switching them on for their sweep to give him a clear view of the front door of the café. He also kept the air blowing on the windscreen as his own breath was steaming it up. Maybe because of the cold and the rain, she was running slightly late today. It was almost 11.05 when he saw her come out the door of the café. He put the car into first gear, keeping his foot on the clutch and moving up the revs slowly. He checked his mirrors, and he could see that there was nothing behind him. He watched her walk between two cars, looking left and right for traffic. He released the clutch and the handbrake to move the car out onto the road just as she started to cross. He accelerated, dropping down into second, and was almost in third gear when he hit her. She'd been looking in the opposite direction and was just turning her head enough to see him come, but not enough for her to get out of the way. Frank had steered the car to hit her dead centre on the bonnet. When he heard the thud as the car crashed into her body, he realised his calculations about her size had been wrong. It had happened so quickly. She 'had no time to react or even to scream or cry out. The impact, instead of hitting her legs, had hit her at waist level. The result of this was that she was swallowed up under the car and he could feel it rise and fall as it rolled over her body at speed. As he expected, because he had to accelerate to hit her, when he tried to brake slowly the car started to slide, but years of stealing, and driving cars at speed paid off. He was able to bring the car under control within 10 feet of where the old woman now lay crumpled behind him. In the rear-view mirror he could see her body lying still, smashed and broken, like the walking stick beside her. He could hear people starting to scream as they saw what had happened. It was time to get out of there. Putting the car into gear, he accelerated away towards the lower falls and the waste ground where Jimmy would be waiting. It had only taken a matter of seconds. Frank could see it all in his mind in slow motion: the surprise and fear in her eyes, the rain on the windscreen and her body smashed on the road. He concentrated on keeping his speed down, even though he knew the car would be damaged at the front, mechanically it was still moving to his commands. Within five minutes, he'd reached the waste ground where Jimmy was waiting. Taking the walkie-talkie and the 9mm Browning with him, Frank helped Jimmy pour petrol over the car, then set it alight. Leaving the blazing car behind they drove in the transit to a safe house in the Beechmount area where they changed into a fresh set of clothes. They handed over the boiler suits they'd worn to the lady who owned the house, so that she could put them through the washing machine. She also took the guns and the walkie-talkies which were to be taken away and hidden by a young, trusted teenager later. After they'd parked the transit van a short distance away, both men then walked through the Beechmount estate to the Wolf Tone Social Club where Brian McNally was waiting for them. McNally ordered three pints of Guinness and led the two men to a corner table to sit away from prying eyes and listening ears. The two men briefed him on what they considered to be a successful operation. When he'd heard everything, McNally told the two men to wait, while he went outside to a nearby phone box and once more dialled the number in the Republic.

When the man with the familiar southern accent answered McNally replied, 'Stage one successfully completed.'

'Good, I'll be up tomorrow,' replied John Jo Murphy, ending the call.

McNally returned to the social club and sat with the two men again.

'That stage is finished, boys. I think you deserve another couple of pints, but not too many as we're going to be busy over the next couple of days.' Both men smiled while emptying the glasses in front of them.

□

CHAPTER 12

MI6 VAUXHALL CROSS, LONDON

It was very rare for Jim Broad to receive a call late on a Friday afternoon. Broad was in his office at London airport. The office was a front for SG9 the special Black Ops team that worked under his command. When he'd answered his phone, it was the familiar voice of Sir Ian Fraser's secretary.

'Can you please come to the office as soon as possible?' she'd said in her clear and perfect English accent. Nothing more, nothing less.

Forty-five minutes later, he was sitting in the office of the director general of MI6, looking out at the grey clouds over the Thames River and London. The rain that had been washing the streets of Belfast had yet to reach the streets of London. Broad knew that the clouds were indicating the rain was on its way. It always amazed Broad how the desk of the top intelligence officer in Britain always seemed so tidy in comparison to his own, which always seemed to be a maze of paperwork. The door to the office opened and Sir Ian Fraser and his secretary entered. The secretary was carrying a tray with a pot of coffee, sugar, milk, and three cups, which she set on the conference table. Then, to Broad's surprise, Caroline Aspinall the head of MI5 the

British Security Service, entered the office. MI5 looked after the intelligence-gathering in the UK while MI6 operated overseas, so the fact that the head of MI5 was here worried Broad. The secretary left them to it, closing the door behind her.

'Sorry to spoil your Friday evening, Jim,' said Sir Ian, as he indicated for him to come and join him and Aspinall at the conference table. Caroline Aspinall started to pour the coffee, leaving the milk, and sugar for the men to serve themselves.

'I need this,' she said. 'It's been one of those days. I hate it when something comes in this late on a Friday.'

'No problem, boss. I was only going out for a show and dinner this evening, nothing important.' Broad smiled. 'So, what's it all about?'

'Something's come up that needs all our input and especially yours as it involves David Reece.'

Broad wasn't sure if he was happy hearing Reece's name in this room once more.

'What's he done this time? You do remember he retired. We can't use him anymore.'

'Caroline and I have been meeting with Sir Martin Bryant, chairman of the joint intelligence committee, and the prime minister this afternoon.'

These words didn't make Broad feel any happier. He waited to hear more.

'Earlier this afternoon, I received a call from Tom Wilson in Belfast. He tells me that the mother of Mary McAuley has been seriously injured in what would appear to be a deliberate attempt to kill her.'

Broad knew that Tom Wilson was the Assistant Chief Constable in the PSNI, the Police Service of Northern Ireland and that Wilson was the head of C3, which in David's Reece's day was the old RUC Special Branch. He also knew that Wilson and Reece were old friends.

'According to the reports Tom Wilson got from his people on the ground, McAuley's mother was knocked down by a car as she crossed a main road in Belfast. The car, which had been stolen, and had false plates, failed to stop, and was subsequently found burnt out on nearby waste ground. They are currently chasing up witness statements and carrying out an examination of the scene where she was knocked down and where the car was burnt out. Wilson tells me his people are not happy. They believe that this was made to look like an everyday accident caused by a joyriding car thief. We saw plenty of those in our day when we were in Belfast Jim. Witnesses at the scene reported that the driver deliberately aimed the car at McAuley's mother, so they're viewing this as attempted murder. Now, the reason he's kept us informed about this is because he obviously knows that Mary McAuley was once an agent working for Special Branch and David Reece. After I spoke with Tom Wilson, I asked him to keep us up to date. I also contacted Sir Martin Bryant, who informed the prime minister, as both are very aware of what David Reece has done for this country and your department. They are both aware of his links to Mary McAuley and through her to her mother. As this incident happened in Northern Ireland, a part of the United Kingdom, it was also thought that we should involve Caroline here and her MI5 teams in Belfast. The investigation, as I say, is still ongoing, and for the moment we don't have the full picture, but from what we know of Mary McAuley's background we can assume that this incident is aimed at her in some way and maybe even through her to David Reece.'

'Why, after all this time, and now that the peace process is in place would they do something like this?' asked Broad.

'That's the thing, Jim. From our people on the ground using our technical means and our human sources we don't think it's anything to do with the peace process or the Provisional Movement,' said Caroline Aspinall. 'Rather, we think it might be something to do with one of the breakaway faction groups such as the Real IRA or the Continuity IRA. Of course, we've sources in those groups as well and we are waiting for any feedback on why this happened. For now, we can only assume it was to get back at Mary McAuley's past. As Sir Ian says, we'll pass any information we get onto Tom Wilson and his team and, of course, to the prime minister's office and to here.'

'Have we anything at all which shows us who's done this?' asked Broad.

Fraser stood, and holding his cup, and saucer walked towards the large bay windows that looked out over London. With his back to the room, he answered Broad's question.

'Everything we've told you so far is all that we have. It's too early in the investigation to know exactly what happened and enquiries are ongoing.'

'What do we do in the meantime?' asked Broad.

Fraser returned to the conference table.

'The only thing we can do, Jim, is wait for more information. But in the meantime, we need to tell Reece and McAuley what happened. This is where you come in. You know Reece better than anyone, and you know his connections to Mary McAuley. I believe, as do the prime minister and Sir Martin Bryant, that you're in the best position to contact Reece and McAuley and speak to them directly. We'll be in a better position once we know what they want to do. If it was my mother, I'd want to be by her side as soon as possible. Can we leave it to you to contact Reece and McAuley and get back to me? In the meantime, Caroline and I have agreed to work together through the six and five teams. For now, the prime minister wants us to treat this as just another family matter, but at the same time, he wants us to keep an eye on things, bearing in mind the background of both these people, and especially David Reece. The British government does not want anything that would endanger the peace process, and this is where I want you to emphasise this to Reece, especially. Is that OK Jim? Do you understand what I'm asking?'

Broad always worried when he heard that the grey suits of politics wanted him to do something. He could feel the anger inside him rising, but he understood that at the end of the day, the politicians, and especially the prime minister, were his masters.

'Do we know how serious the injuries are to McAuley's mother?' asked Broad.

'According to Tom Wilson she's critically ill and on a life-support machine at Belfast City Hospital,' replied Fraser. 'So, you can tell Reece everything you know, or should I say everything we know, for now?'

'Are we going to give them any assistance? Any of our people or any of our equipment?' asked Broad.

'As I said Jim, the PM wants us to treat this as just another domestic incident, a joyriding hit-and-run. He doesn't want any attention brought to the peace process and accordingly the only assistance we'll give to David Reece and Mary McAuley is a sympathetic one. You can help them get to Belfast and arrange accommodation for them if necessary. But for now, we try to stay out of this. It's a personal family matter for McAuley and her mother.'

The more Jim Broad had heard, the more uneasy he felt. The politicians didn't want to get their hands dirty, but at the same time they wanted them to keep an eye on Reece and McAuley. What the bad guys did came second to anything else.

'I think I understand what you're saying,' said Broad, as he stood to leave.

'I'll head back to my office, so any more information you both have please pass on to me. I'll contact Tom Wilson to let him know that I'm going to call Reece and McAuley. But you know David Reece as well as I do. He won't stop until he finds out who's behind this and once he does, God help them.'

When Broad left, Caroline Aspinall poured herself another cup of coffee. 'You and I both know that Jim Broad is right. God knows what Reece will do if these people get in his face. Once we know they're heading to Northern Ireland, I'll give my teams the heads up to keep an eye on them.'

'Each one of us needs to keep the other in the loop, or this could get out of control very quickly. When Broad gets back to me, I'll update Bryant and the PM, and you can have a word with Wilson,' answered Fraser.

The rain Broad had known was coming was now battering the windows of the office. Looking out at the dark clouds, Sir Ian Fraser wondered how bad this day would be.

CHAPTER 13

MALTA

The weather in Malta, compared to Belfast, and London, had been balmy. Today it had been sunny and warm.

At the Villa Joseph in Quawra, Reece, and Mary were in the middle of dinner. They had been enjoying a good day, having been to Valletta to pick up the ring. Then a nice glass of champagne in the midday sun overlooking the grand harbour of Valletta, before returning to the villa to make love and relax. Mary was already planning to call her mother later and tell her the good news of their engagement. Then they'd to book the flights and a visit to Belfast the following week. Mary cooked the dinner which didn't need much cooking as it consisted of fresh tomato and green salad with plenty of the island's delicious king prawns and the Maltese bread Reece loved so much. Reece had picked the wine, a crisp white local Green Label which they both liked. Mary couldn't hide her excitement. She kept talking about looking forward to introducing Reece to her mother and to showing her the ring. She was convinced her mother would be happy for her, knowing the problem she had in the past with her previous husband who was now languishing in jail for an armed robbery. Leaving the place he was robbing, he ran into the arms of a waiting police patrol that Reece had put in place, ready for him. Mary divorced Brendan McAuley when he was in prison. His favourite pastime had been to take out his temper on Mary, which on one occasion had led to Reece stepping in. He had stopped Brendan using his fists on Mary when the couple were on a night out in Newry town. On that occasion Brendan had found himself lined up against a man rather than a woman, a man whose fists were quicker than his, and who laid him on his back staring at the stars. Mary's mother had never liked Brendan McAuley. She'd seen the bruises far too often on her daughter's face and prayed for the day when she'd left him. But Mary, like her mother, had been raised a Catholic, which meant she tried to hold on to her marriage vows. When Mary had met Reece and had decided she'd enough of violent men, she started by working for Reece against the tyranny she saw around her. The feeling for her Special Branch man would change from working against all she'd known to trust, and eventually love.

As they were finishing their meal Mary had brought a notebook to the table and started writing down her plans, from calling her mother later to planning their trip to Northern Ireland, and what she needed to bring and pack. Reece took another sip of the local wine as he watched her, the pen in her hand working fast across the paper. He didn't know how many times he'd told this woman that he loved her. Sometimes he wondered if he'd loved her from the very start, from that first day, when he saw her while carrying out surveillance of IRA targets in Newry town. Watching her now, he knew how excited she was and how much his commitment to her meant.

'You're going to have to watch, or you'll set that paper on fire.' He laughed.

'There's so much to do, so much to remember. I must write it all down or I'll forget,' she replied.

'Don't worry, I'll go over everything with you afterwards, then we can get the flights booked for next week. I think we should stay in a hotel to make the whole thing more enjoyable. Make it more like a special occasion, which it is,' said Reece.

Before he could say any more, his phone on the coffee table started to buzz.

'I wonder, is that your mother? I always said she knew before anyone, so she'd know what's happening without you telling her.' He laughed.

But when he picked up the phone the smile on his face disappeared when he recognised the call was from his ex-SG9 boss Jim Broad. Mary watched the change in Reece's face and stopped writing her notes.

'Hello, boss, how are you?'

'I'm fine, David,' said Broad, getting straight to the point. 'I'm sorry, but I had to call you to let you know that Mary's mother is in hosp—.'

'She's in hospital?' interrupted Reece. 'Why? What's happened?' He held up his hand as Mary stood up.

'It would appear she was knocked down by a hit-and-run driver while crossing the road in Belfast.'

'How is she? Is she OK?'

Broad seemed to take an age to answer. 'She's in the City Hospital in Belfast. She's critically ill and on a life-support machine. All the information I have has come from Tom Wilson. It happened this morning, and he asked me to call you and Mary to let you know. David, I'm sorry. Tell Mary I'm here for you both if you need anything.'

Reece looked at Mary and beckoned her towards him and put his arm round her shoulder.

'Your mother's been hurt in an accident and she's in the hospital.'

The tears started to fall down Mary's cheek. Reece went back to the call.

'Thank you for letting us know, boss. We'll obviously have to travel to Belfast as soon as possible. Did they catch the person who did it?'

'Not yet, as far as I know. Tom Wilson will be able to tell you more when you get there. Do you need any help with the flights or accommodation?'

'No, thank you. We can take care of things from here. Thank you for letting us know.'

'No problem. Remember, David, I'm here for you if you need me.'

'Thank you,' replied Reece, ending the call.

'What happened? What happened to my mother?'

'She's had a bad accident. The boss said she's been knocked down by a hit-and-run driver in Belfast. He said she's critically ill and in the City Hospital.'

A strange sound came from Mary's mouth, like a cat crying. The tears were still coming, and Reece held her close.

'But why? Why?'

'We're going to find out, Mary. First thing we do is call the hospital to ask how she is. The next thing we do is book flights to Belfast in the morning. When we get there, I'm going to pay a visit to Tom Wilson. His teams will know what's going on. But your mother and her recovery are the most important thing for you now, so let's make those calls and get things moving.'

Mary took a deep breath. Pressing her hanky against her eyes, she dabbed the tears from her cheeks. She always looked at David in a crisis. Over the years, she knew the calmness in this man and the clarity of his thinking in a bad situation.

'I still have the hospital's number on my phone from when my mum was there for her hip operation. I'll give them a call now.'

'You do that, and I'll get on to the airport and book some tickets for the morning.'

Mary went into the bedroom to make her call, leaving Reece to call the airport. When Mary came back out, her face was showing pain and concern at the same time.

'My mum is on a life-support machine. They say she has a fractured skull and some internal bleeding, and they're going to operate later tonight. Oh my God, David, she might die! What am I going to do? What if she dies, David? What am I going to do?'

Reece held her. Brushing his hand through her hair, he kissed her on the forehead.

'I'm sure they're doing the best they can. I know if she's anything like her daughter, then she's a strong woman. I've had to book two flights for tomorrow. The earliest plane goes to Liverpool, then

Liverpool to Belfast. We will be there before lunchtime. I also booked us into the Hilton Hotel in the city.'

'We don't need the hotel, David. I have my house on the Lisburn Road where Mum was staying. We can stay there. It'll save us the money.'

'No, it's on the wrong side of the city to the police headquarters at Knock, and it will save us time when I meet with Wilson. I can meet him on my own after we see your mother in the hospital in case you need to stay. Until we know more about what exactly happened, I think we should stay away from your house.'

'Why do you think someone did this deliberately?'

'I don't know. Until we do, we take precautions. I still don't trust the bastards over there. For now, let's pack a couple of small bags and try to get some sleep. I think it's going to be a busy couple of days and your mother needs us to be strong for her.'

'I don't know about you, but for now I need a strong drink. Where's your bottle of Bushmills?'

Reece produced the bottle from the drinks cabinet and poured a generous measure of the Irish whisky into two glasses.

'Maybe you're right. It can only help us sleep later.'

They took the Bushmills out onto the patio and sat looking at the stars. As he sipped the familiar flavour, his thoughts were of Belfast, a city he loved, and hated in equal measure. He had been born there, worked there, and loved there. But on many occasions, he'd almost died there. To Reece, Belfast was now a place to visit, to have a drink, and get out, to leave behind, only returning when he had a reason to do so. He knew Jim Broad, and his gut feeling was that he'd only given him the basic facts and not the full story. He was sure there was more to it than a simple hit-and-run. For Mary's sake, her mother's, and his own, he was going to find out what really happened.

The next morning, Reece, and Mary took the first available flight to Liverpool, then a flight that got them into Belfast just before lunchtime. Reece had paid for the flights with his own credit card, as he didn't want to take Jim Broad up on his offer of help unless he really needed to. From experience, Reece knew that people like Broad always preferred to be in control of the situation and for now, Reece needed to be in control. It seemed like Mary hadn't stopped crying, the silent tears always on her cheek. All night she'd lain close to him as he stroked her hair. On the journey to Belfast, he found he had to constantly reassure her that her mother would be well, even though he knew within himself there was a danger that she wouldn't recover from her injuries.

At the Aldergrove International Airport outside Belfast, Reece hired a black BMW saloon car from the Hertz car hire desk. He drove directly to the City Hospital between the Donegal and Lisburn roads in Belfast. Getting there just after lunch, he found the car parks busy. It took some time to find a parking space. After a short conversation with the receptionist, they were directed to the third floor of the hospital and the surgical ward for critically ill patients. At the nursing station, the senior nurse directed them to the private side ward and Mary's mother. Reece hated hospitals. The smell the constant noise always reminded him of his own visits and the pain from when he had bullet fragments removed from his shoulder after being shot by Sean Costello. Some were still embedded there to remind him now and then.

Then the leg wound he was still recovering from the shrapnel from the bomb that had killed Rachel Cohen. Reece was expecting the kind of scene that he knew would scare Mary. The woman in the bed was looking old and frail, with dark purple bruising showing up on her forehead and cheek. She was hooked up to several machines, one of them helping her to breathe, another monitoring her statistics. There was a drip fed into her right arm. Mary had stopped crying but was taking short, deep breaths as she held her mother's hand. The nurse that was caring for her mother told them that even though her mother was in a coma, they should only speak positively around the bed, as sometimes it was believed the patient could hear exactly what was being said. She reported that her mother had come through a long operation to stop internal bleeding affecting her spleen, which had been removed. The nurse tried to be reassuring, telling Mary they were doing everything they could for her mother. All they could do now was monitor her in the hope that she'd make a full recovery, but it would take time. Mary spoke to her mother to let her know that she was there. For some reason she also told her about her engagement and of her new ring. Reece felt it was her way of letting her mother know that she now had a reason to get well. Reece hated hospitals, and he was sure most sane people felt the same. Anytime he'd ever been in one he'd been in pain, and he knew it was the business of hospitals to deal with the sick and the dying. He stayed by the bedside with Mary for an hour, but he sensed she wanted to stay longer.

'Why don't you stay with your mother a little longer? I can go and book us into the hotel and call on Tom Wilson at the police headquarters. He may have more information on what happened. Are you OK with that? Do you want me to get you anything before I go?'

For the first time in the last 24 hours, he saw a smile cross the lips of the woman he loved.

'Yes, you do that. I'm OK for the minute. If I need anything, I'm sure she's in good hands here. So, I could nip to the toilet or the canteen if I need to.'

Reece kissed her on the cheek. 'If you need anything, give me a call. I'll try not to be too long.'

By the time Reece booked into the Hilton hotel and drove across the city to the PSNI headquarters on the Knock Road in East Belfast, it was late afternoon. He had phoned ahead to make sure Wilson was there and to let him know he was coming. Feeling hungry, he stopped on the way to grab a burger in a McDonald's.

The badge at the entrance to the PSNI headquarters was different from the one he'd served under when it was the RUC Harp and Crown. The word had obviously been sent down from the top floor of the building that he was expected.

With a cursory glance at his driving licence by the guard on the entrance gate, Reece was directed to the visitors' car park and told to report to the reception desk on the ground floor of the building that covered most of the three-acre site that was now the police Headquarters for Northern Ireland. As Reece walked towards the main building, he could see the RUC George Cross Gardens of Remembrance. He had visited the site not long after it had been created. He remembered the water that poured like a small stream down the middle of the site which was surrounded by black marble slates engraved with the names of the police officers who had lost their lives serving the people of Northern Ireland. Many of the names he knew personally. Men and women who he'd worked with and lived with through terrible times.

The Portacabins that had contained the operation rooms of the special surveillance teams operating out of there during the war against the IRA and other terrorist groups had been replaced by a new state-of-the-art complex.

He walked up the short drive and through the front doors of the main headquarters building. It was as he remembered it. Three floors high. It was fit for purpose. To the left, as he entered the lobby, were the offices of the chief constable. To his right there was a glass cabinet containing a large book which was opened each day to a different page which contained the names of officers killed on that date.

At a reception desk on the ground floor, a young policewoman was on the phone. Putting down the phone, she looked up at Reece. 'Mister Reece, ACC Wilson is expecting you. He will be down in just a moment if you'd like to wait,' she said, pointing to the chair beside the Book of Remembrance Cabinet.

The headquarters building hadn't changed much from the days when Reece had worked there during the last ten years of his police service. The building itself looked like an old-fashioned secondary school from the outside. Reece had walked every corridor of this building during those years. Especially the third floor, which had been the operational floor for Special Branch. The floor contained not only the operational offices but also a vast registry of files and documents showing the terrorist and criminal threats to the country of Northern

Ireland. Some documents stored were stored before the country came into existence in 1922, after the War of Independence. The country of Ireland had been split into the six counties of Northern Ireland, and the twenty-six counties of the Irish Free State, which was now known as the Irish Republic, or the Republic of Ireland. Reece saw Tom Wilson coming down the stairs. He was wearing a dark uniform with the insignia of the PSNI showing the rank of Assistant Chief Constable. Reece had to admit that the tall silver haired Ulster man looked fit and healthy. His slim body carried no excess weight, and Reece thought he was either a runner or a gym visitor, or both.

'You're looking well, Tom. The rank seems to sit well with you.'

'Thank you. From what I heard about your last operation in London, you're looking better than I thought you would.' Wilson had the same sharp blue eyes and spoke with the same mid-Ulster accent as Reece.

'I might look good on the outside, but you should see on the inside.' Reece laughed.

'Come, let's go to my office and have a chat.'

Reece followed up the familiar staircase to the third floor.

They still don't have a bloody lift in this building, he thought.

Walking down the long corridor that led through the double doors from the third landing, Reece could see that nothing much had changed. The office doors on the left and right were still there, still the same, but with different names indicating the new occupants. Halfway down the corridor was a door on the left with the sign ACC C3. Reece followed Wilson into the office, which was small with a desk, two filing cabinets, and three chairs. Wilson took the chair at the desk that faced the door. The large window behind Wilson reminded Reece of the operational office he'd worked in a few doors down. That office had two of these large windows looking out onto the same lawn below. He could remember how the windows increased the heat from the summer sun. So much so that they used to grow tomatoes on a pot on the windowsill. Sitting in one of the two chairs facing Wilson was a woman. Reece sat in the chair beside her.

'Would you like anything to drink, David?' asked Wilson.

'No, thank you.'

'David, let me introduce you. This is Detective Chief Inspector Heather Black. She heads up one of my teams in the city. I've asked her to investigate the circumstances of what happened to Mrs Smith. Heather, this is David Reece. An old friend and colleague. We worked together for many years. I don't think there's anything you can teach him about the business we work in.'

'Pleased to meet you, David. I've heard quite a lot about you.'

The woman had short blonde hair and dark-brown eyes. She was slim and dressed in a brown tweed jacket the buttons open showing a blue blouse underneath. What surprised Reece was that someone of her rank was now sitting in the office of her boss wearing tight-fitting blue jeans and white trainers. To Reece, this indicated this woman didn't care about what others thought. They had to take her as she was, whether they liked it, or not. The clothes could also indicate she was hands-on surveillance, ready to work with her teams. All this was a positive for Reece. *Then again*, Reece thought, *maybe I'm just a bit old-fashioned.*

'Pleased to meet you too, Chief Inspector.' Reece nodded to her.

'Before we start, I want you to know we're here for you. Anything that you need, just ask,' said Wilson.

'Thank you. We only want to know what happened. Mary is at the City Hospital with her mother, who is critically ill in a coma and on a life-support machine.'

'Understood. Heather, what have we got?' asked Wilson.

DCI Black turned her body to face Reece, her eyes looking straight at him.

'First, David. Can I call you David?'

'Yes, of course.'

'As the boss says, I know a bit of your background, so you'll understand something of the resources that we've been putting in place to try to get to the bottom of this. Our enquiries so far show that what happened to Mrs Smith was not a simple case of a joyriding hit-and-run. We have interviewed people at the scene, and looked at CCTV, but we haven't been able to identify the driver. The fact that the car was burnt out on waste ground not far from the incident may indicate that the driver had a back-up vehicle or someone waiting for them to assist a getaway. Any self-respecting joyriding car thief would simply drive the car as far away as possible, but somewhere near where they lived, or could hide, before abandoning the car, and leaving on foot. This has all the hallmarks of a planned and deliberate attempt to either seriously injure or kill Mrs Smith. Now, because we are looking at this as attempted murder it gives us the power to use all our resources to get to the bottom who is involved. At any other time we'd be baffled as to the reason why, but on this occasion, with the fact that she's the mother of Mary McAuley, previously your agent, code name Mike, we must consider that may be a reason for this incident. You will understand it's still early days in this investigation. Apart from the interviewing of witnesses and looking at the CCTV, we are in contact with our intelligence sources who are looking for any more information as to who may be involved. Photos from the CCTV don't give us much, only what appears to be a male driver wearing a baseball cap.'

She gave a grainy picture of the suspect to Reece. The DCI stopped giving an update. Then, looking at Wilson, she nodded.

From experience, Reece knew how the investigation would be running. He also knew because of who Mary was, it would be receiving a lot of attention from those in higher authority.

'Thank you, Tom. Thank you, Chief Inspector. Like you, I'm suspicious about what has happened. No offence to you both, but these days I don't like to come back to this country in any circumstances, never mind one that seems to be aimed at Mary and possibly myself.'

'I understand you, David, and I would like to talk to you about that. For now, do you have any questions for Heather? Otherwise, I think she should get on with things.'

'No. No questions. Obviously, if you get any more information, Chief Inspector, you'll let me know,' said Reece.

'In that case, I'll let the Chief Inspector get on with her work. If you get anything more, let me know right away, Heather, and I'll pass it on to David.'

'Of course, sir,' said the DCI, standing to leave. 'I hope Mrs Smith recovers. It was good to meet you, David.'

'Thank you, Chief Inspector,' said Reece. 'It's good to meet you too.'

After she'd left, Reece had a feeling that Tom Wilson had more to say, and what he had to say was not for the ears of his Chief Inspector.

'OK, Tom. What do you want to talk about?'

'Are you sure you don't want something to drink?'

'No. I'm OK, thanks.'

'David, I've some idea of how you and Mary may be feeling about this whole thing. But you must remember that my job as head of the PSNI intelligence-gathering operations is to find out if this is connected in any way to one of the terrorist groups in the country. Unfortunately, it's looking very much like that's the case. I can assure you we're leaving no stone unturned to find out who did this. I've been contacted by Jim Broad who has asked me not only to investigate and find out who has done this, but to watch over you as well.'

'Watch over me? You mean keep me on a leash? I don't care who gets these bastards. What I need to do is to keep Mary and her mother safe. Hopefully, you can do that, but if you can't I won't stand by and let them hurt the people I love. I saw too much of that during the war, when these bastards got away with doing things like this because the politicians were too afraid to take them on.'

Wilson leant across his desk to make sure Reece heard every word.

'I'm your friend. I know exactly what you're talking about, and I went through that war with you. As a courtesy, it's my job to let you know that I'll investigate this and catch these bastards, as you call them, and I'll do everything in my power to protect not only Mary and her mother but you as well. That's my job. Not only as the head of police intelligence, but as a police officer. I know the skills that you have, and I understand that if we need to protect you, then you have the skill to protect yourself as well. I hope things don't come to that, because in that instance I might have to be the policeman and not your friend. Jim Broad is obviously concerned that you and Mary are at risk. Ideally, he doesn't want you to be here, but he understands why. As for the politicians, they're only interested in keeping the peace, and I know that as far as the Provisional Movement is concerned, they want to keep that peace as well, and anything that would put that at risk needs to be nipped in the bud. I can tell you, it's for that reason and from the intelligence that I'm already getting from our sources, both human, and technical, that the Provos are not involved in this. As you're no longer working for Jim Broad, you'll understand that just telling you this bit of information is breaking the official secrets act. But hopefully you'll take this as a sign of our continued friendship and trust. I think it also shows you that this is a priority for me to get whoever did this quickly, and that you're all safe.'

'Have your people been able to find out the reason why this happened?' asked Reece.

'No, not yet. Like you, we can only speculate at this time that's something personal against you, but more likely, Mary. We must assume that whoever it is might know that Mary has worked for us in the past. They may even know she was your agent and who you are. By assuming this, we should expect the worst. That this was the reason they tried to kill Mrs Smith, either because she's Mary's mother and they wanted to hurt her, and through her you. Or they're planning something worse, maybe the capturing of Mary, maybe even you yourself. That's why am telling you to be careful, David. We don't have the full picture yet and we don't know who is involved in this, but we'll find out. Where will you be staying while you're here?'

'I've booked us both into the Hilton hotel and hired a car. Mary wanted to stay at her own house where her mother lives on the Lisburn Road, but I thought it would be safer staying in a hotel until we find out what this is all about. For the next few days, I don't see us doing much more than travelling back and forward to the hospital. You have my number, so anything at all, let me know.'

'Will do, David. In the meantime, I'll have extra police patrols cover the hospital grounds and the area of the hotel. Leave me the registration of the hire car so they'll know it's you. It was good to see you again. I'm sorry it was under these circumstances. As Heather said: I hope Mary's mother recovers and gets well soon. Maybe then we can all have dinner together.'

'That would be nice, but by the look of the injuries Mary's mother has, that might be some way down the road. We just got engaged, and we were about to tell her mother when all this happened, so hopefully she has something to live for now.'

'You old dog, congratulations! In the circumstances, I hope everything goes well. You should get back to the hospital. But be careful, David, these people aren't finished yet, I'm sure of it. Do you have a weapon?'

'No, now that I no longer work for Jim Broad, I can't carry it out of Malta.'

Wilson opened the top drawer of his desk. He took out a box and handed it across the table to Reece.

'I thought that would be the case, so this is for you, but be bloody careful, David. Only use it if you really need to. I could be crucified just for giving it to you.'

Reece opened the small box. He removed the contents, a Walther 9mm PPK pistol, a box of thirty rounds of the same calibre, two magazines, and a holster that would fit snugly onto his belt. Wilson watched as Reece lifted the gun and handled it, turning it from side-to-side Reece pulled back the slide to make sure the gun was empty.

'Are you sure about this, Tom? Are you not taking a risk?'

'I would rather there were some dead bad guys lying in the street than you or Mary.'

Reece lifted a magazine and opened the box of ammo, then removed seven rounds. His hands moved easily as his thumb pressed down on each round, pushing seven in total into the magazine. He pushed the magazine flush into the base of the handle. he slashed the slide once more to allow the top round to pass into the chamber. The Walther PPK was the first gun Reece had been trained in when he'd joined the RUC. It was a compact small gun, easily concealed, and packed a hell of a punch. Although Reece was a marksman with a pistol, he'd always remembered to be careful when firing the Walther as a novice. The slide was inclined to cut a small nick in the fleshy part of the hand holding the gun if you held it loosely. Reece knew that if he held it with a strong grip and pointed low at his target when he pulled the trigger, the front of the gun would rise slightly. This helped to hit the target square in the middle, just where he wanted.

'I appreciate you taking this risk, Tom, but what if I'm stopped while carrying it?'

Wilson reached into the drawer once more. This time, he withdrew a small, laminated card and passed it across the desk to Reece. Reece read: *Certificate to Carry* in one corner, and the crest of the PSNI in the other. Below this were the words, *Authorised to carry a firearm.* At the bottom of the card was a scrawled signature and in print beside it, *Chief Constable.*

'As you can see that card is signed by the chief constable. It's a new thing, mainly because 'we have so many visitors who've worked here before and now want to visit places of interest. This way, we don't have to give them twenty-four-hour protection. We've never had someone use one so far, and they've always been returned, so don't use it unless you really need to.'

Reece stood and slipped the holster onto his belt before inserting the Walther into it. He then loaded the second magazine with seven rounds, then put it with the box containing the rest of the ammunition into his jacket pocket. Reece felt a trust had been placed in him.

'Tell me something Tom, in all your days on the job have you ever heard talk of a high-ranking officer in Special Branch who may have been working with the Provos, most likely in the Newry and South Armagh area?'

Wilson sat back in his chair once more and took a few seconds before he answered.

'There were always rumours, but nothing concrete. Sometimes we found it was just bad feeling between two senior officers. Jealousy and lies can be spread easily. You know the game we were in, David. Lies and treachery were all part of it. The only people we could truly trust were ourselves. I heard some of those rumours, but as I say, nothing concrete, no definite names. Why do you ask? Have you heard something?'

'Because of your trust in me, Tom. I have something to tell you. What I'm going to say must be between you and me. No one else must know for now, understood?'

Wilson nodded.

'You are aware of some of the operations I've been involved in with MI6. These operations have brought me into close contact with Mossad officers both active and retired. One of these retired officers recently told me that during the Troubles he was in contact with the RUC as a liaison officer for Mossad. When he was in Ireland, he was briefed by his opposite number in the Israeli Embassy in Dublin. This Mossad officer was running an agent in the South Armagh, Dundalk Provos. This agent had given them information to say that a senior RUC Special Branch Officer, he thought, with the rank of DCI, was working with the Provos. This officer had tipped off the Provos when we had covert operations working in South Armagh and Newry. In this way, the Provos were able to avoid capture by either cancelling or abandoning their operations. The Israeli officer was able to say that as far as they knew, no police or army lives were lost because of the information that was supplied to the Provos. The reason my contact told me this was to make me aware of an extra risk when I visited this country. I don't know who the rogue guy is or whether he's still in the police or retains connections to the security services.

'I'm telling you this because of what you've done for me here today, to protect you as much as you want to protect me. If this guy is still in the mix, he could be a danger to both of us. We share the same past. We both worked at times in the same areas on covert operations and running agents, so this guy would have been around at the same time. Because of what has brought me here, I thought that you should be aware of it. Any information about who this man is will be important to us both. That's all I know for the present. But I'm just a little concerned about who is involved in this hit-and-run, and if, as is expected, his target is Mary, and me, all we'd need is a policeman from our past interfering in the present.'

'If I hear anything, I'll let you know right away. In the meantime, you get back to Mary and her mother. I think Mary will need you now more than ever.'

When Reece left the office Wilson made two phone calls. The first one to DCI Heather Black, who was now at the Belfast TCG office running operations in the city. He told her that Reece had just left the office and gave her the registration number of the black BMW hire car he was driving. He knew that Heather Black would be in radio communication with her surveillance teams, passing on the car details for them to follow Reece. The second call he made was to Caroline Aspinall at her MI5 office in Thames House in London. He gave the details of his talk with Reece, except the part about the rogue Special Branch Officer. For the second time that day, he let her know that he understood the political pressures of not letting anything happen that could cause problems for the peace process. After finishing the call, he sat back in his chair. Knowing David Reece as he did, this could get very messy, very fast. Now Wilson would take the short walk to the ground floor to brief the chief constable, who he knew, could be more political than the politicians, always worrying about his pension and a knighthood when he retired. Just like his conversation with Aspinall he wouldn't be telling him about the rogue officer, although he'd have to tell him that Reece now had a gun and what he could do with it if he was in danger.

CHAPTER 14

BELFAST CITY HOSPITAL

Before Reece had crossed the Albert Bridge that passed over the River Lagan into the heart of the city, he'd spotted at least two of the surveillance cars following. Reece had been trained in surveillance and anti-surveillance by the best in the E4A unit of Special Branch and the MI5 watchers' team. Being trained this way had saved his life on a few occasions. He had been watching for the surveillance teams since driving out of the PSNI headquarters and then turning left down the Newtownards Road. He had expected them. If he was Tom Wilson, he'd have done the same thing and set a team on him. Reece knew that anyone following would use the four-corner box type surveillance pattern: two cars ahead, two cars behind him, and a further two cars in reserve. He had spotted one of the front two cars and one of the ones behind. He wasn't worried if they were there, it was a form of protection, so he didn't try to deviate or lose them but instead drove straight through the City Centre and on to the Lisburn Road and the City Hospital entrance where he parked up. He found Mary sitting beside her mother's bed. There didn't seem to be any more tubes or any less for that matter. Mary's tears had stopped though her face was pale. Looking up she smiled when he walked into the room.

'How is she doing?' asked Reece.

'No change, although the doctors say she's holding her own. Oh, David, I'm glad to see you, it's so quiet in here.'

'I told you she was a strong woman.'

'The doctor's just been in, and he says we won't see much change for at least twenty-four hours. She seems so peaceful…if it wasn't for the tubes and machines.'

Reece put his hand on Mary's shoulder and, bending down, kissed her on the top of her head.

'I think there's not much we can do here now. we both need to rest. Let's head to the hotel, we can come back anytime you want, and we are not far away if there's any change.'

Mary stood up and held her mother's hand for a few seconds.

'I'm not going to be far away, and I'll see you again in the morning. Love you, Mum.'

Reece put his arms around her. He could see that she was exhausted, and she needed some rest.

'We can get something to eat at the hotel and then it's a shower and some sleep for you, my girl,' said Reece.

'I won't argue with you there. Suddenly I'm famished, and very tired.'

When they left the ward they stopped at the nurse's station and Reece gave them his contact telephone number to call any time. Mary told the nurse they would be back in the morning after nine. On the drive to the hotel Reece told Mary about his conversation with Wilson.

He left out the part concerning the rogue police officer. Mary wasn't happy that he was carrying a gun again.

'Do you really think we're in danger, David? If what you're saying is true, someone tried to kill my mother and through her, maybe get to me, and you. Are the surveillance teams still following us?'

'If they're as good as I think they are, then yes. That might not be a bad thing for now, at least we've some form of extra protection. I don't think Tom Wilson or Jim Broad would like anything to happen on UK soil while the politicians are breathing down their necks to protect the peace process. Try to relax if you can and for now, let's concentrate on getting your mother well again.' Reece tried to lighten the mood. 'After all, her daughter's going to get married to the most handsome man in the world. And she can come and recuperate with us in the Malta sunshine.'

'I do hope so, David. I really do.'

The surveillance that was following were getting better, they'd begun to learn his driving routine: if he would indicate or not when making a turn or go through traffic lights on orange. He only spotted one surveillance car and wasn't a hundred per cent sure on that, but he hoped they were there, anyway.

The receptionist in the City Hospital who had taken details of the car when Reece had passed on his details, and the fact that he was visiting a seriously ill patient, made a note, and placed it into her handbag before leaving work that evening. She finished work at 5 PM and the traffic was heavy as she drove up the Falls Road and parked up in the Beechmount area. She then walked the short distance to her nephew's house on Beechmount Parade. When she knocked, the door was answered by Brian McNally.

'Hello, Aunty. Come in, come in. I've just put the kettle on.'

The woman sat in one of the two wing backed floral patterned chairs by the fireside that matched the settee opposite and waited while her nephew brewed the pot.

'Are you still off the sugar?' he shouted from the kitchen.

'Yes, I'm sweet enough, and I have my figure to think about.'

He brought a pot of tea and one cup on a tray with a small milk jug.

'You want me to pour, or you do mother yourself?' he asked.

'No, just let it settle a bit and I'll pour it myself,' she replied.

'Well, Brian, I can see you keep a tidy house even though you're on your own,' she said, looking round the room.

'I try my best. The only time it's untidy is when the Brits call to give it a search.' He laughed.

She poured herself a cup of the tea, adding the milk afterwards. Lifting the cup to her lips she blew gently on the liquid before taking a sip.

'I need this, it's been a busy day,' she said, placing the cup back in the saucer.

'I'm sure it has been. Have you anything for me?' he asked.

She lifted her handbag and after searching around inside, produced the note she'd written before leaving work. Her nephew had called to her house in Andersonstown yesterday. He had asked her to keep an eye out for an elderly patient who had been knocked down in a car accident and specifically to get details of anyone visiting the patient.

The fact that her nephew knew she might have an elderly patient who had been knocked down and be on one of the wards didn't surprise her. She knew not to ask too many questions and was always willing to help when her nephew asked.

'Just as you said, an elderly lady is in intensive care after being knocked down yesterday. She's only had two visitors today: a man and a woman. I believe the woman is her daughter and the man appears to be her partner.'

'Have you any names?' he asked.

'The patient's name is Rosie Smith and I think she comes from somewhere on the Lisburn Road. Her daughter is called Mary and her daughter's partner registered a BMW for our long-term patient parking under the name of David Reece. He had to show me his driving licence for proof of identity.'

McNally spent some time going over what she knew. She didn't know where exactly in the car park he parked his BMW. She described the man as being almost 6-foot-tall, dark hair and blue eyes. She remembered he was wearing a Barbour jacket with an open-necked shirt and, she thought, blue jeans. To her own eyes he was fit and healthy. The woman had long black hair; she was pretty, and was well dressed in a floral dress. McNally showed her the old IRA picture of Reece, and she confirmed it was the same man only older.

'Did they say when they would be back?' he asked.

'Not to me, but I was able to speak to one of the nurses on the ward who told me the daughter was very upset and had said she'd be back each day. The man left a telephone number with the ward and with reception.' She handed the note to McNally. 'I've written down everything that I know, including the number. It's there for you in the note. I don't know that I could do anymore without bringing attention to myself.'

'No, don't worry, Aunty. You've done more than enough. Leave the rest to me.'

She knew better than to ask any more questions, and realistically she didn't want to know anything else. It would be better for her if anything went wrong or anything happened.

'Right then, that's me off home for ma dinner. I'm famished.'

McNally kissed her on the cheek and escorted her to the door.

'Are you at work the rest of the week?' he asked.

'Yes, why?' she replied, worried about what he was going to ask next.

'Don't worry, Aunty. It's just in case I need to get in touch with you quickly, and I'll know where you are.'

'Just be careful, nephew. The world is a dangerous place out there.' She smiled.

'And you, Aunty.' He smiled before closing the door behind her.

After she'd left, McNally went to the same phone box on the Falls Road he'd used in the past. He made two calls. One to John Jo Murphy. He told him his guests had arrived and that he could expect visitors within the next couple of days. Murphy told him he'd prepare the accommodation. The second call was to Frank Walsh. He told Walsh to meet him in the Wolf Tone Club at eight o'clock that evening and to bring Jimmy Bailey and Bailey's sister Mariad with him. As he walked home, a plan was now formulating in his mind. Brian McNally began to smile.

CHAPTER 15

HILTON HOTEL BELFAST

The Belfast Hilton hotel had been built after the Troubles. The hotel overlooked the Lagan River that runs through the city to the Irish Sea. Like all Hilton hotels the world over, the design was simple, yet classy, and functional at the same time. Reece liked the room on the third floor as it overlooked the river. Across from the large windows, they could see the two giant cranes of the old Harland and Wolff shipyard, indicating the site where the famous ship Titanic had been built. They had both showered and, with only towels covering them, they'd slept on top of the bed for an hour.

'Are you sure you switched the charger on when you plugged your phone in?' said Mary, opening her eyes.

'Yes, don't worry if they try to get us, I've also given the hospital our hotel number. If anything happens, they'll let us know.'

Reece was lying back with his hands behind his head, looking at the ceiling. Mary turned over and lay her head on his chest. He could smell the freshness in her soft dark hair. Her body was cool against his skin and although, like always when they were in this position, he felt like making love to her, he knew that was not what she needed at this time.

'I know, David, I'm just worried that Mum's there all alone with all those tubes. I'm glad you're here. I don't know what I'd do without you.'

Reece pulled her closer and tried to change the subject. He knew she was worried, and he also knew she must be strong. His mobile phone started to buzz. Reece left the bed and taking the phone off the charger lead he looked at the screen and could see the call was from Tom Wilson.

'Hello, Tom, what's up?'

'Hi, David. I'm just calling to see how you got on today. How's Mary and her mother?'

'Both doing OK in the circumstances, thanks for asking.'

'Where are you now?' asked Wilson.

'I think if your team are as good as I think they are you know exactly where we are, in the hotel.' He smiled to himself.

He could hear Wilson laughing. 'I told them you would spot them. How long did it take you?'

'Not long, but they're good. But it's good to have them there all the same. Thanks for that.'

'You're welcome. Just checking in to make sure you're all right. You have my number if you need to get in touch with me. I'm heading home now for the night. We can catch up tomorrow, but before I go, can you let me know when you'll be leaving the hotel so that my teams don't have to start too early?'

'Will do Tom and thanks again. Have a good night.'

'What was all that about?' asked Mary.

'Just Tom Wilson making sure were tucked up safely in bed for the night.'

'That's nice of him. I'm only realising now when we last ate. My belly thinks my throat's been cut,' she said, smiling.

'Let's get dressed and go down to dinner. I believe the views at night from the hotel's Riverfront Restaurant are spectacular. So whether they are or not, if you're there with me the food will taste spectacular as well.' Reece laughed.

The changes in Belfast since the end of the Troubles and the instalment of the peace process always amazed Reece anytime he returned to the city. New hotels, conference centres, theatres, shops, bars, and restaurants. Belfast had become a cosmopolitan city once more, but more modern than in the past. They'd rebuilt it from the rubble. As Reece looked out of the large restaurant windows that overlooked the river, he couldn't help but remember the days when, as a young policeman, he'd worked for one week a month in what was called the bomb transit. The job of the officers in the transit was to race to bomb calls to clear buildings and streets of civilians before a car bomb would explode, wrecking those buildings, and lives. Sometimes the week's duty in the transit would be quiet. at other times, they could be attending calls once or twice a day every day. It was during one of these calls that he came close to losing his life. The 999 caller had said a bomb had been placed in a grocery store at the top of the Donegall Road. As they drove up the Donegal Road, they could see a police Land Rover above the shop stopping traffic coming down the road. They pulled the transit across the road beside a garage to block traffic travelling up the road. Unknown to Reece and the other officers in the transit, the terrorists had placed a bomb in the garage as well. The owners had run out and seeing the police Land Rover thought they were sealing off the road for their bomb. As they'd got out of the transit and started to stop traffic, the bomb in the garage exploded. Luckily for Reece and the men in the transit, the blast went upwards rather than outwards. The memory of those few moments would always be the same: the blast lifting him off his feet and blowing him backwards, slamming him against the transit. As he travelled through the air, everything seemed to be in slow motion. Looking to his right, he could see a policeman on his knees with his hands over his head as pieces of glass fell like rain on his hands and cap. None of the officers were injured, but they were slightly shaken up. Reece later noticed a tear in his trousers: his knee had been cut by the flying glass and would need a few stitches later. He had been slightly deafened by the blast and just as the officers got their senses back, the second bomb went off in the grocery store that had been the reason for the original call. The terrorists had placed two bombs in two separate buildings before making their getaway. Another memory of that incident always made Reece smile. While stopping traffic from getting onto the road after the blast and the clean-up, one stupid driver tried to drive through Reece to get onto the road. Reece put up his hand, shouted three times for him to stop, but he kept coming. Eventually Reece put his hand on the gun on his belt and shouted that he would shoot him if he didn't fucking stop. That did the trick. The driver and his nervous legs somehow found the brakes.

'Penny for your thoughts?' asked Mary.

They had enjoyed the meal and the views from the restaurant window. Each table with its small vase of fresh flowers and lighted candle added just that bit of class that made the experience more intimate, more personal. There hadn't been much conversation as everything came back to Mary's mother in the hospital bed. Reece had continually tried to steer Mary away from thinking about her mother. The bottle of Chablis was still half full, which, being their favourite wine, was unusual. Mary wasn't in the mood for drinking and Reece needed to keep a clear head in case they had to drive back to the hospital at a moment's notice.

'Just thinking about how the city looks now, compared to the old dark days when we raced around trying to stop people from killing each other.'

'I remember how bad it was then before I married Brendan and moved to Newry. Newry wasn't much better. But I agree with you, the city looks lovely now. A place for people to come and enjoy themselves in peace and quiet.'

'I believe it's very popular with stag and hen parties. The flight from England on EasyJet are relatively cheap. At the weekends, bars, and restaurants are full. There is a whole new generation out there who hasn't got a clue of what it was like. They don't really know that there are still some bastards around who want to keep it all going. That's basically why I moved to Malta. I wanted to get away from this place as far as I could.'

'I know what you mean. If it wasn't for what happened to my mother, I wouldn't be here either. Malta and you are my home now and I only hope that after my mother gets well, we can all go back there to live in peace.'

They took what was left of the wine back to the room. Leaving the curtains open so they could see the light shining on the river, they both fell asleep.

CHAPTER 16

BELFAST

They woke early. The sun was shining, sparkling off the surface of the river. Reece phoned down for a continental breakfast for both. They took their time getting ready, putting on fresh clothes, which, with the good night's sleep, left them feeling refreshed for the day. Mary was wearing a black two-piece trouser suit with a white blouse underneath. She felt that sitting for a day in a hospital, the way she was dressed, would make it more comfortable. Reece had no worries about comfort. He dressed casually in jeans and a shirt, the order of the day. Reece phoned Tom Wilson to tell him they would be leaving the hotel about nine thirty. Wilson thanked him and told him the surveillance team was already out on the ground.

'I hope Mum has had a good night's sleep as well,' said Mary.

'Well, no phone call is good news,' answered Reece.

Before he put on his Barbour jacket, Reece checked the Walther Pistol. It was a habit he'd carried out over the years. Make sure the magazine fits snugly and there was a round in the breech ready to go. Reece put the gun in the holster on the waistband of his trousers, then lifted the car keys off the table. Mary watched him. She didn't like the fact he was carrying a gun again, but somehow, she felt safer that he did.

'OK. Let's go and see how your mother's doing.'

Driving through the city on a crisp sunny day, when the rush-hour traffic had died down, was a nice experience. They could see all the new buildings they'd talked about the night before, the sun bouncing off the many windows looking out on the streets below. Reece had promised himself that he wouldn't look for the surveillance and just try to relax. But the professional in him was still watching, ever vigilant. He spotted two of the vehicles a black Volkswagen Golf and a red Toyota. The drive to the hospital only took 20 minutes. The lights and the traffic were in their favour. Even finding a parking space was easier than it had been. While Reece registered the car at the reception, Mary went ahead, eager to be with her mother. When Reece got to the ward, he found that Marys mother had been moved to a bed in a four-bed ward on the same floor. Mary had resumed the same position as the day before, sitting beside the bed, holding her mother's hand. Reece noticed that one or two of the tubes that had been attached to her mother's body had been removed. A young nurse came in to check the patient's pulse.

'Your mother had a good night, which is always helpful. Her signs are showing she's fighting back. The doctor will be around later to check, and he'll be able to tell you more, but try not to worry, he'll tell you more than I can.'

Reece pulled up the other chair and sat quietly beside Mary. Reece hated hospitals. They always reminded him of painful times. He always thought the quiet noise created by people moving about and talking in the corridors and on the ward made him sleepy, just like one of those self-help tapes or CDs designed to do just that.

'I still think she can hear us,' said Mary.

'I'm sure, keep talking to her. Tell her everything. Tell her about us and Malta, our engagement, and that the sun is shining today.'

Mary did just that. She talked quietly, telling her mother everything Reece had mentioned. Hospital chairs were never comfortable. They were not meant for people to sit for long periods of time.

'I think I'll go to the canteen and get a cup of coffee. You want one?' asked Reece.

'Oh yes, that would be nice, and a biscuit if you can find one,' she replied.

Reece left for the lift that would take him down the two floors to the canteen. When the lift doors opened, a nurse coming out almost bumped into him. The nurse smiled as she stood to one side, allowing him to enter the lift. He noticed she was wearing a different – coloured uniform to the ones on the ward: blue instead of light green. He thought maybe she was one of the nurses who specialised. As the lift door closed and he started to descend he remembered the nurse wasn't wearing a hat.

The nurse had continued to the ward where Mary was still sitting with her mother. The nurses' desk outside the ward was empty now that the nurses were carrying out their rounds in other wards and preparing the medicine trolley.

'Excuse me, are you Mrs Smith's daughter?' the nurse asked as she entered the room.

Turning, Mary could see the young, attractive nurse with blonde hair tied in a ponytail.

'Yes, I'm Mary.'

'I wonder, could you come with me? The consultant would like a quick word about your mother's progress. He's down in his office on the bottom floor, and I can show you the way.'

'Can we wait for my partner? He's just gone to get some coffee.'

'No, I'm sorry, the consultant needs to see you now as he only has a few minutes between his patient rounds.'

'OK, lead the way.'

The nurse walked in front of Mary towards the lift. Mary quickly sent a text message to Reece.

Going to see a consultant.

Inside the lift, the nurse pressed the button to the basement floor.

'Have they told you how your mother's doing?'

Mary noticed a small bead of sweat on the side of the nurse's face.

She's young and maybe in training, she thought, which is making her a little nervous.

It had been a while since she'd heard such a strong Belfast accent.

'They only say she's holding her own. I'm glad they took out a couple of those ugly tubes overnight,' replied Mary.

The lift came to a halt, and when the doors opened, the nurse turned left, and Mary followed. The corridor was quiet apart from two men dressed in a porter's uniforms pushing an empty bed trolley towards them. The nurse stopped walking, and standing to one side, she let Mary pass. Mary's thoughts had been about her mother's condition and the questions that she was going to ask the consultant.

Looking ahead at the two men, she began to realise that something was wrong. She couldn't see any office doors in the corridor, only the exit door behind the two men. As she got closer to the men, the realisation that something was wrong became stronger. The men were wearing baseball caps. They let hold of the trolley and started to walk towards her. Mary turned to walk in the opposite direction, but her way was blocked by Mariad Bailey. Mary opened her mouth to scream for help when a sudden explosion of pain went through her body, sucking all the breath out of her, followed by a darkness as she fell.

The stun gun did its job. Frank Walsh had jammed it into Mary's neck, and as she'd started to fall Jimmy Bailey supported her body before she hit the floor. When Brian McNally had given Walsh the stun gun, he told him she'd be out of it for only a few minutes, so time now was of the essence. Walsh handed the stun gun to Mariad Bailey while he helped Walsh lift Mary onto the bed trolley. All three quickly pushed the trolley through the emergency doors and out to where Walsh had parked the transit. They opened the rear doors and the men lifted Mary's body into the back of the vehicle. Mariad Bailey and Jimmy got into the back with Mary. Walsh closed the doors behind them and, jumping into the driver seat, drove the transit through the main hospital car parks and, turning left, out through the Donegal Road exit. In the back of the transit Mariad tied Mary's hands in front of her using plastic cuffs. Walsh made sure he drove at a safe speed. not bringing attention was important now. Mary started to come round. the pain in her neck and shoulder started to subside. Taking a deep breath she opened her eyes, the headache forcing her to close them again.

'So, Mary McAuley, you're our patient now. Lie still and keep quiet. There's plenty of electric charge in this little device to help you sleep a little bit more if you don't,' snarled Jimmy Bailey.

Mary opened her eyes slowly this time. She remembered the man in the hospital porter suit. the same man was now kneeling above her. Turning her head, she could see the pretty nurse who had walked into the corridor with her. She didn't panic, there would be no use in doing that now, she decided to say nothing. She felt sick and fought to keep from gagging.

This wasn't the first operation that Mariad Bailey had been on. Now 28 years old, she'd been a member of the women's IRA, the Cumann na mBan. At nineteen she'd joined the Provisional IRA, then after the ceasefire, and peace process, with her brother, she'd crossed over to the Real IRA. When she'd met with Brian McNally the night before in the back room of the Wolf Tone Club she was not surprised to be asked to take part in the operation to lift the tout, a traitor to the cause. She'd done the same two times before and both the touts had ended up lying on a border road with a bullet in the head. McNally explained the operation and had brought with him a bag containing the nurse and porter's uniforms for them to wear. He gave Walsh the stun gun and explained its use and effect. McNally had also told the two men that one of their people would deliver two pistols to the garage before they left for the hospital. These guns were only to be used if things went bad. The main danger being the ex-Special Branch man David Reece. McNally had said that it would be ideal if they could capture both Reece and McAuley, but the main target was Mary McAuley. She was a tout, and she'd to be dealt with.

Reece had a deep-seated instinct for danger from his days in Special Branch. The same instinct that had got him out of trouble and saved his life on a few occasions. As he stood in the queue at the coffee counter his mind was working overtime as he tried to understand why he was feeling a sense of that same danger now. He kept asking himself, what was it that was making him feel this way? His thoughts raced over what had happened that morning. His phone buzzed in his pocket, and he read the text message from Mary. Suddenly, he understood, and started to run back towards the lift.

CHAPTER 17

BELFAST

The lift was in use, but Reece didn't have time to wait. Still running, he took the stairs three at a time, up the two floors to the ward. Mary was nowhere to be seen. Her mother was still lying peacefully on the bed, her eyes still closed. Reece tried to call Mary, but her phone seemed to be switched off, the call going to her answer phone. He left a voice message for her to call him back and sent a text message to the same effect.

He searched two of the nearby wards before he found a nurse in one of the small side rooms.

He questioned the nurse, but in his stomach he already knew what the answers would be.

'No. I've been doing the rounds, and I haven't seen her since I spoke to you both this morning when you came in. Why, is something wrong?'

'Maybe, I don't know. can you get somebody from security to come here now?'

'Yes, right away,' the nurse replied before locking the medicine cabinet and going to the nurses' station where she dialled an internal number on the phone.

'Can you send someone from security to ward C3 immediately, please?'

'I'll check the ladies' toilets just to make sure she isn't there,' said the nurse, putting the phone down. When she left, Reece dialled the number for Tom Wilson on his phone. His gut instinct told him that Mary wasn't in the toilets. She wouldn't even be in the building.

'Mary's gone,' Reece said when Wilson answered the phone.

'What do you mean gone?' replied Wilson.

'She's gone. I think they have her. I went for coffee and when I came back, she'd disappeared. The hospital nurses don't know where. They don't know what happened.'

'I'll get our surveillance people to block off the exits and search vehicles leaving. You understand because it's a hospital we must let people come and go. I'll get the local police to send a couple of uniform cars to take over from the surveillance people. If we are lucky, she's still there, but if I know these people, they'll already have gone. I'll get Heather Black, and we'll see you at the hospital in twenty minutes. Then we can decide where to go, and what to do. In the meantime, you continue looking around where you are, asking people if they saw anything. We need to look at the hospital CCTV and speak to hospital security as well.'

'I'm already on it. I have the security people coming to the ward and I'll get them to have the CCTV set up for when you get here.'

'I'll update the chief constable. He will implement a plan that we've in case one of our officers is kidnapped. It basically closes the roads into the estates in West Belfast and the roads going south. I'll see you in twenty, will have the blues, and twos on to get us there quicker.' The line went dead.

When an overweight security man arrived on the ward Reece told him what he thought had happened. He told them that the police would be checking vehicles leaving the exits from the hospital and that he needed to see their CCTV right away. The security man didn't ask any questions.

'I'll only need to talk to the hospital chief executive and let her know what is happening,' said the security man.

'I don't care who you talk to, but we need to move fast. Where's your control room? Where's the CCTV?' asked Reece.

'Follow me. I can call the chief executive from there, it's on the top floor.'

Reece got into the lift with the security man. He could smell the sweat from the man, who he suspected was the type who got nervous easily. Reece knew the man was already nervous as he was being thrust into something that had probably never happened to him before. He would have to keep pushing the security man's buttons to get him to move quickly. When the lift stopped on the top floor they went through double doors directly opposite. There were no windows in the room and one other man was sitting in front of a console of TV screens showing the views from the CCTV cameras around the hospital. The man with Reece told the man in front of the screens what had happened, and that they needed to look back over the footage right away. Reece didn't want to go too deeply into his own and Mary's background. These men didn't need to know of their connections to the police and security services.

'This woman may have been abducted from the hospital. She's not a patient. she was visiting her mother. I need to see the footage of the last 20 minutes showing all exits from the building and from the car parks. Do you understand?'

The man in front of the consoles nodded. Using a small joystick, he moved the screen video around and Reece could see the timer on each one recording twenty minutes.

They watched as the black and white images moved forward again at normal speed on all four screens. Each monitor was split into four separate screens, the total showing fourteen door exits and the two exits from the hospital. It was Reece who saw one of the screens show two men wearing porter uniforms accompanied by a nurse with a blonde ponytail and no hat pushing a trolley carrying what looked like a woman. They could see the men were wearing baseball caps. They lifted the woman into the back of a white transit. Leaving the trolley, the nurse and one of the men got into the back of the transit, while the other closed the doors then got into the driver's seat to drive out of the camera's view. Reece told the man at the controls to freeze what he'd just seen, then check the hospital exit cameras for the transit leaving, then try to get a registration number. Reece knew he'd just seen the abduction of Mary. The memory of seeing the nurse in a blue uniform came back into his head.

'Where does that camera cover?' asked Reece.

'The ground floor delivery door at the back of the building,' answered the man working the joystick.

'Is there a camera inside where they came out through the doors?' asked Reece.

'No, just the outside,' replied the security man.

'When I was going down in the lift for coffee, I passed a nurse coming out. Do your nurses wear blue uniforms?' asked Reece.

'Just the nurses that work on the maternity ward. most of the other nurses wear light green. The nurses at the Royal Victoria hospital wear blue.'

'Can you blow up the screen to show the two men with the trolley and the nurse when they lifted the woman into the transit, and can you slow it down please?' said Reece, now using a softer tone to his voice. He knew people would react better if they felt they were being asked rather than ordered.

'Sir, that looks like the transit leaving by the Donegal Road exit,' said the security guard, working the joystick, and pointing to one of the screens. They could see the transit turning left on the Donegal Road, driving away from the city.

The security guard was speaking to the chief executive of the hospital on the phone.

'She wants to speak to you,' said the guard, handing the phone to Reece.

At least the woman sounded like she knew what she was doing, asking him all the right questions. It didn't take Reece long to explain what had happened, what they'd seen on the CCTV, and that the police would be checking vehicles leaving the hospital. He told her that a senior police officer was on route from police headquarters, and he would be able to explain more. The woman seemed happy with this, and she asked Reece to put the security guard back on.

'Thank you for that Mr Reece,' said the guard, putting down the phone. 'The chief executive says we are to give you any help you need.'

'Thank you. I'm sorry, but I forgot to ask your name.'

'It's John, the man at the desk is Stephen.'

'Thank you, John, and you too, Stephen, I'm David.' Reece tried to keep his voice under control even though he felt like he wanted to scream, run somewhere, or just punch someone. He knew if he showed the panic, he felt to these two men then things could be missed, and it wouldn't help the situation. 'It's obvious from what we've seen on your CCTV that my partner has been abducted by these people and now this is a police matter. As I told your chief executive, there's a senior police officer on the way, he'll take over the search for my partner. The best we can do is to have all these screenshots saved and ready for him to see. They will be here in 20 minutes, so, as there's nothing else we can do. I'm going to take a walk down to that corridor and the back door to see if they left any clues behind. I'll be back before the police get here. How do I get to the corridor?'

'You take the lift to the basement, then turn left when you come out of the lift,' said Stephen.

Reece didn't take long examining the corridor and the doors out to where the transit had been parked. It was then that he saw what he knew was Mary's phone lying smashed on the road. It was obvious that the phone had been deliberately placed under the wheels of the transit that took Mary. He knew the men were likely wearing gloves, most likely surgical gloves, to help with their disguise as porters, and the fact that they wore baseball caps and kept their heads down showed they were aware of the CCTV. He was sure the woman who posed as a nurse had no gloves on and there was a chance she may have left fingerprints behind. Reece was careful not to touch where he thought there could be prints but he knew deep down there wouldn't be any. Experience told him these bastards would be making every effort to get Mary across the border, where they could work on her in relative safety. He could feel his heart rate pumping faster in his chest and the metallic taste of adrenaline in his mouth. He had felt the same sensation many times before when the covert operations brought sudden danger, and most of all he knew time was against him. He had to try to control the anger inside him, the anger that wanted to kick in every door in West Belfast until he found her. The professional side was kicking in. He knew it would be a waste of time to jump into his BMW and drive up the Donegal Road to chase every white transit he saw. He agreed with Tom Wilson that the best plan for now would be to seal off the estates and roads going out and into West Belfast. The kidnappers would be desperate to get Mary to a safe location in the South of Ireland, somewhere close to the border with the North where they could work on her. Reece had worked with the southern police, the Garda, and he knew from experience they never wanted to rattle the Republican terrorist's cages. Thoughts of his time in Special Branch, when based in Newry a few miles from the Irish border, he'd seen the aftermath of the IRA torture team when they left a body on a border road after they'd interrogated them. Again, his pulse started to race at the memory. Many of those victims had admitted to being informers working for the security forces, but he also knew under torture many of them had admitted what the terrorists wanted to hear rather than take any more pain. Their final pain was a bullet in the back of the head. Torture teams or the Nutting squad as they were known, would sometimes leave explosive booby traps near the bodies to try to kill the security forces responding. Because of the suspect traps this led to long delays, until the ATO could clear the area before the bodies could be recovered, which only led to more pain and suffering for the families of the deceased. He tried to push these thoughts to the back of his memory. Now was not the time to think the worst but to try to concentrate and get Mary back safely.

Reece returned to the control room. He could see that Stephen knew how to get the best quality pictures out of the videos. He had transferred a running video with large still photographs to one screen. The face of the nurse was clear in the pictures. Because the men kept their heads down, the caps blocked any clear view of theirs. Reece knew any kind of mask would have brought unnecessary attention to them. He also knew they expected to be well away and in a safe location before the alarm could be raised. The PSNI were likely to have their faces on record, and the clear shots of the nurse might help to find them quickly. Again, Reece felt the pressure of time. The control room phone rang, and John answered.

'That was the chief executive. She's on her way up with your police officers,' he said, putting the phone back down.

Reece thought the chief executive looked younger than she sounded on the phone. She was dressed for business, wearing a dark blue trouser suit and dark rimmed glasses on a face that Reece would have described as oval, while her black hair was tied in a ponytail.

'Hello, Mister Reece, I'm Erin Johnson, the chief executive of the hospital,' said the woman, holding out her hand. 'Mister Wilson and my security people have told me what's happened. I think it's awful. I'm truly sorry and, of course we'll give you and the police whatever help we can.' Her accent was soft, almost lowland Scottish.

'Thank you. This is not yours or the hospital's fault. The people who did this have no respect for anyone. We have been looking at the CCTV and we've narrowed down the pictures you need to see. Stephen here has produced a rolling screenshot of what happened, plus the important still photographs of the people involved.'

Wilson and Black walked to the back of the room and asked Reece to join them so that they were out of earshot of the others.

'As I said on the phone, David, we've instigated a planned operation to seal off certain estates and locations in West Belfast. Because we've acted quickly, I'm sure they would have anticipated this, and will be hiding out somewhere in Belfast, instead of making a run for the border, which for the moment, is too far away, and full of dangers they don't want to run in to. We will search a few locations, but this will take time to set up and cause a lot of problems on the ground. I'm sure you remember from your own time on the job, the locals will react to any closing down of their area. It won't take long for the stones and petrol bombs to start flying. When that happens, the politicians will put pressure on the chief constable to pull out. Heather has her surveillance teams working to identify our suspects and to find where Mary is being held. I've also instructed our agent handlers to contact their people as soon as possible for any information they can get.'

'What do we do in the meantime? You know that every second counts and they'll be trying to get Mary across the border to work on her in some fucking shed where no one will hear her scream.' Reece could feel his stomach tense once more.

'You and Mary always knew the risk. For now, we are doing everything we can to get her back. I've asked Heather here to work with you and keep you updated every step of the way. For now, we'll send a copy of these photographs to our teams at HQ to see if they can identify these people quickly. I'll head back to headquarters to monitor everything and keep you both updated. Stay with Heather. She will be out on the ground keeping in touch with me and her own people using our secure comms.'

Heather Black sat down beside Stephen at the computer screens, plugged in a USB, and began to download the pictures he'd saved. When she'd completed the download, she plugged the USB into a tablet she was carrying, then pressing a few buttons on the tablet, she transferred the file.

'That's the file sent to headquarters. They will work on the photographs and video to try to identify them. Hopefully, it won't take long for us to identify them, but the men may take longer because of the baseball caps. Then we'll have something concrete to work on. From what I've seen, I'm pretty sure that the woman, the nurse, is Mariad Bailey, the sister of Jimmy Bailey. If it is her, then I must tell you she's one nasty bitch and anyone she's with will be just as nasty. We have run a couple of operations against both in the past. Her hair is black, I think that's a wig. If I'm right, then one of the men could be her brother,' said Black.

'Then we should hit their houses right away,' said Reece not feeling any better from what he'd just learnt.

'We will, but we both know they won't be home and there won't be any evidence to show what they're up to. By showing their faces they know we'll be after them and it's obvious that they'll be willing to go on the run and live somewhere south of the border out of our reach for now,' said Wilson. 'OK, Heather, take David here, and skirt round some of the estates where I have no doubt these rats are hiding. Your teams might get lucky and spot something. You can pull your people out of closing the hospital exits. I'll head back to headquarters to update the chief constable and keep an eye on what's going on. I've no doubt that as this is a public building, someone will have noticed the police activity, asked questions, and contacted the press. Before this gets out of control we need to move fast.'

Reece followed the DCI back to her car, a dark blue Audi. The car had been fitted with all the up-to-date surveillance equipment, from the hidden mic in the ceiling to the hidden camera showing the road ahead on a screen in the middle of the dashboard. Black had a running commentary going with her team. Reece could identify the callsigns. They hadn't changed much since his own days of operating surveillance in the city. He soon picked up most of the terms. The callsigns all reported they were covering the estates in West Belfast, Andersonstown, Ballymurphy, and Turf Lodge. Reece kept quiet as he listened to Black communicating with her operators and the control room back at headquarters. A radio message had broadcasted the registration number of the white transit van. There was no surprise to Reece or Black when they reported back that the plates were false and that they referred to a plumbing company in East Belfast.

Black asked HQ to look at any street CCTV to see where the van went after it left the hospital. Reece was surprised how quickly the reply came back. The van had gone up the Donegal Road and crossing over onto the Falls Road, it had last been seen passing Milltown Cemetery and heading towards the Andersonstown Estate. Black asked control to direct all resources towards that estate. Control confirmed the nurse fitted the description of Mariad Bailey but couldn't confirm the men.

Uniform search and arrest teams had been directed to go to the home addresses of the Bailey families and associates. Reece knew that if these people were as good as he thought they were, no one would be home. He asked Black to take him to Andersonstown, where the van had last been seen heading. It had started to rain heavily, and Reece remembered the old saying that rain was the policeman's best friend when it came to riot situations, the one thing rioters always seemed to hate more than the police was getting wet, it would keep them off the streets.

'Control to Red1,' Wilson's voice came over the radio. He must have put the blues and twos on to get back to headquarters that quickly thought Reece.

'Go ahead, control,' answered Black.

'Just to let you know, as expected, the press is onto what's going on. Our headquarters press office is getting enquiries from the Belfast Telegraph and BBC Radio Ulster. The teams need to be aware that there may be cameras out on the ground looking for trouble. I would think someone in the hospital has tipped them off.'

'Roger that. Understood,' answered Black. She looked across at Reece and raised her eyebrows. Both knew that once the press knew, politicians would know, and questions would start to fly, and answers demanded from the people back at headquarters. The pressure would be brought for them to pull back and avoid clashing with the communities in West Belfast. The politician's precious peace process was more important than Mary's life. This meant they didn't have much time. They drove around for another hour and despite the rain, the young hoods of West Belfast were coming out. Not only were they looking for police to throw the stones and petrol bombs at, but they were trying to stop cars which they would then hijack and set on fire. To try to stay undercover in such an area would be a mistake.

'I think we're wasting our time chasing our tails looking for these people. They will keep their heads down until things quieten down,' said Reece. 'My time would be better spent back at my hotel making a few phone calls. Can you drop me back at the hospital to pick up my car?'

'Yes, no problem. I'll let the boss know, and then I'll get back out to link up with my teams and see what we can do. I can pull them back to the edge around Andersonstown, so we can pick up on anything that looks suspicious moving about. I'm sure the boss will keep you updated. Try not to worry, David, everyone's out on the ground and we'll do everything we can to get Mary back safely. When I drop you off, I'll give you my number in case you need to get in touch.'

Reece nodded and forced a smile. He knew she was honest in what she'd said and that they were doing everything they could to find Mary, but he felt he needed to move things himself and that required a couple of private phone calls.

CHAPTER 18

ANDERSONSTOWN, BELFAST

They had reached the garage before the police road stops had been put in place. Jimmy Bailey had jumped out and opened the doors, allowing Walsh to reverse the transit into what realistically was a large hay shed which could have taken three transits. The shed was at the end of a lane that backed off the main Andersonstown Road and the estate which ran under the main Belfast to Dublin M1 motorway. Brian McNally had kept this building in his back pocket for just such an operation only known to himself and those involved. On the way to the shed, Mariad Bailey had put a gag around Mary's mouth. The gag almost made Mary retch. she could taste car oil on it, and she imagined it must belong to one of the two men. The woman in the nurse's uniform, who had now removed her wig showing her black hair underneath, seemed to be enjoying herself, grinning as she pulled Mary by the hair, she led her to a chair. The woman tied Mary's arms behind her, then each of her legs to the front of the chair, before removing the gag.

'Who the fuck are you? Why are you doing this to me? Let me go.'

The woman in the nurse's uniform came right up to Mary, then leaning over her, slapped her.

'You would be better to keep your tout mouth shut. We are not interested in your bleating,' the woman spat the words into Mary's face. Mary felt the sting of the slap and wanted to cry but biting her lip held back. she didn't want to show any weakness to this bitch.

'You had better do as she says and keep quiet. No one can hear you here anyway, so you'd be wasting your breath. If you're a good girl, we might give you some water and something to eat later. In the meantime, there's a bucket in the corner if you need to go to the toilet,' said Walsh.

Mary looked around her. The building they were in appeared to be an old shed or somewhere that farming machinery would be kept. She could hear the constant noise of traffic moving at speed and guessed they were near a motorway. It was dry and had three lit electric bulbs hanging from the ceiling. There were three made-up camp beds in the far corner of the shed with a card table and four chairs. Mary felt that it would be a waste of time trying to shout for help, as it looked like the shed had been well prepared for her arrival. The windows had been covered with sheets of PVC board.

'Can I have a drink of water? I can still taste that rag you stuffed in my mouth.'

Without saying anything Walsh took a small bottle of water out of a holdall sitting beside the table, unscrewed the top, then poured a small amount into Mary's mouth.

'Thank you.'

'You're welcome. Just to make sure you know what happens next, it's our job to keep you well until we deliver you to our friends south of the border. We are under orders to speak to you as little as possible and that you're well enough to make the journey, which might be a little uncomfortable for you. So, if I was you, I would save my breath and energy for what comes next. You're going to need it.'

Her arms and wrists ached where they were tied. The woman seemed to take pleasure in pulling them even tighter when she'd sat Mary in the chair. Mary tried to concentrate. She tried to keep her head clear even though it was buzzing with the whole experience. She had an idea of what they were planning for her, but she couldn't let herself think about that for now. She knew David and the others would be looking for her and wondering if these people were going to hurt her. For now, she'd do everything in her power to prevent that hurt coming sooner rather than later.

'You to keep an eye on her. I'm going to call the boss to let him know everything is on schedule,' said Walsh as he left by the smaller of the two shed doors. He walked to the bottom of the lane that joined the main road, then walked another 200 yards to the call box. When McNally had briefed the three of them in the Wolf Tone Club the night before, he'd given Walsh the telephone number of the club and said he'd be in the bar and to call there when they'd lifted the tout. The phone had rung out three times before it was answered. Walsh asked the man answering for Brian McNally. A minute later Walsh heard the familiar voice of his boss.

'Hello, what have you got for me?'

'First part done, but we only got the woman. We are back safe in the den. What do you want us to do now?'

'As we thought, the opposing team is bringing a lot of pressure to bear in our half of the pitch. We're going to have to play defence for a couple of days before we can move forward. You have everything you need in the den to play safe and lie low. Call me here again tomorrow at one. By then, we'll have a clear picture of what the opposition is up to. In the meantime, preparations are being made for the transfer to the next team below the line. Remember, they want her fresh, undamaged.'

'Understood. Until one tomorrow,' Walsh replied putting down the phone.

When he returned to the shed, Walsh sat at the table with the brother and sister. He told them of his conversation with McNally and that they would have to stay in the shed for the next few days.

'For fuck's sake, do you mean we've to clean that bitch's backside for the next two days?' asked Jimmy Bailey.

'You know better than I do, Jimmy. You don't disobey orders. If the boss had heard you now, he would blow your kneecaps off himself,' answered Walsh.

'Frank's right, Jimmy, and anyway, you don't have anything better to do. I know your love life,' said Bailey's sister.

'Right, we can keep her in the chair during the day and at night we can tie her to one of the beds. But one of us will be awake at all hours. We have the Browning pistol, which we'll use if we need to, but other than that we keep her fresh and well, as the boss said,' said Walsh.

Walsh left the table and walked over to where Mary was seated.

'Your friends are looking for you, but they won't find you here, so to be on the safe side we want to keep you happy and well for a couple of days. So, you be a nice girl and we won't hurt you. But any fucking about and who knows we may have to break a bone or two. Just nod if you understand.'

Mary nodded, but in a way, she felt relieved that she was going to be here for another couple of days.

CHAPTER 19

HILTON HOTEL

The rain was coming down faster than ever when Reece parked the car back at the Hilton. He was still alert to any surveillance watching him. Not just the police surveillance, but anyone else, especially after what happened to Mary. He ordered a pot of coffee for his room and sat down at the dressing table to make two phone calls. The first call was to the office of the director of SG9, Jim Broad. When he was connected, the secretary put him through to Broad's office immediately.

'Hello, David,' answered Broad. 'I've been expecting your call. Caroline Aspinall and Tom Wilson have both been in touch to update me about what has happened. Have you any more news?'

'Probably no more than you already know. They have Mary and we must get her back. It's as simple as that. But the longer it takes the more likely she'll be dead.'

'I'm sure Wilson and his team are doing everything they can. I know that Aspinall has been in touch with GCHQ to make sure anything they pick up is passed to you right away.'

Reece had expected that. He knew that they would be using all the resources they had including listening into the terror groups' conversations through their bugging and telephone intercept operations.

'Boss, you know Mary, and I wanted to leave all this behind us, but these bastards just wouldn't leave it alone. Anything you can do to help me get Mary back safely is greatly appreciated.'

There was a few seconds' silence and Reece could imagine Broad either writing things down or speaking to someone else in the room.

'Understood, David. I have C here with me now, and we are both in agreement that even though you put in your resignation from the department, we'll give you whatever help we can to get Mary back. But I have to say, you must understand the delicacies of the shit that the Northern Ireland situation, the political situation, can throw up. Between Caroline Aspinall and the MI5 team and Tom Wilson with his people, we think you have enough there now to get the job done, provided we believe Mary is still in Northern Ireland. At this moment, it's basically an abduction, a kidnapping, so realistically a policing matter. So for now, work through Tom Wilson. To help you, I'm sending Joe Cousins, who can provide the SG9 footprint on the ground. He'll be with you in a few hours. I've booked him into the Hilton so that you can work together, and any feedback can be provided in real time.'

Reece knew that Sir Ian Fraser was in the office with Broad and as the head of MI6 he'd sanctioned the involvement of the SG9 input. To Reece this meant it was being taken seriously and at a high level.

'I appreciate your help, boss. I'll be in the hotel for the next hour or so waiting on calls from Wilson.'

'Good luck. If we get anything, I'll be in touch,' said Broad.

Putting down the phone, Reece looked out the window, the grey clouds and the heavy

Rain seemed to make the whole situation even darker. Somehow, the fact that Joe Cousins was coming to help him made things seem a little easier. Reece had worked with Cousins on a couple of operations recently. Both had ended in people being killed, one of them a female SG9 agent known to them both. He knew Cousins would be a calming and reliable influence on him and that the experience he would bring would be invaluable if they were to find Mary.

The next call he made was on his mobile phone. His thinking was that GCHQ and.

MI5 wouldn't have it bugged yet, or at least he hoped so. Anyway, he didn't care anymore. They either would help him, or they wouldn't. If he had to operate alone, he would. From his recent travels to Israel, Reece knew Tel Aviv was two hours ahead, which meant it was now early evening there. Jacob Lavyan had given him his personal number, so there was no worry about it being an office connection. The international dialling tone sounded at least six times before he heard the familiar voice.

'Hello, David. I didn't expect to hear from you so soon. How are you?'

'I'm well, Jacob. But I have a problem and I hope you'll be able to help me.'

'If I can, my friend. What do you need?'

It was the answer Reece had hoped for before he'd called the number. It would make the conversation easier.

'Thank you, Jacob. My problem is a big one.'

'Go ahead, I'm listening. Are there others listening too, do you think?'

'Probably, but I don't care. This is important.'

'I understand.'

'Mary has been kidnapped by terrorists. We are in Belfast. Her mother was injured in a car accident, which I think they carried out to get us here and while we were at the hospital this morning she was abducted.'

'That's terrible! What are you doing to get her back?'

'That's where I need your help. The police and security services here are doing everything they can, but because of the peace agreement and the political niceties they'll be hindered. When we met you told me of a source your people in Dublin had.'

'Yes, I remember.'

'If these people take Mary where I think they'll take her, that source might be able to identify where.'

'I don't know if the source is still available. I know from my own experiences time is important in these situations. I'll find out right away and get back to you within the hour. Where are you staying?'

'That's great, thank you Jacob, I'm staying in the Hilton hotel but maybe not for long. I'll wait for your call before I do anything else.'

'Shalom, David, shalom.'

'Shalom,' replied Reece, cancelling the call.

He called reception and ordered another pot of coffee. Before it arrived, his phone buzzed again. This time he could see the name Tom Wilson flash on the screen.

'Hello, Tom. Any news?'

'Yes, David, some good, some bad, I'm afraid. The bad news first. We have had to pull back the uniform people on the ground around the estates. As we expected, the young people were beginning to have a field day, attacking them with the usual bottles and bricks. Considering the weather, we didn't expect there to be so many and they appear organised, so that would indicate paramilitary involvement, someone controlling the response. On top of that the politicians at Stormont are bringing pressure on the chief constable and when that happens nowadays, he must consider everything, and try to cool the situation down.'

Reece had expected this but not so quickly. Someone or some organisation was behind this.

'And the good news?' asked Reece.

'For a start, we'll be pulling the uniform people back from the estates, but not out all together. They will set up traffic checks on the roads out of the city, mainly the ones going south. When things quieten down in the estates, Heather Black's team will be able to operate again with drive-through passes on the main suspect locations. We have had one source come in already to say that Brian McNally, the OC for Belfast Real IRA, has been spending a lot of time in the last 24 hours in the Wolfe Tone Club and taking calls. McNally is a nasty piece of work and I'm sure he has his dirty hands all over this. We will increase our surveillance on him and the club and listen in where we can. Two of his favourite men that he uses are Jimmy Bailey and Frank Walsh. So that would confirm who the men were, Jimmy being Mariad's brother, so we've everyone looking for them as well. What I'm saying, David, is that we are doing all we can, and we are starting to see some cracks to look through to help us find Mary.'

'Anything from Five?' Reece knew if MI5 were doing their job, they would already have several locations in the city bugged. They would have everyone on it listening for any scrap of information. If only to report back to their political head in Northern Ireland, the SOS, the Secretary of State.

'Nothing yet, but with them now knowing about our friend McNally and the Wolf Tone Club, they'll zero in on that and hopefully get something soon. Anyway, I'll keep in touch. Will you be staying at the hotel?'

'Yes, I've nothing else planned.'

'Right. Talk later.'

After the call, Reece thought about what Wilson had said. The politicians were getting jittery and putting pressure on Wilson and the PSNI. In his own way, Wilson had let Reece know he was on his side and trying to ignore them. He had also let him know that MI5 had the Wolfe Tone Club bugged, if not the building at least the phones. Reece had always hated the waiting for information when operational. He realised he'd been walking back and forth across the room willing for something more concrete to happen to let him know where Mary was so that he could be more involved. Reece was usually the one pulling the strings, but for now he had to be patient, and he didn't like being patient he was more a man of action. The mobile phone buzzed.

'Shalom, Jacob.'

'Shalom, David. Any news?' replied Jacob Lavyan.

'Nothing yet. We are still searching and hoping for some intelligence as to where they might be holding Mary. For the moment, we still think they have her in Belfast. The politicians and the press are sticking their noses in and that could only make things worse.'

'Do they know who might have her?'

'We have a few names. All not good people. They are knocking on their doors, but nobody's at home.'

'Well, I might have some good news. I've spoken to my contacts in Dublin, and they believe they can still contact the source in South Armagh. He's a lot older now and not as involved as he was, but he should still have his ear to the ground, as you say. So he might be able to point us to where they have Mary.'

'That's great, Jacob. Any help at all is most welcome.'

'In the meantime. I've asked one of my ERM people in Dublin to contact the source and you. His name is Ari, and he was a Katsa in the same business as you and is aware of what is needed. I've given him your number, so expect a call sometime this evening. If you need anything more, call me at any time, night, or day.'

Reece knew that Jacob was telling him that Ari was an ex-Mossad field intelligence officer who was now working for Jacob's company.

'I owe you one, Jacob. All being well, we can get together when this is over.'

'That would be good. I look forward to it, maybe another Bushmills. Shalom, David, Shalom.'

'Shalom, Jacob.'

Reece sent a text to Broad.

Need files on people over here who may have Mary. Can Joe bring with him?

A reply came back almost immediately.

Will send what we've and will contact Tom and Caroline to make sure they provide what they have as well.

Reece drank some more coffee even though his stomach felt like he could throw up at any time.

Chapter 20

West Belfast

'I need to go to the toilet,' said Mary. She couldn't see her watch, and she estimated they'd been here for at least three hours. Her shoulders, back, and wrists were starting to hurt. She needed to move. She needed to get the circulation back.

'No problem, little lady, there's a bucket in the corner you can use,' said Mariad Bailey with a smirk on her face.

'But I need at least to be able to get the circulation of blood back into my arms and legs. The hand ties are tight, and my arms are going numb. My hands and fingers are tingling. If your bosses really want me to be in good condition when you hand me over, then at least untie me and let me walk about for a few minutes. There's three of you with guns, so I would be mad to try anything stupid.'

Walsh stood up from the chair at the table and, standing behind Mary, he examined her hands and arms. He could see the skin around the ties had turned purple and bruised. Taking a clasp knife from his trouser pocket, he opened the blade, then cut through the ties.

'Just remember you're the one who said it would be stupid for you to do anything. I would hate to have to tell my bosses that you tried to escape, and we had to shoot you.'

Mary felt her arms fall loose by her sides. A sudden flow of blood through her wrists into her hands felt like an electric shock. She stood and shook her arms by her sides until she felt the tingling disappear. She turned to look Walsh in the eye.

'I'm not stupid, but I think you all are. No matter what happens to me there are people out there looking for us right now, and they'll find you. When that happens, we'll see who the stupid people really are.'

All three kidnappers smiled. Mariad Bailey walked around Mary slowly. When she stood in front of her, she laughed.

'If your friends are looking for us, and if they find us, you'll never know cos I'll put a bullet in your head before they get through those doors. We don't know why our people want you, but we know you're a tout for the Brits. You might have had a wonderful background working for the Provos during the war. That all adds up to nothing if you're a tout.'

'And if I'm not a tout, what do you think will happen then? The war is over, and the peace process is more important than your little army,' replied Mary.

'Enough of the chat, Mariad. This bitch will get what's coming to her soon enough. We just need to concentrate on what we must do. Don't let her get in your head,' said Walsh.

Walsh grabbed Mary's arms from behind and shoved her back down into the chair.

'We'll tie your hands again if you try anything. Remember, one of us will always be watching you, so as you say, let's not be stupid,' said Walsh.

'Let's all have a cup of tea and settle down for the night,' said Jimmy.

CHAPTER 21

STORMONT

Reece had dozed on top of the bed. The buzzing from his mobile phone woke him. Although it was still late afternoon, because of the time of year, it was already getting dark. He could see the name Tom Wilson on the screen.

'Hi, Tom. What's happening?'

'Hi, David. We still have everybody out on the ground looking for Mary and any information we can get. In an hour, we're going to have a meeting with the SOS at Stormont. I would like you to be there. The more ammunition we've in our back pocket the better. I know that your work for SG9 is still top secret and maybe even the SOS is not aware of the department. The meeting, as far as I can see it, is to bring up two things. The first is to brief him on everything we know so far about Mary's abduction. The second is to get him to use his political influence on the Republican side to show them that it's in their best interests to help find Mary and get her back.'

'Yes, I can be there. Where exactly in Stormont? It's a big place.'

'Not the big parliament building itself but round the side. Where the SOS has his own offices besides Stormont Castle. You will be cleared to get through security, and I'll meet you in reception, see you in one hour.'

The call finished, Reece decided a quick shower and fresh clothes were needed. When dealing with politicians he always felt that appearances and a clear head were important.

The drive to Stormont only took 30 minutes from the hotel. The view of the main building as you drive up the mile long entrance from the Newtownards Road was always stunning thought Reece. The building was the location of the first Northern Ireland Parliament which lasted until it was taken over by rule from Westminster at the beginning of the Troubles. From a distance, the building looks like it's been made of white marble, but it's the paint that was used to make it look that way. Reece knew that when he got to the roundabout, where the Edward Carson statue stands in the middle, that he should go to the road to his right and to the grounds of Stormont Castle. Reece had only been at the castle once before when he worked at Police HQ, and he had to drop off an intelligence report. He knew the castle was where the main civil servants of the government of Northern Ireland work. Beside the castle is the Stormont cottages one of which was the offices of the SOS for Northern Ireland. When he had finished his call with Tom Wilson, Reece realised he hadn't a clue who the SOS was. All he knew was that it would be an MP from the current British government in power at Westminster. He Googled on his phone, so he was able to find out that Gerald Freeman MP of the Conservative Party of Great Britain and Northern Ireland was the current SOS as they were known to the security services. He didn't have the time to research him further. He was waved through the main security gates by the armed

PSNI officers, then through to the castle and the cottage. Wilson, as promised, had called ahead to ensure his clearance, bearing in mind that Reece would be carrying the Walther Pistol he'd given him. Reece parked the BMW in one of the visitor's parking bays. Entering the main reception area he saw another security guard standing just inside the door who nodded for him to go through. Giving his name to the receptionist he was asked to wait for a few minutes as she made a call to someone, letting them know he'd arrived. Within five minutes Reece could see Wilson walking down the long corridor towards him.

'David, I'm glad you're here. The SOS is in his office with a few people I think you know. Follow me.'

Reece followed, feeling like a schoolboy being escorted to the headmaster's office not knowing whether it was going to be good or bad. The corridor seemed very long for a cottage and at the end there was a pair of double doors leading into a small secretary's office where a woman sat typing behind the desk. Wilson didn't stop, but continued to walk through another set of doors, with Reece following. The room was well lit, as despite the large bay windows overlooking a lawn, the early evening darkness had descended, the grass still visible highlighted by spotlights pointing towards the sky from ground level. The office was palatial, with a three-piece leather suite and a large desk with two chairs in front of it. At the side, four people were sitting around a large circular conference table. All four people stood to greet Reece as he came into the room. Two of them, Jim Broad, and Caroline Aspinall, he already knew. *They got here fast*, thought Reece. He also recognised the SOS from his Google photograph, but in the flesh, he looked even younger. The Right Honourable Gerald Freeman MP came around the table and introduced himself, shaking Reece's hand.

'Mr Reece, I'm pleased to meet you, although I'm sorry the circumstances aren't better. Please, join us at the table. I'm sure you know Jim and Caroline here. This is Beverley, my personal secretary. As this is a special meeting, she'll take some notes. I find notes can be easier redacted than tape recordings.' He smiled.

Reece nodded in acknowledgement to the others at the table.

As he spoke while shaking his hand, Reece had the feeling the SOS was asking for his vote. Reece sat at the table beside Tom Wilson. The SOS resumed his seat and Reece noticed that there were yellow writing notepads and pens in front of everyone except Beverley, who held on to her notebook while continuing to write, no doubt adding Reece's name to the list already attending the meeting.

'Beverley has been cleared at the highest level,' continued the SOS. 'David, I can call you, David?'

'Yes, no problem,' replied Reece.

'You can call me Gerald or minister if you prefer.'

'I can assure you everything said in this room stays in this room. The notes will be kept on file but are mainly for my benefit, as I've found that with the many meetings I attend, they help me remember who I met with and what was discussed. I would therefore ask any notes you make yourselves to be left behind for Beverley to file or destroy as I see fit. After this meeting, I'll also be speaking with the prime minister. He has told me you helped deal with the situation in Manchester and that we can be assured of your full cooperation today. I've been fully briefed and updated about this terrible situation and what has happened so far. Tom Wilson has kept me informed via the chief constable of what action the police have taken. He tells me that it would be a waste of time to lift some of these people now. We are not totally sure of who they are or where they are. We don't have enough information to question them, and even if we did lift them, they would say nothing, wasting the time we need to find this lady. Then, to add to things, it could mean more riots on the streets, something we need to avoid at all costs. I was just about to be briefed by Jim and Caroline. Your arrival is auspicious and just in time. Before they start, I think I should tell you a little bit about myself because everything on Wikipedia isn't the whole story. Normally, posting to Northern Ireland as SOS is seen as a dead-end job. Basically, a minister is sent here to keep the lid on things and to stop the two factions from getting back to killing each other.

'To tell you the truth, David, it's like keeping a bunch of unruly children from throwing their dummies out of the pram. You might not know it, but I come from a military background. I was a captain in 2 PARA, which didn't make the Republican side so happy, but the fact that I'd never served in Northern Ireland saved the day. I did two tours in Iraq, so I've some idea of what it takes to operate in a hostile environment and having been briefed by Tom and Jim on your background, and where you come from, and what you've done, I want you to know from the start that you have my full support.

'I know that London and the politicians here are not happy that your friend Mary has been taken in this way. The big worry, and you must appreciate this, is that the peace process needs to be kept on track, so from a political point of view I'll be taking the lead in that respect. Now we were just getting round to your involvement with Mary, so before we hear from Jim and Caroline can you bring me up to speed on how you got to know her, if you could tell me in your own words?'

Reece looked around the table. All the eyes were now on him. Both Wilson and Broad, who knew the background best, nodded for him to continue. Reece felt they were wasting time with back stories. But, from what he knew of politicians they always wanted a fuller story to protect their backsides in case the shit hit the fan.

'Well to save time, minister, I'll give you the short version. During my days in Special Branch, I recruited Mary McAuley as an agent, working close within the higher ranks of the Provisional IRA and their political arm, Sinn Fein. During those years she provided vital intelligence, saving many people's lives. In the run-up to the peace process and the talks they involved, she was able to give a running insight into what the Republican movement was thinking and saying to help move the peace talks along. There may have been other people doing the same thing at the same time, but I think the information she provided was so beneficial, we probably wouldn't be where we are today and have a peace process where both sides put down their weapons and are talking instead of killing.' Reece stopped talking and waited for a response from the minister.

'Thank you for that, David. My own view is that if it was not for agents such as Mary, and undercover officers working behind the scenes such as yourself, we may have taken a lot longer to get where we are today with the peace process. Can I ask you where you are today, I mean in your personal relationship with Miss McAuley?'

One thing Reece was beginning to realise about Freeman was that he took no prisoners. getting straight to the point and wasn't afraid to ask the difficult questions.

'Since the last operation I was involved in, which took place in London, you may be aware of, Mary and I'd hoped to retire to Malta and that's where we've been the last month. The night before her mother's accident, I asked Mary to marry me, and she said yes. So, answering your question, minister, our relationship is one based on solid ground where we both want a future together, hopefully living in Malta into our old age in peace and away from all this shit.'

'Thank you, David. I think we all understand where you're coming from. Now, Jim, as I understand it from the prime minister, both David and Mary played a significant role in saving his life during the recent operation in Manchester.'

'That's correct, minister. David has been working with the department for a few years after having retired as a detective inspector in Special Branch here in Northern Ireland. Just before the Conservative Party Conference last year, his old agent Mary McAuley made contact to say she'd information that there was going to be some sort of attack in Manchester. After further investigation and more intelligence from Mary, we were able to ascertain that the target was the prime minister attending the conference.

'We were also able to discover that the terrorist operation was a joint one between a member of the Real IRA, Sean Costello, and an Islamic terrorist cell led by Sharon Lyndsey. On this occasion, Mary McAuley put herself at great risk in helping spot Costello, who she knew personally from her days working within the Provisional IRA. We now believe that it was during the operation in Manchester that Mary may have been identified as working with us, this information then being passed back to the Real IRA, who we now believe instigated her mother's hit-and-run, putting her in hospital forcing Mary back to Belfast, into the open where she could be abducted. It is also possible that David is a target either for abduction or assassination.'

Freeman raised his hand and nodded towards Jim Broad.

'Just a quick one, Jim. This may be a bit of information that David is unaware of. The brother of Sean Costello is Paul Costello, and he's a senior Sinn Fein MLA or member of the local assembly here in Northern Ireland. So he would be one of the people that I'll be talking to as we try to get Mary returned. I've spoken to him in the past and I find him to be opposed to violence, but in the case of getting revenge for his brother's death, his views may have changed. Please continue, Jim.'

'I have much more to say, minister. As regards to the operation in Manchester, subsequent intelligence we received at the time confirms Sean Costello, who had been a member of the Real IRA after the peace process, had gone rogue, and was carrying out the operation without the sanction of the Army Council. It is our belief that Sean and Paul had both gone separate ways after the ceasefire and the signing of the Good Friday Agreement.'

'Caroline, can you bring us up to date with any new information from the MI5 and GCHQ point of view?' asked Freeman.

Reece noticed Caroline Aspinall had a small file in front of her, which she now opened.

'Thank you, minister. As soon as I was made aware of the abduction by ACC Wilson and our own offices based at Palace Barracks, I immediately requested that anything we had on the Real IRA, specifically the Belfast Brigade, should be forwarded to me, so that I could brief everyone here. From a few telephone intercepts, I can confirm that this abduction has been planned and carried out by the Real IRA, under the orders of Chief of Staff Brendan McDevitt and their Army Council. The police surveillance team has for some time been watching the movements of the Real IRA Belfast Brigade Commander Brian McNally. They noticed recently he was using a public phone box near his home on the Falls Road to make and receive calls. Because of the intercept on this phone in the follow up to the abduction, we noticed he made a call to a number in the Republic of Ireland. He had a cryptic conversation about having a package, which he would now deliver. We recognised the voice of the person in the Republic of Ireland as that of John Jo Murphy. We had his voice on record from when he'd talked previously with Sean Costello during the Manchester operation. On that occasion Costello had set him the task of tracking down Mary McAuley if she was in Belfast, because he believed he'd seen her in Manchester. John Jo Murphy is now a senior member of the Real IRA and we believe he's been put in charge of the operation to abduct Mary, then have her brought across the border for interrogation, and subsequently, no doubt execution.'

While listening to the director of MI5, Reece couldn't help thinking, *no shit, Sherlock*. Reece remembered back to his days in Special Branch and working with the MI5 bugging teams who operated out of the military base at Palace Barracks in Hollywood. He wasn't surprised to hear that they were still working out of the same building, as it was a relatively secure location outside Belfast city. Caroline Aspinall turned over a page of the notes. Pushing her glasses back on the bridge of her nose, she continued.

'Obviously goes without saying that everything I tell you in this room regarding our technical operations and transcripts resulting from them is top secret.' Everyone nodded.

'We have another operation running, which has been running for some time, covering the Wolfe Tone Club in West Belfast. The club is a popular drinking den for all the Republican factions in the city. We have both phones and the bar area itself covered, although you'll understand because of the noise side it's difficult to hear voice conversations sometime. I'm telling you this because although we do not have any voice conversations indicating anything to do with this abduction, we do have a phone call conversation between Brian McNally and an unknown male. The male confirmed that they had the package and were safe at the location. McNally told the unknown male that there was the expected security force's response, sealing off the areas, blocking roads. He told the unknown male they may have to stay where they were for a couple of days but that he'd be in touch to update him.

'We don't know where the unknown male is, but the phone number he was using refers to a call box in Andersonstown. Now that we've his phone number, GCHQ will keep a monitor on it, but from the conversation we expect the unknown male to call McNally again at 1pm tomorrow.

'I've told ACC Wilson the location of the call box and he'll have eyes on it if he can identify the caller and maybe follow him. We will continue to monitor all three phones. The call box used by McNally, and the one used by the unknown male, plus the Wolf Tone Club. I'm sure everyone agrees the conversations all indicate that Mary is being held somewhere in the North of Ireland, most likely still in Belfast. I'm sorry, I can't give you anything more at this time, minister. When we get more, it might give us the opening we need to track down these people, allowing us to react, and get Mary back.' Aspinall tidied up the papers in front of her and closed the folder.

Reece could see the evening being lit up by the spotlights on the outside lawn casting shadows across the grass. The SOS stood and looked at the faces looking back.

'Thank you everyone. David, I hope that what you've heard reassures you that we are doing everything we can to get Mary back safely. I want you to work with Tom and Jim, but please, no heroics on your own. This is a delicate matter and there's more involved here than just the recovery of Miss McAuley, as I'm sure you will understand. Everyone knows what they must do. For my part I'll have the senior members of Sinn Fein, including Paul Costello here for a meeting this evening, after which I'll speak with the prime minister. As for the press and media who are already onto this: my own Press Officer and the Press office at the PSNI will be the only ones to have any contact with them. For now, all we say is we've received a report of a possible abduction of a female, and enquiries are ongoing. Questions regarding the follow-up searches and police road stops in the West of the city can be covered by the usual answer that we are carrying out investigations into dissident activity. Let me not detain you any further. Caroline and Tom, can you stay behind? I need to go over a few things with you before I meet with the Republican politicians. Thank you, everyone. We all have a job to do, so let's get on with it.'

Reece could see Freeman as a commander of men in a military setting, but having nodded to the SOS his understanding, he had no intention of leaving this to a politician. As everyone stood to leave, Broad came round the table and shook Reece by the hand before whispering.

'I'm sorry about all this, David, but as you can see, we are putting everything into getting Mary back. Can I walk you back to your car?'

As they walked back down the long corridor and out into the car park, Broad said nothing more.

'Mine's the BMW,' said Reece, taking the keys out of his pocket and pressing the remote. The side lights flashed, and they could hear a loud click as the doors unlocked.

'So, boss, what is it you want to talk about?'

'That politician in there talks a good talk. We'll have to see if he walks the walk. I wanted to speak to you alone to reassure you of mine and Fraser's full support. We're taking a risk letting you know you can run your own investigation outside the parameters and restrictions of the local political scene. When you get back to the hotel, you'll find Joe Cousins and our friend from the SAS, Captain Geoff Middleton, waiting for you. They travelled over by Puma to the Hanger at RAF Aldergrove at the same time Caroline and I flew from London. Before they left, I briefed them at the SG9 office at the city airport. Everything you heard in there and more is in a file for your eyes only that they have with them. They also have equipment for you that you might need. I'll be available twenty-four seven but, as I might need to head back to London you should proceed as you see fit. I know you gave me your resignation notice but as it wasn't in writing I've told Sir Ian, you're still on the books.'

Broad took a small wallet out of his pocket and handed it to Reece.

'It's your old MI5 get out of jail ID. Only use it if you really need to and don't get caught with it on you or it might bring you more trouble than you need.'

'I don't know if I should thank you or not, but I do appreciate that you're putting your neck on the line. I'm not going to give any guarantee that this will end happily but, I can assure you if people hurt Mary or come after me. Then they'll know what hurt really means. Why are you putting your neck on the line, anyway?'

'Two reasons. The first is through the prime minister via Sir Martin Bryant and C. They all know your past and what you can do, and as they expect you'll do whatever it takes to get Mary back, anyway, they would rather we had some control of that. The second, as I'm sure you're sick of hearing, is the danger that this has brought or could bring to the peace process if it goes tits up and there was a shoot-out on the streets of Belfast between members of the British Security forces and dissident republicans. That is to be avoided at all costs and I suspect that will be one of the points the SOS is now pressing on Tom Wilson and Caroline as we speak. The Republican delegation he'll meet with later will be told the same thing.'

Broad reached into his pocket and removed a mobile phone which he handed to Reece.

'This phone is encrypted. It's the latest Samsung model and won't be picked up by anyone who wants to listen in. It already has three numbers on speed dial, Joe Cousins, Geoff Middleton, and me. If you need to add anyone to the list, feel free to do so, but make sure it's only people we can trust. This operation is off the books, David, as I'm sure you're beginning to understand. You get caught, you're on your own, and we'll totally deny you as having gone rogue. David, you know this country better than any of us. You know what makes these bastards tick, so I'm hoping you'll be able to get inside their heads. You will have noticed that at the meeting we just had, there were no files or photos provided of the people we think are involved. I think in all reality, the politicians are shitting themselves and just want this to go away. That means a body at the border. If it's been done in the Republic, they can do a Pontius Pilate and wash their hands of everything. I'll be in back in London and I'll keep you up to date from there. In the meantime, get back to the hotel and catch-up with Joe who has all the information you need to know about the bastards we think lifted Mary and the ones behind it. Geoff has a Smith and Wesson 59, which has the firepower you like. At least it's better than the Walther Tom Wilson gave you. He wants it back, by the way.'

Broad held out his left hand and Reece placed the Walther with the spare mag into it before shaking Broad's right hand.

'Thank Sir Ian for me. If this goes sideways, I know I'll only have myself to blame,' said Reece.

'If this goes sideways, we are all fucked for the future, but we all need a little bit of excitement now and then, and the one thing I've found since I got to know you, David, is that there's always a little excitement just around the corner.'

CHAPTER 22

HILTON HOTEL, BELFAST

Joe Cousins and Geoff Middleton were sitting at a table in the hotel's main bar. It was Cousins who spotted Reece and waved him over.

'Normally, I'd say it's great to see you too, but under the circumstances…I'm glad you're here anyway,' said Reece, pulling up a chair.

'Good to see you too.' Cousins smiled. 'We just got a round in. Do you want one?'

'That would be good. It's been one bitch of a day. Thanks, Joe.'

'The usual?'

'Yeah, Bushmills, make it a double, thanks.'

Reece leant over to shake the hand of the SAS man.

'I'm glad your both here Geoff. I've just been to a meeting with the SOS for Northern Ireland and the security people involved and I'm glad to say we are starting to get some information on where this is all heading.'

Cousins returned and handed the whisky to Reece, who took a large gulp before setting the glass down.

'Thanks, Joe, I needed that,' said Reece.

'So, I see, but don't drink it too quickly. Have you seen the prices in here?' replied Cousins.

'London briefed us, and we've a file in my bag here for you to read later,' said Middleton, pointing to the grip bag beside his leg.

'Yes, Jim Broad told me, and I believe you have something a bit heavier as well.' Reece smiled.

'Also in the bag,' replied Middleton. 'We have booked into the hotel, but we're sharing a twin room. I hope he doesn't snore too loudly.'

'Let's finish these drinks and go to my room for a catch-up on everything. I think we are going to have a busy day tomorrow,' said Reece.

The three men talked for over an hour. They discussed what had happened so far and with the help of the file that the men had brought from London, Reece was able to quickly bring himself up to speed with the people they were up against. It had been a while since he'd interested himself so closely with the Republican Movement in Ireland and the main people involved. The file had one page of information on each of the named people he'd heard about and a couple he hadn't. Names, DOBs addresses, and places frequented with aerial photos and maps, and up-to-date full-face photos attached to each briefing sheet.

Now he knew what McNally, Walsh, and the brother, and sister Bailey looked like. Then at the back of the file, more information. this time the breakdown of the Real IRA high command including Brendan McDevitt, John Joe Murphy, and finally the MLA Paul Costello. Setting the file on the bed and spacing out the photos, Reece wiped his tired eyes.

'A nice bunch,' said Middleton.

'Yes, we've been over the file a few times on the way here. I don't think there is one of them who shouldn't be six foot under,' said Cousins.

'And this might be what's needed to do the job,' said Middleton as he reached into the grip bag and handed the Smith and Wesson with two mags to Reece.

Reece felt the familiar weight. He pushed one of the mags into the handle before pulling the slide back, allowing a nine mil parabellum round into the barrel before putting the gun into the right pocket of his Barbour jacket lying on the bed. It was always the way special forces carried a weapon, one in the barrel ready to go. He slipped the spare magazine into his trouser pocket.

'I have a few extra boxes of ammo in the bag as well if we need them,' said Middleton before lifting out an ear Mike. We have these for close comms, and the frequency won't be picked up by any nosey people.'

'So, David, we know from the files and today's updates who these people are. What happens next? What are we going to do?' asked Cousins.

'To tell you the truth, Joe, I don't have a clue. I would like to kick McNally's door in and squeeze the truth out of the bastard, but two things are stopping me. He would probably laugh in my face unless he knew I was serious about killing him, which, believe me, I would love to. The second reason is that whatever we do from now on in we've to be aware that these same bastards are under surveillance from a very good police team and maybe even MI5 watchers, so if they spot us we may become the targets taking the pressure off McNally and his friends.'

'In my past I did a little surveillance in and around the city. I don't know it as well as you, David, but from what I've seen coming from Aldergrove it's changed quite a bit. But as we all know from Manchester, a city's a city, and you can get lost or lose a tail within a few streets, so I say let's get out there tomorrow and shake the tree to see what falls,' said Cousins.

'I agree Joe, we won't get Mary back sitting here waiting for news. News we might not get, if I know how these politicians operate. They believe in one thing only and that's knowledge is power. The SOS has already shown everyone that for this operation and the protection of the peace process he's in control of everything, and that will include what he wants us to know,' said Reece.

Reece lifted the file off the bed and looked through the pages. Cousins and Middleton both tried to read his thoughts as they watched his eyes scan the notes.

'You're both right. It's going to be a risk, but I'm not prepared to wait on any tidbits of information we might get. Jim Broad will do his best to keep us informed. Both him and C are putting their necks on the line by giving us the go ahead to find Mary. I think they understand there might be trouble if these bastards get Mary to a place where they can beat the information she has in her head out of her. If that were to happen, I don't think the SOS realises the damage it could do to his beloved peace process. Let's get a good night's sleep and meet back here in the morning about seven and we can go through a plan then.'

'I don't know about you Joe, but I'm famished, so I'm going out to find a decent chip shop and grab me a fish supper, said Middleton, walking to the door.

'Wait up Geoff, I'm coming with you,' replied Cousins. 'See you in the morning, David.'

After both men left Reece called down to reception and asked them to send up a double Bushmills.

CHAPTER 23

THE HAYSHED

'I really do need to go to the toilet and if it means that bucket you can turn your heads away,' Mary said loudly.

'Now don't you worry your little head. We have seen it all before.' Laughed Walsh.

'Let her piss in her pants,' said Mariad Bailey.

'OK, that's enough, Mariad, stop messing about. There's a small toilet at the back. Take her there but keep the door open and watch her,' said Walsh.

Mariad stood behind Mary and prodded her in the back with the Browning pistol to make her stand, then followed her to the back of the building, where there was what Mary could only think was another small bucket, but this time made of porcelain with no seat. It looked like it hadn't been cleaned in years.

'Sorry, but if you tell us what we need to know we can provide an upgrade,' said Mariad as she waved the gun upwards, a look of hatred on her face.

'For what I need that will have to do,' said Mary.

The woman held the gun and watched, never taking her eyes away until Mary was finished. Then, pointing the gun at Mary, waved it to direct her back to the chair.

'We are going to be here overnight, so let's all try to get some sleep. We will take turns to watch, three hours each. I'll take the first three hours, then you, Jimmy, and then you, Mariad,' said Walsh, who then turned to Mary. 'You. Get over to the bed in the corner and stay there. Sleep if you can, but if you can't, don't worry, you'll be sleeping soon enough. For good.'

Mary lay on the top of the blanket that was covering an old mattress. She could smell the sweat and urine from years of use and could feel the iron springs beneath the bed. *It must have come from an old doss house or hospital*, she thought. Walsh was standing beside the bed before he stooped down to tie a small metal chain around her ankle and pulled it tight before attaching the chain around the bed's metal leg with a small padlock.

'There now, all settled for the night. Do you want me to tell you the bedtime story of the wicked witch?' He laughed.

'No, thank you,' replied Mary before turning to face the wall. Her back to the room and her abductors, she struggled to hold back the tears.

CHAPTER 24

BELFAST

All three men had breakfast together in the large hotel restaurant. Reece introduced Cousins and Middleton to the famous Ulster Fry, which, although both men had worked in Northern Ireland in the past, neither had tasted. *Probably*, thought Reece, *because both had been billeted on army bases, so had to put up with military food.*

'Now that's what I call a breakfast,' said Middleton.

'I agree,' said Cousins, as he burped loudly.

'It will keep us going. This is going to be a long day, and God knows when we'll be able to get another bite,' answered Reece.

'What's the plan for today, then?' asked Middleton.

The table Reece had picked for breakfast overlooked the city, and was away from other diners, so he could speak normally without the danger of others overhearing.

'I've been thinking about that. After breakfast, I'll call Wilson then Broad for any updates and check up on what they're doing so that we don't interfere with their plans.'

'Plans?' asked Cousins.

'Yes. I have no doubt, as I said last night, that they'll have surveillance teams out watching McNally, the Wolfe Tone Club, and the phone box used by his unknown male contact yesterday, so we don't want to expose ourselves for now. I think we need to get to know where McNally lives and the other two locations without bringing attention to ourselves. According to McNally's file, he always has lookouts watching over him, so if we need to get to him it will have to be done very carefully. The usual tourist maps are no good as they don't cover West Belfast, especially Andersonstown. First thing this morning I went to a newsagent across the road and bought two maps. On one side is the whole of Belfast, on the other is the rest of Northern Ireland down to the border showing Monaghan and Louth in the Republic,' said Reece, handing one of the folded maps to Cousins.

'I've already circled in red ink McNally's home and the Wolfe Tone Club. you can familiarise yourselves back in the car. What car do you have anyway?' Reece asked.

'It's a Toyota Avensis. Dark blue supplied by the military surveillance unit based at Aldergrove. It has local plates, and it has a local security radio, so we'll be able to monitor what's going on. It's not armoured but should be good enough for what we need,' answered Cousins.

'Good, I'll be in a hired black BMW. I'll take mine today and you can work in the Toyota. The encrypted phones will help us communicate alongside the ear mics, especially if we need to be on foot. So, I suggest we get out and spend a couple of hours getting to know West Belfast before McNally gets his one o'clock call. When that happens, if we are lucky, the surveillance teams will be able to follow the unknown male to where they're holding Mary. In the meantime, let's just stick to the tried and tested call signs. I'm Alpha One. Joe, you're Two, and Geoff, you're Three. If any of us has McNally on the move, we call him Tourist One and if we identify his unknown male contact, he's Tourist Two. Joe, are you sure these ear mics will work?'

'They'll be OK over short distances. I have two handheld walkie-talkie radios in the car, which cover a larger area. I don't know if they can be picked up by MI5, if they are, as we expect, listening in for any radio traffic.'

'That's good. We'll have one in each car and only use them in an emergency if we lose each other at an important time. Before they tie us down, whatever will happen will happen anyway,' replied Reece. 'For now, let's get out there, and get to know the land, then meet up in about two hours to catch-up.'

'Geoff can study the map as we are driving. I know a bit of the West Belfast area, at least the main roads which, I'm sure, haven't changed too much,' said Cousins.

The next few hours passed as Reece had expected, joining in with the traffic on the main roads and making sure they did not bring attention to themselves, especially when they drove through the heartland areas of the Falls Road and Beechmount where McNally lived. Then, keeping conversation to a minimum, they drove past the location where MI5 had indicated the phone box used by the unknown male during his call with McNally. Reece couldn't spot any surveillance on either, which was good. He knew they would be concentrating their eyes on anyone approaching the phone box, so he made sure to pass it at a consistent speed in case they spotted his hire car. Either way, he only made one pass and didn't care if Wilson got in touch to ask what he was doing in the target area. He would tell him he wanted to know the area a little better just in case he could help in any way. Wilson had no idea that he'd be working with Cousins and Middleton with the blessing of SG9 and MI6. As the saying went, need-to-know, and Wilson didn't need to know. The biggest danger, as Reece could see it, was a blue-on-blue situation if they ran into the surveillance teams at the same time they were moving on McNally and his crew. They had agreed to work by the Israeli rule only to use their weapons if their lives were in danger or someone became an enemy combatant by their actions. Until then, their weapons would remain concealed.

The weather had been kind. Even though there were dark clouds threatening impending rain, it had stayed dry, but a cold breeze was keeping the temperature down. Reece was remembering the streets and routes before they came to him. The traffic, as in any city, meant he kept his speed down. When he drove off the main Falls Road and into the Beechmount area, the streets all appeared to contain the same red-bricked, small, terraced houses. Some with fenced-off front gardens, others with the doorstep right on the pathway passing the house. At the rear of the houses, there were long alleyways, or ginnels, as they would call them in England. It was through this alleyway system that IRA killers were able to attack army and police patrols during the Troubles before escaping out the back and entering another house on the other side of the alley. Then exiting on a completely different street to make their getaway complete. The satnav included with the hire car was ideal, in that it would show streets that were a dead end, where, if he'd entered them, he would have to turn to come back out. He knew from his days of surveillance this was dangerous in two ways: people living in the streets always noticed strange vehicles turning and not stopping. Also, they were ideal for boxing someone in for an attack.

Reece spoke into his mic. 'Let's take a break and meet for a coffee. There's a Starbucks on Boucher Road just the other side of the motorway. See you there in about twenty minutes.'

'Roger that,' came the reply from Middleton.

Reece remembered Boucher Road as a long straight road with a mixture of large retail stores, storage units, and some small shopping malls. The entrance to Windsor Park, the Northern Ireland national football stadium, was near the Donegal Road end of the road. Boucher Road was ideal for them to meet and catch-up, as it was just outside West Belfast but had easy access routes into the area they'd been working in.

Reece reached the car park of the Starbucks in ten minutes and used the time to phone both Broad and Wilson. The time was 11 a.m. In two hours, the unknown male was to make his call. Reece wanted to make sure there was no change to what was going to happen before he met with Cousins and Middleton. Broad assured him that there'd been nothing more to report and Wilson would only say his people were out on the ground but nothing unusual yet and that he'd let him know if anything changed. Wilson asked Reece where he was, and Reece lied when he told Wilson he was walking around the shops in the city centre. This seemed to please Wilson and Reece didn't care if it did or not.

The coffee house was busy, filled with the standard chairs and the smell of coffee Reece always felt that with the noise of the chattering customers and the large coffee machines, specialist coffee shops were a safe place to meet and talk. Most of the customers in the queue were getting their coffee to take out. Reece ordered his usual medium Americano with cold milk on the side and sat at a table by the large window just in time to see Cousins and Middleton park up. Five minutes later all three men looked out at the car park from the same table.

'Have you been all right finding your way around?' asked Reece.

'Yes, no problem. Joe knows the place better than he thought, and the maps are good,' replied Middleton.

'We did a drive-pass on the Wolfe Tone Club, the phone box, and McNally's home address. All quiet for now,' said Cousins.

'Yeah, me too,' said Reece. 'I think if things go as we understand them, then this whole thing could be over by two. We should park up just outside the areas where we think the surveillance teams will be operating. I'll cover the area where the phone box is and you two the Wolfe Tone Club. That way, we should be able to give further back-up if needed, but remember we are not supposed to be here, so we are in a wait and see situation for now.'

Joe Cousins nodded before speaking. 'We only did one drive past in Beechmount where McNally lives. We noticed a couple of things. There were two young lads obviously doing lookout. That's why we only did one drive through. We didn't want them to clock us. Then when we drove down the street Geoff spotted a security camera on the wall of the house which would cover the approach to the front door. If he's that security aware, then you can be sure he'll have one covering the back of the house.'

Reece let this information sink in before he spoke. 'I spotted the lads when I did my drive through as well. Because I was keeping my eyes on the road and the car at a constant speed, I didn't see the camera, so I want to change the plan. You two sit outside the area of surveillance at the Wolfe Tone Club. If, as I suspect, the lads doing lookout will be lifted when McNally is away, then I'll break into his house at the back.'

'What? Are you mad?' reacted Cousins.

'Probably. But I'm thinking, what if something goes wrong? What if the surveillance team loses the unknown male and they don't find Mary? If I'm in his house, I might find a clue to where she is and I could be there waiting for McNally when he gets home to question him myself. If Wilson's people find Mary and let me know, I can leave the house before McNally returns and we lose nothing by my having been there.'

'What if McNally returns with others or you get caught in there? Or there's a camera at the back?' asked Middleton.

'It's a risk I must take. No back-door camera, then I'm good to go. That's where you both come in. If I don't hear anything positive from Jim Broad or Wilson, I'm depending on you two confirming where McNally is and if he's with anyone.'

'What if he stays in the club? We can't hang around forever,' asked Cousins.

'If we've no word on Mary either by the surveillance or MI5 and GCHQ, then we'll have to go with my plan to wait for McNally to get home.'

Cousins looked at Middleton before replying to Reece.

'I still say you're mad. If everyone, including us, are the other side of West Belfast looking at McNally and the phone box you'll be on your own without back-up. If you're spotted or challenged, you're on your own. To be honest with you, David, it's a plan I'm not happy with.'

'That's why I must do it. No one, not even Wilson and Broad, will expect it. They'll be concentrating on McNally and if, for some reason his plans change, then we need to be ahead of the game. If we don't find Mary alive and well today, then I want to make sure Brian McNally gives me answers. We all know that if the local police lift him, he'll smile back at them over a desk saying nothing and his Republican-supporting solicitor will get him free after shouting about the violation of his human rights. McNally doesn't give a shit about human rights, and that's why Mary is in the danger she is now, if she's still alive.'

Reece felt he was raising his voice in frustration trying to get his argument across then remembering where he was, he continued speaking softly enough for the two men to hear him.

'Yes, gentlemen, I've had to think the worst that, if she's not dead already she will be soon and that will only be after they've tortured the life out of her. So, Joe, I'm going to be waiting for McNally if we don't find Mary this afternoon. Where you can help is to confirm when he's going home and if he's on his own. Then you can stay in the area where, if I need you, you can come quickly. I hope that we won't get that far, but it's something I must do.'

This time it was Geoff Middleton's turn to speak. 'We can see you're going to do this with or without our permission, or anyone else's, for that matter. So, of course, we'll be with you on this, but if you're going to have that face to face with McNally, make it quick, and quiet. We don't want a shoot-out on the streets of Belfast. We all know what that will mean. If we get out alive, we'll probably end up in jail and you might have started another war.'

'I know the risk, Geoff, and what I ask of you. But I ask it because we've been in those kinds of situations together not so long ago, and I can't think of any other people I would rather have backing me today.'

Both men nodded back at Reece.

'OK, thank you. We need to make sure our communications are working well. 'We'll have need of them before the day is out either way. We should leave the secure phones open when you have information on McNally. Switch them on and have the Bluetooth linked to the radio so I can listen into what's going on. Ideally, we'd have a team of twelve, but this will have to do.'

Once again, both men nodded. All three left. They split up, with Reece heading towards the Beechmount area of the Falls Road and Cousins and Middleton heading towards the area around the Wolfe Tone Club.

CHAPTER 25

SG9 CONTROL ROOM, LONDON CITY AIRPORT

Sir Martin Bryant hated this place. He hated having to drive out of the capital to the offices of SG9 at the business section location of London City Airport. but today was one of those times when it had been necessary. The prime minister had insisted he be there to oversee what was happening in Belfast. Apart from the two communications operators manning the vast array of technical equipment in front of them, which included video feedback, the only other person in the room, sitting next to him, was Jim Broad. The large clock on the wall showed 12.40. They could hear the radio traffic from the Belfast surveillance teams. They had reported McNally leaving his home in Beechmount Parade and walking to the Falls Road where he flagged down a black cab which then took him to the Wolfe Tone Club in the Turf Lodge area of West Belfast. McNally seemed to be alone on his journey, without minders or lookouts. Broad had told Bryant it was probably because the operation McNally was involved in would be of the highest secrecy, and the less some of his people knew the better, in case they were lifted by the security forces. The prime minister, like all politicians, didn't like things being out of their control or blowing up in their faces. Having Bryant there would help insure, if things went sideways. The finger of blame wouldn't be pointed back at him. Jim Broad knew exactly why Bryant was there, and after he'd spoken to Sir Ian Fraser, the Director of MI6, they'd agreed with him that if things did go wrong in Belfast. He would have to throw David Reece to the wolves as an ex-agent gone rogue completely out of their control.

'Now we wait,' said Broad.

'I'm sure this is the part you hate,' replied Bryant.

'Yes, every time, and it never gets better with experience, either.'

'Do 'we have control of Reece?' asked Bryant.

'The Belfast MI5 team put a tracker on his car last night. One that only we here can see on the computer map of the city on the wall,' replied Broad pointing at a large screen which had a red line electronically drawn through the map.

'The red line shows where he's been and is now. I know he told ACC Wilson this morning that he'd be walking about the city centre shopping while he waited on word from him. But as we both know Reece is not the kind of man to wait. And, as I suspected, that's not the case. As you can see if you follow the journey of the red line, he's spent most of his morning in West Belfast, passing by two of our locations of interest before most recently parking up on Boucher Road.'

Bryant crossed the room and standing with his arms folded across his chest he stood to get a closer look at the large screen in front of the operations desk. Broad walked over to stand beside him before speaking slowly so that Bryant would understand every word he said.

'As you can see. The surveillance car we provided for Cousins and Middleton has a built-in system that also provides live feedback on where the car is. That's the green line on the map. We know from that feedback that they've also been moving around the target areas in the West of the city. It parked up in Boucher Road at the same time as Reece, probably for a quick coffee and a chat about what happens next if I know Reece. Both vehicles are heading back into West Belfast and although we've this feedback, because of the distance between us here and Belfast, it has a delay of five minutes, so we'll always be slightly behind.'

'But what about the police surveillance teams? Will they not spot your people?' Asked Bryant.

There it was thought Broad the use of the words, your people, another pointer to the ass covering of the politician.

Broad took a deep breath before he answered.

'Reece and the other two are well trained and have been involved in this kind of operation many times. They know how to avoid being spotted and from the tracking we've seen, apart from them doing one drive past of the target locations, they've stayed just outside the circle of police surveillance covering each of the targets. You must remember this is West Belfast, and even the police surveillance teams will have to treat the area as working in enemy territory. Their concentration won't only be on their targets, but also in avoiding detection themselves, which could blow the whole operation. A car driving once by their target won't raise any suspicion and our people know that.'

The clock on the wall showed 12.50. Both men knew in ten minutes the route this operation was taking would be decided. For now, silence, apart from the odd bit of radio traffic coming over the airwaves. Although the operation room was large, for those minutes to Broad, it seemed the smallest room in the world.

CHAPTER 26

ANDERSONSTOWN, WEST BELFAST

Mary had found it hard to sleep. The bed was uncomfortable, feeling lumpy, and she could feel some of the springs and smell stale sweat. She was sure she'd been bitten on the back of her hand at least twice by something that was sharing the bed with her. She'd not been alone in the bed. She'd heard her captors swap over for their stint of guard duty during the night, whispering to each other as they did so, and then there was loud snoring. To her surprise, when she looked to see who it was, the woman lying on her back gave out another large grunt as she breathed ever-more loudly. Eventually dawn started to break and all three of her captors were up using what ablutions there were. Walsh made tea and from a holdall produced sandwich packs.

'I hope you're not a veggie, as I could only get ham or chicken,' he said, giving Mary a choice of the two packs he held out to her.

Mary didn't want to, but she was starving, not having eaten anything since breakfast in the hotel the day before. She silently took the chicken pack, and unwrapping it, took a large bite.

'Easy now, we don't want you to choke yourself. You might have a bit of travelling to do today,' said Walsh.

The rest of the morning passed slowly for Mary. They had placed her back in the chair in the middle of the shed, this time using one of the plastic ties to secure her right leg to the chair leg. She wasn't running anywhere soon. The woman tried to engage her in conversation, but always with a sneer and a sarcastic comment, so Mary ignored her. She wasn't going to waste her breath. Walsh and Jimmy Bailey sat at the table making conversation which Mary couldn't hear, but she knew by their body language and the way they kept their voices down they were discussing her and what was going to happen next.

Walsh looked at his watch and moved towards the door.

'Right, you two, keep a close eye on her. I'm away to call the boss. In the meantime, get packed up here in case we need to move quickly. Any nonsense from our guest, you have my permission to give her a good slap.'

Mary could see that Walsh was in charge and the other two knew it as well, so she had no intention of giving them an excuse to give her a slap.

Walsh walked down Owenvarragh Road with the large Roger Casement Park to his right and the Andersonstown Leisure Centre to his left. At the main Andersonstown Road, he watched for surveillance, noting the people walking about, what they were wearing, and where they were walking. He checked the cars and vans that passed him and any that were parked up with people inside them. He pulled the hood of his parka coat up, not only to hide his face from observers, but to protect him from the rain that was falling at a steady pace. Because of this, there were few people out and about, even though it was the lunchtime period. When they'd met with Brian McNally in the Wolfe

Tone Club, he'd briefed Walsh on his own. Apart from putting him in overall control for this part of the operation he'd set out two scenarios which he called Plan A and Plan B.

Plan A was the abduction of the tout and if things were all right security-wise, they could have brought her straight from the shed down the main Dublin Road out of Belfast then hand her over to their people on the southern side of the border.

That plan had to be cancelled due to the quick and large security-force response sealing off West Belfast and the Dublin Road routes. They knew this was a possibility, so McNally had agreed a Plan B, which included them having to delay until they were sure they could move. This time, when Walsh came to the main road, he'd turned right and walked in the opposite direction to the day before. The traffic was busier, and he kept his head down to avoid the spray from the passing vehicles. He walked about two hundred yards to a Chinese takeaway where he went in and ordered four chips and rice with curry sauce. While the food was being prepared, he made a call from the public phone on the wall of the waiting area. It was 1 p.m. exactly. After the call he collected his order and leaving the carry out, once more he turned right and walked another two hundred yards to reach his destination, the West City Car Dealership. Walsh stopped and, pulling his hood tighter, he quickly looked behind him. He was alone on the road; the rain keeping other walkers from the streets. Satisfied he wasn't under surveillance he walked through the forecourt of the dealership and, entering the main sales room spoke to the receptionist just inside the main doors.

'Is Frank Connor about?'

'Can I ask what it's about, please?' asked the receptionist.

'He's expecting me. I'm picking up a car,' replied Walsh.

'Mister Connor is in his office, just go through,' said the receptionist, pointing to a glass-partitioned office at the rear of the showroom.

Walsh walked to the office. Knocking on the door, he entered without waiting for a reply.

Standing looking at a white board showing sales figures on the wall was the owner of the dealership, Frank Connor. He was a short bald and overweight man wearing a tight-fitting grey suit. The man turned to see who this was entering without invitation and intruding on his concentration.

'Can I help you?' he asked Walsh.

'I hope so. Brian McNally sent me,' replied Walsh.

That was all that was needed. The words, by the look on the man's face, struck him like a thunderbolt but with a resignation of understanding.

'I was told you might be coming, but I hoped I wouldn't see you,' said Frank Connor.

'I've been told you have what I need,' said Walsh, not wanting to get into a long conversation with this man.

Connor looked as if he was going to be sick, his face white, and now showing beads of sweat under his chin.

'Well? I don't have much time,' said Walsh.

Connor fumbled as he opened the top drawer of a small filing cabinet and after a search, he produced a set of car keys and handed them to Walsh.

'It's parked at the back. A black Range Rover with the dark-tinted rear windows and a full tank of fuel as requested.' He realised he was talking fast, but he wanted this man out of his building as quickly as possible. The Real IRA Commander had sat down beside him a few nights before when he was in the Wolfe Tone Club for a quiet pint after work. McNally had spoken to him like the Don in the *Godfather* movie. 'I want you to do me a favour. You might never have to do it, but if you do, I'll owe you one.'

The favour was to provide a clean vehicle, which someone would call for. It was to be fully fuelled and have tinted rear windows. If there were no problems, he'd get the car back in its original condition. He would be told where to find it. If there were any problems, all he had to say was that it had been stolen. He knew who McNally was and his reputation. He wasn't going to argue. Walsh took the keys and left without saying more. Frank Connor sat down at his desk and felt he was going to be sick in to his bin.

Walsh always loved to drive top of the range cars and the Range Rover was exactly that, right down to that special smell you only get in brand-new cars. Despite what Connor had said, he checked to make sure the petrol tank was full. It needed to be, as they had a bit of a journey later. Walsh drove back to the shed and parked about twenty yards from the entrance.

'Right, here's some food, get it inta yeh right now, then get ready. I've spoken to the boss, and we'll be going for a bit of a drive and bringing our friend here with us,' said Walsh as he entered the shed.

'But they'll have details of the van. We'll get spotted,' said Mariad Bailey.

'Don't worry, we won't be using the van. I have a clean vehicle outside. Over lunch, I'll bring you up to date with what the boss's Plan B,' replied Walsh.

CHAPTER 27

WEST BELFAST

When the secure phone buzzed, interrupting the comms connection with Cousins and Middleton, Reece knew it could only be Jim Broad.

'Yes, boss,' answered Reece, looking at the G-Shock watch which showed 13.05.

'David, a bit of bad news I'm afraid.'

'Tell me.'

'Our friend McNally received the call we expected at one on the dot. It was the same man's voice asking for him. The police surveillance teams had the phone box, but he didn't call from there. Five and GCHQ are trying to track down the location he made the call from, but I'm sure he'll be well away when they identify where.'

'For fuck's sake. What did they talk about?' asked Reece feeling angry, wanting to punch somebody, anybody.

'There we have another problem. The only conversation came from McNally who told our unknown male to go to Plan B immediately, to which the male replied understood. That was everything, no more I'm afraid.'

'What are the police and Five doing now?'

'Not much they can do. They still have the border roads and crossings sealed off with surveillance and road stops, and Five will continue to monitor all its resources. We don't know what Plan B means. It could mean anything from keeping Mary in a safe location in the city to trying to get her across the border,' said Broad.

He didn't want to mention the third option, that they may have already started to torture her and would shortly leave her dead body on a country road outside the city. He knew Reece would be thinking along the same lines.

'What about the politicians? What happened with the meeting the SOS had with the republicans and especially Paul Costello last night?'

Broad could hear the anger in the question and looking across the room at Martin Bryant he tried to pick his words carefully.

'Not much feedback. As far as I know, the minister laid down the law that Mary must be freed unharmed and if they knew anything about her abduction, they could tell the police anonymously if they wanted. Apparently, the Republican delegation wasn't too happy with the security forces' reaction, and they tried to say there was no evidence that republicans were involved at all. Costello was one of those leading with that argument. The minister left it with them that the British government would see it as a threat to the peace process if anything happened to Mary. I think that's as tough as he could be with them.'

Bryant nodded his approval at what Broad had said.

'Nothing more than I expected,' replied Reece. From the way Broad's voice was coming across, Reece felt he was being cautious. Instinct was telling Reece that someone was looking over Broad's shoulder, listening to the conversation. He sounded too formal, keeping straight to the point, which was unlike him.

'I've told ACC Wilson what I've told you, and I've let him know I would be telling you the result of McNally's phone conversation with our unknown male. You might get a call from him asking where you are. If he's the kind of policeman I think he is, he won't want you out there working on your own. Where are you now, anyway?'

'If he asks, you don't know. If he asks me, I won't tell him. It's now a need-to-know situation, and he doesn't need to know. I know the risks, but it's now time for you to let me get moving on these people.'

'That's why we sent you the back-up. We always knew this could go this way. I'll help in whatever way I can from here and anything I get, you'll get. But remember what I told you last night, David. If you're caught, you're on your own, and if you must shoot your way out of any situation, you will be classed as rogue.'

'Nothing new there, then. Understood, and thank you for the help.'

The line went dead and Broad could see the look of concern on Bryant's face.

'I'm not happy, Jim. I know Reece has the skills and we've used them to great effect to our benefit in the past, but this way we don't have complete control of him. I'm worried as I'm sure the PM is, to have him out there doing God knows what to get Mary McAuley back.'

'You're correct in saying we don't have complete control, but we've some. Cousins and Middleton are backing him up, and will be able to keep me updated as well. Personally, I wouldn't want anyone else out there tracking down the movements of these bastards other than David Reece.'

Bryant walked to the door of the operations room where he turned to face Broad.

'I'm sure you're right, Jim. But just in case, I'll speak with the prime minister in the hope this doesn't turn into a disaster.'

When Bryant left, Broad looked once more at the electronic wall map. He could see the red line that now showed Reece parking up in the Beechmount area of West Belfast and he thought, *Don't fuck this up, David, or we're all fucked.*

CHAPTER 28

BEECHMOUNT PARADE

Reece parked up on the main Beechmount Avenue just off the Falls Road. He made sure not to park directly outside any of the driveways in the Avenue, but instead between two of the houses where he'd bring less attention to himself. Reece had been born in the Royal Victoria Hospital on the Falls Road not far from where he now sat in the car observing the street around him. All was quiet. there was no sign of lookouts or window curtains twitching, the rain keeping people indoors.

'Alpha One to Alpha two,' spoke Reece into the secure handheld radio.

'Alpha two send,' answered Cousins.

Reece informed Cousins of his conversation with Broad and the information that Tourist Two was in the wind.

'What's happening with Tourist One?' asked Reece.

'He is still in the club and the surveillance teams seem to be concentrating their focus on him for now.'

'As we decided this morning, I'll make a visit to his home location. When he moves, keep tabs on him and keep me updated by the secure phone. If he heads for his home location, I have the ear comms when you're close. That will give me time.'

'Roger Alpha One, be careful.'

'Will do.'

Reece left the car, gripping the handle of the gun in the pocket of his Barbour jacket. He felt a bit more secure in what he was going to do. He knew strangers in West Belfast could be spotted quickly and suspicions passed to the local IRA unit for investigation, so he didn't intend to hang about in the open. He crossed the road from where he'd parked his car and pulled the peak of the flat cap he was wearing tight down on his head. He turned into the long alleyway which stretched the full length of three hundred yards at the rear between the houses of Beechmount Parade on his left-hand side and Clowney Street on his right. Each house was protected by a ten-foot brick wall with a door leading into a back yard. Reece had raided many of these buildings in his RUC uniform days when he was stationed in Belfast as a young constable. The yards beyond the doors used to contain the outside toilets but were now most likely empty or a storage shed. Once inside the alleyway, he was protected from view. The high walls giving him protection from any prying eyes. If anyone else had been in the alleyway, it would have been difficult to avoid eye contact and the likelihood would be that he'd be challenged and asked who he was and what he was doing there. Again, the rain seemed to come to his aid. There was no one about, and the only noise were the footfalls made by Reece's canvas boots. He counted the doors in his head and when he reached what he thought was McNally's home he had it confirmed by the number 43 painted in white on the black door. The black refuse bin standing in front of the door with the same white painted number confirmed it. The door was made of wood and looked like it had been in place since the houses had been built nearly seventy years ago. Despite there being a Yale lock, Reece felt the door open with the slightest of pressure from his shoulder. He opened the door, slowly looking around for the telltale signs of cameras or alarm systems. He saw none, so pushed the door wider. No dog either. He stepped into the yard and closed the door behind him.

McNally's file showed that he lived alone and that his main security was his use of lookouts in the area when he was at home. The back door of the house with another yale lock and four panes of glass in the top half keeping it secure. The glass was single pane. None of the usual double glazed. Reece removed his cap and, placing it directly over the pane above the lock, used the butt of the Smith and Wesson to tap it gently. The glass broke easily and fell inside the door. Reece waited for a few seconds to see if there was any reaction to the noise, which was minimal, and with the rain hardly audible. He placed his hand through the broken window and reaching down inside, turned the lock, and opened the door. Once inside, he closed the door behind him and stood still, listening for any sound, for any movement. Again, he could see no sign of security cameras or alarms. He kept the gun in his hand, pointing it in front of him as he moved slowly. The kitchen was clean and tidy with dishes drying on the rack by the sink. Everything was quiet except for the buzzing of his phone in his pocket, which he ignored until after he checked the front living room, which was all clear.

'Hello.' He spoke quietly, noticing Broad's name on the screen.

'Hi, David, just an update. Our friend McNally has made a second short call using the phone in the Wolfe Tone Club. GCHQ tells us it was to the number in the Republic of Ireland that he's called before, speaking to the same man, who they identified as John Jo Murphy. All McNally had to say was that the package was on its way and will be at the handover at six tonight. Murphy only replied that in that case he would remain where he was to await the package and arrange things at his end. That's all we've for now, so they'll be transferring Mary as we speak.'

Reece felt as if someone had given him a kick in the stomach. Broad continued to speak, but Reece had difficulty hearing what he was saying. His head was spinning with thoughts of what to do next. Was being here the ideal place for now?

'Sorry, boss. What did you say?'

'Wilson's people are staying on McNally until he goes home, then they'll be moving about West Belfast and the motorway network, trying to pick up what they can, but I'm afraid it's a needle in a haystack for now. If I know anything about people like McNally, he's kept his distance from the operation, so he'll be heading home until he hears more. Do you want me to get Wilson to lift him and try to squeeze him?'

'No, not for now. Even if he did get something from him, it would take some time and we don't have time. And if he did talk, the bastard would probably lie to send us in the wrong direction. We couldn't believe a word that came out of his mouth.'

'You're the man on the ground, David. What do you suggest?'

'Leave this to us. Let the police do what they normally do, but if you can, keep them away from McNally for now.'

'Understood, whatever you do from now, be careful. I'll keep you informed if I get anything this end.'

The phone went dead, and Reece checked the two bedrooms and the bathroom. Everything in the house was neat and tidy, which was strange for a bachelor living on his own. Maybe McNally had a relative or cleaner who came in and looked after the place, although there was no mention of anyone in McNally's file. He went back to the living room and made himself comfortable in the large chair facing the front door. He rested the gun on his lap and took his time looking around him, noting the pictures on the wall and the top of the unlit fireplace. There was a framed copy of the Republican Proclamation, the one that had been read out by Patrick Pearse on the steps of the GPO in Dublin, at the start of the uprising in 1916. That had eventually led to the War of Independence, Civil War, and the formation of the Irish Free State, now the Irish Republic. The window that looked out on the street was covered with a set of net curtains, making it difficult for anyone to investigate the house but easy for looking out. The room was warm but not hot enough to force Reece to remove his Barbour jacket. His stomach was still turning, but now under control, the professional in him taking over. The red light on the handheld radio, which was on silent, began to flash. He pressed the answer button.

'Alpha One come in, over.' It was Joe Cousins.

'Alpha One send, what have you got?'

'Tourist One just left the club. We can hear the comms of the surveillance teams following. He got into a black cab. He's on his own. Might be heading your way, over.'

'Roger Alpha Two. You're probably right but keep a listening to the comms and head closer to my location so we can use the ear mics.'

'Roger that, understood. On our way.'

Reece felt the gun in his hand and aimed it at the door.

'Now Mister McNally, let's see what you think when you have to face a man instead of a woman.'

CHAPTER 29

BELFAST

Because Walsh had told them to have everything prepared, the brother and sister Bailey were ready to move.

'Do you need to use the toilet before we go? It might be some time before you'll get the chance again.' Walsh asked Mary.

'No I'm OK, but I'd rather stay here if you don't mind. You all go ahead and enjoy yourselves,' replied Mary, thinking that a little gallows humour might help her situation. She was still in the chair, her ankle strapped to the leg.

Mariad Bailey didn't want to miss the opportunity. She strode over to Mary and slapped her.

'That's enough,' shouted Walsh. 'She's only trying to goad you. Leave the beatings to our friends in the south. Remember she's not supposed to be harmed by us.'

'Well, the bitch is being smart mouthed,' snarled Mariad. 'And besides I don't like her anyway. A smack in the mouth is to little. She deserves a good kicking.'

Mary stared back at the woman. She desperately wanted to cry, and she could feel the blood trickle down the side of her lip and chin, but she wasn't going to let this bitch see the hurt. Instead, she just spat the blood on the floor and smiled back at her.

'Jimmy, cut her free from the chair before tying her hands in front of her.' Said Walsh. 'When we get to the car Mariad and I'll sit in the front, I'll drive. Jimmy, you sit in the back with her. If she plays up, gag her. Shoot her if she tries anything serious. Just so you understand bitch, we don't like your jokes or you. If you put any of us at risk, you're a dead woman earlier than you need to be.'

Walsh checked there was no one about before pressing the key fob to open the doors of the Range Rover, then signalled to his companions to move. Jimmy Bailey pulled Mary by the arm and pushed her roughly into the back seat before jumping in beside her. Mariad sat beside Walsh in front as he started the engine.

'This is the only way to travel. Sheer luxury, if only I owned it,' said Mariad.

'You never know. When we deliver our package we might get it as a bonus,' answered her brother.

'Let's deliver the package first. Keep a close eye on her,' said Walsh.

He drove down the Andersonstown Road onto the Falls Road, then through the West Link that connected the motorways through the city. Instead of turning right and taking the M1 towards the south and Dublin, he turned left, and headed for the M3, passing the George Best Belfast City Airport. They passed the towns of Hollywood and Bangor before driving down the coastal route away from the city. This way they travelled in the opposite direction to the one the security forces would expect. Mary watched as the familiar villages and towns passed.

She knew the rear-tinted windows blocked anyone seeing into the back of the Range Rover. Jimmy held the Browning pistol on his lap, the barrel pointed in her direction. They were now travelling south on the Ards Peninsula. Mary knew it well and that the further south they travelled the less chance they would run into trouble. She'd travelled all over the area of the Peninsula in the past, from beach holidays with her parents to hotel stay overs with her husband. She'd travelled the full length of it, from Belfast down its east coast path to where it separated at Strangford Lough from the North Channel of the Irish Sea. If they continued to stay on this tourist route down the coast of Northern Ireland, instead of the direct route from Belfast using the motorways, she knew they would avoid the likelihood of running into a police roadblock. They had already passed two police cars that were travelling in the opposite direction, paying them no attention. The further they travelled from the city the more she noticed her three captors relax. Walsh had switched the radio on and tuned into BBC Radio Ulster. She noticed when the news bulletin came on there was little mention of her abduction, only that police enquiries were continuing.

'Even the local radio isn't interested any more,' said Walsh, looking at Mary in the rear-view mirror.

Mary didn't reply. Instead, she was trying to locate where they were and where they were going. The nearest area that boasted Republican sympathisers was South Down, but they were lightweights compared to the people in her old town of Newry, and then further into South Armagh, both of which they could be heading to. To get there by road they would have to cross Strangford Lough on the car ferry from the town of Portaferry to Strangford village itself, a ten-minute crossing where she hoped she'd be able to attract attention.

CHAPTER 30

WEST BELFAST

'That's his cab approaching your location Alpha One.' It was the voice of Joe Cousins coming through strongly in the ear mic, making Reece jump. At least the equipment was working and now he knew that not only was McNally almost home, but Cousins, and Middleton were near enough to give him whatever support he needed. He pressed the button on the earpiece.

'Roger Alpha Two, I'm ready for him. Keep an eye out for any trouble.'

Reece sat up in the chair. He heard the cab pull up and one of its door's slam before it drove away. He heard the key in the front door, then it closed before McNally opened the inner door into the living room. The room was dark enough to make McNally stop and look twice to allow him to focus on the shape sitting in his living-room chair. He first identified the figure of a man and then the outline of a semi-automatic pistol pointing at his chest. He didn't know the man personally, but he knew his face from the pictures that John Jo Murphy had shown him. The one he'd said was the RUC Special Branch man, the one who had killed Sean Costello.

'Who the fuck are you, and what the fuck are you doing in my house?' he asked, pretending he didn't have a clue why Reece was there, his face an angry snarl.

'Oh, I think you know exactly who I am, Brian, and why I'm here. Now be a good boy and sit down,' answered Reece calmly, using the barrel of the gun to indicate for McNally to sit on the settee opposite him.

Knowing the man's reputation, McNally decided to play safe, and do what he was told, for now. He knew his lookouts would be back on the street soon.

'I'll ask you once again. What do you want?'

'You don't get it, do you, Brian? I ask the questions, you answer them, and you better answer quickly and truthfully, because we both know time is important.'

McNally didn't reply. The longer he dragged this out, the more likely his bitch girlfriend would be with John Jo in the south and his own minders outside knocking on his door. Given the extra time, he might have two rats in the trap.

Reece had sat across the interview table too many times with people like McNally. He could read his thoughts. The problem was McNally was thinking in the past. He was sure McNally had sat on the other side of those interview tables many times, knowing time was on his side. He would have known he'd have to be released without evidence against him, provided he kept his mouth shut.

'I know what you're thinking, Brian. The longer you keep me here the more likely the woman your people abducted will be dead, and maybe even me, captured, and dealt with by your scum friends. But as I don't have the time, I'm afraid I'm going to have to insist you answer my questions quickly. I have this gun for a reason. I'm willing to use it, as I'm sure you know. This won't be anything like the soft interrogations you had in the past.' Reece pointed the gun at McNally's right knee. 'You know the damage and pain a bullet can do to someone's kneecap. I know from your file you've pulled the trigger yourself.'

McNally's eyes narrowed, staring at the barrel of the weapon only feet away. He tried to calculate the distance between both men, but from a sitting position he knew it was too far and he knew the man pointing the gun would know that as well. Now he just stared back with hatred for the man in front of him.

Reece continued. 'As I said, Brian, I know we don't have much time, so I don't intend to keep you company much longer.'

In one swift movement Reece lifted a cushion from behind him and placing it in front of the barrel of the gun, fired a shot into the settee inches from McNally's thigh. The noise inside the room was loud, but the cushion had acted like a gun silencer which would sound outside just like someone hammering a nail into a wall. The black scorched hole in the middle of the cushion smoked but didn't catch fire. The smell of burnt material filled the room. Reece knew the kind of fear that McNally had spread throughout the community, especially with his neighbours. If any of them did suspect that it was a gunshot, they wouldn't come running. Reece also knew that the lookouts and minders were not in place yet, otherwise he'd have been given a heads up from Joe Cousins.

'Jesus, are you fucking mad?' shouted McNally.

'I told you, Brian, I don't have time for you to fuck me about. The next one goes straight in the kneecap.' Reece pointed the gun at McNally's left knee. 'Where is Mary?'

McNally looked at the gun, then at Reece standing above him with the cushion in his other hand. He could see a darkness in the man's eyes. He knew he meant what he said. He had seen men like this before where he couldn't decide if they were sane or mad. *This one was mad*, he thought. He also knew if his men were on the lookout positions and heard the shot they could come rushing in the door. This man was prepared to kill anyone getting in his way, including him. Again, he estimated the distance between them, which was now a lot closer, but he knew he couldn't move faster than a bullet.

'You can't do this. You're the law, you don't shoot innocent people,' said McNally.

'You see that's where you're wrong, Brian. I'll let you into a little secret. When it's war, the law comes last. So once again, and this time if you don't answer, you don't tell me the truth, you'll be one kneecap down. Where is Mary?' Reece said the last bit slowly and clearly.

McNally decided to play for time. 'Look. I don't know and that's the truth.'

Reece moved closer and placed the cushion over McNally's left knee, pushing the barrel of the gun into the cushion. McNally thought once more about making a grab for the gun, but he knew the man holding it could pull the trigger faster than he could react.

'Wait, wait,' shouted McNally, raising his arms above his head. 'OK, OK, I'll tell you what I know.'

Reece stood back, but kept the gun pointed at McNally's knee.

'Start talking. Answer the question, and don't waste my time anymore. Don't fuck me about.'

McNally dropped his arms and sat further back in the settee, trying to create more space between his body and the barrel of the gun. He pushed his right hand down the side of the settee arm.

'Are you looking for this?' asked Reece. Dropping the scorched cushion he took a knife out of his pocket, the serrated edge shining in the light of the room.

'I'm not that stupid, Brian. Bastards like you always try to have a back-up. Let's face it, I would too if I was in your shoes. Of course I searched the room when I came in. I also found the one that matches this down the side of the chair.'

It was then that McNally decided his only chance was to go for it. This man was going to kill him anyway. He used his dropped hands to give him the extra leverage to push himself up and with all his weight slam into the man standing in front of him.

Reece had expected McNally to try something, but the speed with which he moved surprised him. Reece knew from McNally's file that he'd been a champion boxer as a young man in West Belfast. He had used that skill to fight his way to the top of the Terrorist gang he was now in charge of, beating one victim to death along the way. Although he was older and looked to be slightly overweight, when he jumped against Reece it wasn't just body fat, but muscle. The force of McNally's lunge knocked Reece off balance, and he fell backwards knocking over a small table of ornaments, which crashed as they fell, the sound reverberating around the room. Reece fell back and felt the whole weight of McNally across him as he fell to the floor, McNally on top of him, his hands grabbing for the gun in Reece's hand. It was then that Reece heard McNally give a loud grunt, as if the wind had been knocked out of him with a punch. He rolled away from Reece onto his back, his hands now searching for the knife wound in his side. Reece realised that in McNally's own action of using his weight to force Reece backwards and grabbing for the gun, he'd forgotten about the knife in Reece's other hand.

Reece hadn't deliberately stabbed McNally. In a way, he'd done it to himself by jumping into the blade. Reece stood above the man lying on the floor, who was now taking quick, sharp intakes of breath. He could see the blood pumping in sequence with his heartbeat pouring through his fingers. His face was sweating, the skin pale.

'You're a stupid man, McNally,' said Reece putting the gun back in the pocket of the Barbour jacket and throwing the knife onto the settee before kneeling beside him.

'You fucking stabbed me,' said McNally through clenched teeth and short breaths.

Reece pulled McNally's hands away from the wound to get a better look at the damage.

'I'm not an expert Brian, but it looks bad. If you get help quickly you might live, but until you give me the answers I want, I'm willing to sit here and watch you bleed. At least that way I'll have the satisfaction of knowing you won't be lifting anymore women off the street for torture.' Reece searched for and found McNally's mobile in his trouser pocket before he sat down on the settee and waited. It didn't take long.

'The people that have her, have already taken her out of the city, she may even be across the border by now. That's all I know. You need to get me an ambulance.'

McNally could feel the wet blood flowing through his fingers. The pain of the wound and the difficulty in breathing made it hard to talk. He knew the man kneeling beside him didn't care, but he also knew if he didn't get help soon, this man would let him die.

Reece could see the small pool of blood under McNally's body getting larger with every short breath he took. He thought the knife had punctured McNally's lung.

'You're right Brian. You haven't much time, so tell me how are they getting her out of the city and across the border? What kind of car? How many of them? You need to talk fast otherwise you'll be dead, and I'll be gone. Tell me what you know, and I might just phone an ambulance. Your choice.'

McNally tried to get up, but the energy was draining fast, and he knew it, falling back down.

'There's three with her, two men, and a woman. I don't know what route they're taking. I only know it won't be by the main road. They already have a head start so you're too late.' McNally tried to smile his answers coming in short difficult breaths. The blood was now coming out of his mouth and down his chin. Reece knew McNally wouldn't tell him anything more, and whatever he did tell him would probably be a lie anyway.

Reece found the hole in the settee where the bullet had entered and using the knife he cut down to find it. He put the used bullet in his pocket and picking up the ejected casing he did the same. Stepping over McNally he went into the kitchen and wiped what prints he could off the knife handle and the door before returning to the living room and kneeling once more beside the man on the floor.

He quietly slid the knife under McNally's body.

'There now, Brian. I'm going to leave you now. I'll phone for an ambulance when I leave. They should be here within twenty minutes if they're not on an extended lunch break, so you should be all right, provided you don't exert yourself shouting or trying to stand.' Reece knew by the look of the blood loss already the man would be dead within ten.

'Please hurry. Call them now. I need help now,' McNally said gasping through clenched teeth.

'Don't worry Brian, I'll give you the same chance you give everyone else. When the emergency services come you can tell them you got injured fighting off a burglar. Then you'll be the hero bastard once more to all your friends.'

McNally could only grunt in reply, his eyes closing.

Reece left by the back door and walked back the way he came. He pressed the button on the earpiece.

'That's me out and on the way back to the car in the Avenue. Meet me there.'

'Roger,' replied Joe Cousins.

The human being inside of Reece felt sorry for McNally and he knew that if he'd phoned for an ambulance right away, he would probably be OK. But knowing what McNally would have done to him, and what had happened to Mary, he knew the world would be a better place without the likes of McNally in it. It would be hours before someone would find him, his minders, or a visitor, and by then he'd be long dead. Local police would describe the scene exactly as Reece had told McNally: a fight with a burglar had resulted in his death. Reece had an idea that knowing how those police investigators would feel about McNally they wouldn't be trying to find out what really happened.

When he got back to his car the other two SG9 men were parked behind him. Cousins, sitting in the passenger seat, pressed the button to open the car window. Reece quickly told both men what happened.

'Let's get back to the hotel. I'll contact Jim Broad and update him. All we can do for now is head for the border and hope he has something for us.'

Before you go anywhere, David, you need to change your jacket or wash that blood off,' said Middleton, pointing to the fresh stain on the pocket of the coat.

'Another reason to get back to the hotel. I'm sure Mary has left some face wipes in the bathroom. Let's meet back in the lounge once we all have a quick freshen up.'

CHAPTER 31

HILTON HOTEL

On the drive back Reece spoke to Broad on the hands-free car phone. Broad didn't seem surprised to hear what had happened to McNally.

'I'm sure he got what he deserved, David. From what he told you, it would add up that his friends have a head start.'

'I know. There are dozens of roads crossing the border and we'd have to be lucky and need an army to find them and stop them before they get over,' replied Reece.

'I'll contact the PSNI and get as many of their people out, stopping as many vehicles as possible if they're not already doing that. We might be lucky, and God knows we need some luck. What are you going to do now?' asked Broad.

'I'm heading back to the hotel. I have no choice. I need to get after them. I need to close the distance before it's too late. I have McNally's phone, so if anyone tries to speak to him, I should know who it is at the same time you do. That might give us a slight advantage.'

'I agree, David, keep our two friends with you and in the loop. What might help is there has been a call monitored by GCHQ.'

'What?' asked Reece feeling impatient. *This whole thing was taking too long,* he thought, and he felt the politicians didn't care either way what happened.

'After the SOS spoke with the Republican MlAs we had a call going from Paul Costello to John Jo Murphy. He wants a meeting with him in Dundalk before they do anything to Mary. Of course, he didn't use those words exactly, referring to Mary as the package, but it was enough to indicate that's what the conversation was all about.'

'Did they say where in Dundalk?'

'No, but the meet is at ten tonight in the drinking hotel. Something that might help is the hotel these people used in the past. The Imperial Hotel is right in the centre of the town. I'll send you the details of Costello's Silver Ford Sierra. If you get there in time, Murphy might bring you to where they're holding Mary. We can't tip off the southern government or police. We can't trust them. From experience around the border and Dundalk, we know there were members of the police in cahoots with the IRA.'

'Thanks, boss. From my days in Newry, I know the Imperial. I know you're sticking your neck out for me.'

'You don't know how far, but you've been there for me when I needed you. Good luck. If I get anything more, I'll let you know.'

The line went dead just as Reece was pulling into the Hilton car park. Cousins and Middleton were already in the lounge with a large pot of coffee in front of them.

Reece quickly told them the details of the call with Broad.

'We have a little time. Not much, but a little. If what the boss tells me is true, Costello is putting some sort of hold on the kidnappers until after he meets with Murphy at 10 p.m. If that's the case and we are there, it might be our only chance to find Mary in time.'

'So, the boss is still backing us on this if we go across the border?' asked Cousins.

'Aye, but under the usual deniable rule if we get caught. Then we're on our own. I'll understand if either of you doesn't want to take the risk.'

Both men looked at each other before Cousins replied.

'We are with you all the way. We have Costello's details in the files we brought and his photo.'

'Thank you, guys,' answered Reece.

Before Reece could say anything more a shadow of someone standing above them blocked out the light across the table. The man looked lean and fit, about six-foot-tall, and he had that appearance of age that was difficult to tie down. Reece thought between thirty and forty. He was clean shaven with fair hair that looked untidy and long to his neck and shoulders. He was casually dressed in jeans, a polo sweater, and a brown leather jacket. He looked like he was heading to a rock concert.

'Excuse me, gentlemen, but is one of you Mister Reece? David Reece?' The accent was Mediterranean, and the tanned skin wasn't local.

Reece stood to face the stranger. 'I'm Reece.'

The man offered his hand. 'I'm Ari. Jacob Lavyan sent me.'

Reece shook the man's hand. The grip was firm.

'Ari, welcome, please join us. You may be just in time.'

Reece introduced Cousins and Middleton before he waved to a nearby waiter and asked for two more cups before pouring for himself and then Ari.

'Did Jacob bring you up to date with what's happening?'

'Only that your agent has been abducted by the Real IRA and you and your team might need some help to get her back.'

Reece couldn't help but smile at the understatement.

'You could say that. All we know is that they might already have the agent, as you call her, over the border in the Republic of Ireland. We understand that they'll do nothing to her until at least 10 p.m. tonight because they're awaiting a meeting between a Republican politician from here and one of her captors. The politician wants to question her himself. The agent's name is Mary, and we're engaged to be married. So you'll see why I'm determined to get her back. We were just about to leave when you introduced yourself.'

'I'm ready. I have my own car outside. What's the plan?'

'Can I ask if you have experience in this sort of thing? What's your background?' asked Middleton.

Ari's eyes seemed to narrow before he answered.

'If it's important to you, I'll tell you. I would want to know if I was in your position. I'm a retired Israeli Defence Forces, the IDF, officer. And, as Lavyan has told me to be honest with you, I was with Mossad for a while in the Kidon teams. I've been working with Jacob for the last three years.'

Middleton seemed impressed. 'Sorry, I had to ask.'

'That's quite all right. I would have asked the same of you, but Jacob has told me that anyone working with David is to be trusted.'

'I trained with the IDF and your Kidon unit in the past. I'm currently with 22 SAS. Have you worked on any kidnap situations like this?' replied Middleton.

'Yes, once, when a young IDF soldier was kidnapped by terrorists in Gaza. They held him for five days before we rescued him. We killed the terrorists.'

Middleton nodded his understanding of the briefness of the reply to his question. Such operations were not always successful. Reece cut into the conversation between the two men.

'We have our own GCHQ people monitoring the enemy's phones. We are going to head to Dundalk just across the border and hopefully spot this politician meeting with one of the abductors, John Jo Murphy.'

Ari smiled at the name. 'I know Murphy. He's been of interest to us for some time. I'm sure Jacob told you of my purpose in this country, that our organisation works through our embassy keeping an eye on people who may be a threat, and Murphy fits that category.'

'Then I don't need to tell you more, just that we need to move. The fact that you're aware of Murphy will be a great help. Do you know him personally? Do you know what he looks like?'

'Yes, I've observed him in the past. I know what he looks like. Can you excuse me? I must make a quick phone call before we go.'

Ari walked towards the hotel reception before using his mobile.

The three men watched him. At the same time Reece spoke quickly to Cousins and Middleton, briefly explaining who Ari was and his connection to Jacob Lavyan and the Israeli intelligence community.

'Whatever he brings to the table can only be of help and God knows we need all the help we can get. I'm sure if he comes from Jacob Lavyan, then we can trust him.'

Ari finished his call and sat at the table once more.

'I know Jacob has told you we have an old agent who knows the area and the people in South Armagh. He's been in cold storage for some time, but I've just called him and told him I want any information he has and to meet me at midnight. David, I know you have much experience in running agents. Would you like to come with me?'

Reece wasn't sure. Time was limited. 'Yes, I will, but first, we should concentrate on this meeting in Dundalk between Costello and John Jo Murphy. We must hope that one of them will take us to where they're holding Mary.'

'The meeting in Dundalk is at ten. It may only last one hour. You know surveillance as well as I do, David. It's risky at the best of times when you have a large team and plenty of back-up. But there are only four of us and a couple of cars operating in an area where we could lose our quarry very quickly. I'm not meeting up with the agent until midnight in the Ravensdale Forest, not far from Dundalk, so we can do both,' said Ari.

Reece probably knew the area better than anyone at the table. He had worked for many of his Special Branch years in South Armagh and on a few occasions across the border to Dundalk and Ravensdale Forest itself.

'OK, then I'll travel with you, Ari. We have two more cars outside. Geoff can take mine and Joe the other. That gives us three vehicles to watch John Jo and Costello. If we lose them, I'll go with you to meet the agent at midnight.'

This seemed to please Ari, and he nodded his agreement.

'OK. We need to let Joe and Geoff book out of the hotel. I'm going to keep my room on because I intend to find Mary and come back here, then we can get this show on the road. Ari, meet us down here in 10 minutes,' said Reece.

Fifteen minutes later all four men stood in the car park of the hotel. Reece pointed out the two cars that they'd been using.

'The one Joe will be driving is government issue and has some sophisticated kit in it so if we must leave it behind, we burn the shit out of it. We can't let it fall into enemy hands. They would use it for propaganda purposes, and it could scupper the whole peace process. It's for that same reason we can't leave any one of us behind. We bring everybody home dead or alive.'

No one was smiling. All understood.

'In that case you need to see my little baby,' said Ari, pointing towards a parked dark blue Nissan Izuzu.

The vehicle looked huge parked beside small cars. It was the type with the passenger compartment in the front half and a covered flatbed on the rear. Reece noticed it also had bull bars covering the front radiator.

'Let me show you the luggage compartment,' said Ari as he pulled the tarpaulin that covered the rear of the vehicle slightly to the side.

Looking under the tarpaulin, the three men could see what Ari meant by his baby. Inside, there was an arsenal of weapons. Reece could see at least four AK-47 assault rifles, an RPG7 rocket launcher, and boxes of ammunition, a few of them marked *Explosives.*

'As you can see, I've brought everything we'll need 'to carry out an assault and rescue mission behind enemy lines.' Ari smiled.

'Holy fuck,' exclaimed Cousins. 'If you get caught with that lot you'll be doing a life sentence.'

'Don't worry, my friend, both the vehicle and I have diplomatic immunity.' Laughed Ari.

'Joe, get Ari an earpiece and then we can all hear and talk to each other,' said Reece.

When Cousins returned, Ari pushed the device into his ear. The earpiece, because of its colour and size, was barely visible, and with Ari's long hair, completely invisible.

'For the rest of this operation, we'll work the comms through our phones and the earpiece. As we'll be close to each other, I don't intend to lose anyone to the people who have Mary. It's going to be dangerous. We will be on our own when we cross the border. If anyone goes down, we'll bring him home with us no matter what. For callsign purposes we'll use the NATO mnemonic alphabet with our first names. So, Ari is Alpha. I'm Delta. Geoff, you're Golf and, Joe, you're Juliet,' said Reece.

They all laughed, except Cousins, who just smiled, and nodded. Reece continued. 'Mary will be Mike, which was her code name, anyway. Geoff, take care of the hire car. If we need to, we can leave it behind and damage to it will come out of my pocket, so try to return it without a scratch. I'm sure MI6 wouldn't appreciate the bill if it got shot up in a foreign country. I'll travel with Ari. Unlike him, we don't have diplomatic immunity to cross the border with weapons, but once over, it won't matter. Joe, Geoff, give me your weapons to keep in the back of Ari's truck until we are over the border, then we can pull in somewhere and return them to you.'

Both men followed Reece to the rear of the Izuzu. There they handed over two British Army issues 9mm Browning pistols with two spare magazines they were carrying, a total of forty-five rounds. Reece placed them under the tarpaulin cover.

'Right,' said Reece. 'Let's get on the road. We can link up just over the border. I just remembered. There's a lay-by just outside Killeen village just on the south side. We can do the handover there and check our times for the centre of Dundalk and the Imperial Hotel for Costello's 10 o'clock meeting with John Jo. Ari and I'll cut through Newry town. You two stick to the main Dublin Road. The lay-by is just outside Killeen. If you're there before us just wait, we still have plenty of time.'

CHAPTER 32

WARRENPOINT

At the very moment the SG9 team were leaving the Hilton hotel Mary was being bundled down a boat jetty and forced at gunpoint into a small boat. The journey had brought them to the town of Portaferry on the northern side of Strangford Lough. There they'd queued with other cars before boarding the small ferry which made a 10-minute journey across the Lough to the village of Strangford. Mary thought that she'd be able to raise the alarm and escape from her captors. But the pressure of the gun being pressed into her side ensured she kept quiet. There were only about twenty cars and a small van on the ferry. The crossing was smooth. Walsh drove them off the other side through the village of Strangford and onwards towards Downpatrick. After driving through Downpatrick and Hilltown they took a long straight road through the Mourne mountains down through Rostrevor and on to Warrenpoint. The winter fading light made the mountains look even darker. With the mountains behind them they pulled up at a small slip road in Warrenpoint leading down to the waters of Carlingford Lough. It was almost 6 pm and Walsh had timed his arrival perfectly. The Warrenpoint main harbour could dock large container ships but just outside the main harbour and nearer the main town square there were a couple of small jetties and slipways to accommodate smaller vessels. At the bottom of one jetty was a small boat. The owner was tying it off, making it secure against the side of the sea wall. The man had the look of someone who knew what he was doing. if anything, he reminded Walsh of the actor in the captain Birds Eye adverts. He was wearing dark overalls and a baseball cap, his face covered with a grey, almost white beard that made him look like the hardened sailor that he was. The man stood and without speaking nodded. He knew who they were as the two men and two women walked down the jetty towards him.

Gabriel Murphy had used this 19-foot fibreglass dory to catch lobsters in the Lough for the last 10 years. The boat had a 115 hp mercury engine and a small two-berth cabin under the bridge. Walsh nodded back. nothing was said as all four people boarded the boat. Once more Jimmy Bailey stayed close to Mary, making sure she was aware of the gun that was sticking into her back. Mary frantically looked around to see if anyone could see them but with the darkness descending and the cold rain falling there was no one. She even considered throwing herself over the side once they got onto the Lough. But that idea was soon thwarted when Jimmy and his sister pushed Mary down into the cabin, both sat facing her. Mariad had hated to leave the beautiful Range Rover behind. Walsh had left the keys in the ignition, keeping his promise that Frank Connor could get it back in good condition. Gabriel untied the ropes. jumping into the cabin beside Walsh he started up the mercury engine.

'Do you know what's next?' Walsh asked Gabriel.

'Yes, I'm to give you a lift across the Lough to Omeath where a van will be waiting to take you on. Any more than that I don't know, and I don't want to know.'

Gabriel Murphy had answered a knock at his front door the previous night to find his cousin John Jo Murphy asking to come in. Gabriel had never been involved with the Republican movement. His life was spent dropping off and picking up his lobster pots in a daily run along the shores of the southern side of Carlingford Lough. The lobsters he trapped in the pots would never make him a millionaire. The ones he did catch provided him with a simple life living in a cottage close to the shoreline and drinking in his local pub at night, joining in some of the singsongs that broke out when people were in the mood, known to local people as a bit of craic. John Jo had asked this favour ensuring him that he wasn't in any danger and that it would mean John Jo would owe him in return. He could have said no, as he had so many times before. John Jo knew that Gabriel only wanted the simple life, but Gabriel agreed only to this simple task knowing it would put John Jo in his debt. A debt he could call in if ever he should need it. The small boat easily cut through the light waves. The journey took just over ten minutes. No one spoke, the only noise being the outboard engine and the waves cutting through the bow. When he pulled into the jetty in the small harbour at Omeath in the Irish Republic, all was quiet. A dark blue Toyota Hiace van was reversing slowly along the top walkway above while Gabriel was tying up to the jetty wall. Once the boat was secure all four passengers left the boat and quickly walked up the jetty to where the Hiace was now waiting. Still no one spoke. Everyone seemed to know what their job was, although Gabriel did notice that one of the women seemed reluctant to move, being forced to keep moving by the man who had sat below with her on the journey across the Lough. When she leant back into him, it was then that Gabriel noticed the black handgun being used by the man to prod the woman, encouraging her to keep moving forward. All four got into the rear of the van, the doors being held open by the man who had reversed it before. Within thirty seconds everyone was in, the doors closed, and the van moving away, its headlights cutting into the darkness disappearing into the distance. Gabriel returned, untied his boat, started the engine, and steered it in a direction along the shoreline that would take him to his cottage, where he'd tie up for the night. After lighting the log fire inside he'd open a bottle of Jameson whisky, job done.

The journey for Mary continued, but now she knew she was in the Republic of Ireland across the border. Her stomach was turning. she could taste the fear in her mouth. Although it was dark in the windowless rear of the van the front driver's cab, windows gave enough light as the headlights of cars coming in the opposite direction lit up the inside of the rear. When they did, she could see Mariad, and Walsh whispering to each other and Jimmy holding the gun and smiling back at her. She tried not to show her fear, instead staring back at her captors when she caught them looking at her. There were no chairs in the back of the Hiace, so everyone sat on the floor. This was OK when they were on the main roads, but she felt the hard bumps when 'they'd driven onto what she thought were country lanes a couple of times. She estimated they'd been driving for almost an hour when the road changed once more to one of those hard pothole filled tracks, which seemed to go on forever, then suddenly stopping, braking sharply to a stop.

Jimmy jumped down from the back of the van first and waving the pistol he indicated that Mary should be next. Mariad decided to help her down by shoving her in the back. Mary landed on her knees in a muddy hole that saved her from any leg damage.

'For fuck's sake Mariad, would ye catch yourself on?' shouted Jimmy.

Mariad Bailey was laughing. 'She lost her balance.'

Mary struggled to get to her feet, but on the way she grabbed mud in her hand and threw it straight at the bitch as she was laughing. She caught a full mouthful of the mud before she could close her mouth.

'Not laughing now, bitch,' said Mary.

It took all Jimmy's strength to hold his sister back.

'You asked for that, Mariad. Now stop it. She'll get what's coming to her, so stop it, for fuck's sake.'

'When you get that bullet in the back of your head, I'm going to be the one pulling the trigger,' said Mariad, wiping the mud from her face.

Looking around her, Mary could see they were in the large yard of what looked like a farmhouse, with two large barns one at each end of the house. The whole yard was lit by the beams from two lights on the house roof and one of each on the barns over the doors. Two men came out of the farmhouse and walked towards them. Mary recognised both John Jo Murphy and Brendan McDevitt. Her blood ran cold. She knew of McDevitt and that he was now the head of the Real IRA, but it was his other nickname, Doctor Death, that reminded her of the stories she'd heard of how he liked to torture his many victims before killing them himself. It was McDevitt who spoke first.

'Ah, at last Mary, you're here. I hope you had a comfortable journey?'

To Mary the crooked grin was as unpleasant as his guttural voice. She tried to put a brave face on it.

'Why have you brought me here, Brendan? You have no right to do this.'

'Ah, now let's not get into all that now. We will have plenty of time to talk. We will be asking the questions, and you'll answer, one way, or another. Right, John Jo, show Mary to her new quarters while I get our Belfast guests something to eat. They have had a long day and I'm sure they're starving. Kevin, you watch over her.'

Kevin had been the driver of the Hiace that brought them here. As Murphy led Mary by the arm towards the barn to the left of the house entrance, Kevin went over to a Land Rover parked outside the barn. The only other car in the yard was a red Volkswagen.

The Land Rover looked like it belonged on a farm, the paint rusted, and the bodywork covered in bumps and scratches. Kevin opened the rear door and took out a black Armalite rifle before following John Jo and Mary into the barn. Everyone else followed McDevitt into the house.

Looking around her, Mary could see two chairs placed in the middle of the large space. The inside of the barn was well lit by two large arc lamps on stands. Along one wall there appeared to be empty cattle stalls with a feeding trough in front of them. On the opposite side there was what appeared to be a large steel tank filled with water which stood on top of two oil drums. Above the tank attached to one of the beams was a pulley of sorts made with ropes and chains and a large hook on the end. John Jo spun Mary around and sat her down in one of the chairs facing the barn doors. He quickly tied her hands behind her back with plastic cuffs and then an ankle to each leg of the chair with the same type of cuffs.

'There now, Mary, all comfortable. You won't need a gag as no one will hear your screams here.' He smiled. 'Now, Kevin here will keep you company and we'll be back later for that little chat. I must meet up with an old friend, but I'll be back later.'

Looking back, Mary decided not to answer. It would only inflate his ego. Kevin took the other chair and, placing it so that he could see Mary and anyone coming into the barn, he sat down. Placing the rifle across his lap, he said nothing.

Chapter 33

Dundalk

Reece and the rest of the team had no problems crossing the border. They had all been waved through at the PSNI traffic checks on the main Belfast to Dublin Road just outside Newry. The traffic being held up had slowed them down to a crawl in line. This gave the officers manning the checkpoint time to note the number of people in the vehicles, or if one of them was a woman, note the registration which would then be flashed through to the PSNI HQ Control in Belfast. At the same time they would still pull in the odd vehicle for a search and question stop. Reece knew if they were on the ball it wouldn't be long before Tom Wilson knew that one covert military car and his hire car had just crossed the border and into the Republic. Wilson would call Jim Broad, who Reece hoped would then tell him to forget what he knew. Then in the future, if he was asked, he could deny all knowledge. When they'd parked up in the lay-by just outside Killeen on the Republic side of the border, the lay-by was empty. They were protected from view and the car headlights passing on the main road by a row of fern hedges. Reece had used it years before to pick up and drop off agents. Ari handed all three SG9 men their personal weapons and at the same time invited them to take something more powerful in case they ran into serious trouble, which was to be expected. Joe Cousins took his time before selecting an AK47 and two full magazines.

'This is going to be fun,' he said, placing the weapon in the back seat of the BMW. Geoff Middleton looked the weapons over and made his selection. An Armalite rifle and two magazines. One he inserted in the rifle and pocketed the other as a spare then he placed the rifle in the well of the front passenger seat.

Ari turned to Reece. 'Do you see anything you would like, David?'

'Plenty, but not for now,' replied Reece, looking over the small arsenal.

'OK everyone, let's get into Dundalk, and find out the lie of the land. Costello or Murphy may be early so we need places where we can observe and not be spotted. I don't need to tell you how to suck eggs. You have all done this before and we are only going to get one chance at this. Joe and Geoff, you might have to stay with Murphy on your own while I go with Ari to meet his agent at midnight. Try to keep the comms short and to the point. Thanks again guys, be careful.'

They drove in convoy fashion until they reached the outskirts of Dundalk. Reece and Ari branched off to take a circular route into the town while Cousins and Middleton continued along the main route to the centre of the town. The hotel was on Park Street, one of the main thoroughfares through central Dundalk. When they drove past, Reece could see the hotel had been upgraded from the years when he used to visit the local Garda Police station to liaise with his opposite Special Branch officers in the Irish Police. That had all stopped when two senior RUC officers had been ambushed and killed by the PIRA on their way back from a meeting in the station just after they'd crossed the border into South Armagh. It was felt they'd been set up by someone in the Garda station who tipped off the Provos.

The hotel front now had a Continental-looking outside café with a dark blue slate finish to the front entrance. Although the rain had stopped and it was cold, there were still a few customers in the outside café, the hardy ones with thick coats and scarves. The surrounding area, with restaurants and bars, was busy, and finding a suitable parking space was difficult. Ari drove on, continuing for a short distance before turning to come back the way he had come. Then a car pulled out, leaving Ari a space to reverse into that had a good view of the front door of the hotel. Reece looked at the time on the dash. It was 21.25, so a good thirty minutes before their targets would be meeting. Because of the cold air, there weren't too many people hanging about. Reece lowered his window by an inch to prevent the windows misting up.

'Delta. Juliet in town centre. Where do you want me?' asked Joe Cousins on the radio.

'Roger Juliet. I'm watching some cars turn into the car park at the rear of the hotel. I just realised they probably have a rear entrance to the hotel as well. Can you go in and find somewhere to discreetly park and observe? If you find you're being compromised come back out, but at this time of night it should be busy enough with coming and going to give you the cover you need,' replied Reece.

'Roger. On my way,' answered Cousins.

Then the voice of Geoff Middleton.

'Delta that's Golf in town, where do you want me?'

'That's great Golf. We have the front and rear of the hotel covered for now. Can you park up on the road going north out of the town centre as that's the most likely direction our targets are going to come in and leave by, so you can give us a heads up?' answered Reece.

'Roger, Delta, will do,' replied Middleton.

'I think we've it well covered, David,' said Ari.

Reece watched as Cousins, driving the BMW, turned off Park Street, and into the rear car park of the Hotel.

'Delta, that's Juliet parked up with plenty of cover from other vehicles. Waiting for my Romeo,' announced Joe Cousins two minutes later.

'That's a good one, Juliet. Everyone, let's give JJ the code name Romeo and our visitor from Belfast, Hamlet,' answered Reece.

'Romeo and Hamlet it is, then,' replied Cousins.

It didn't take long for things to start moving. Ten minutes later it was Geoff Middleton who spoke first.

'Everyone. Hamlet is coming into the town from the north.'

'Roger Golf. Good job we were here early,' answered Reece. 'Stay in position Golf. Romeo might not be far behind.'

'Roger, will do.'

Five minutes later Reece and Ari could clearly see Paul Costello slow his Silver Sierra and turn into the rear car park of the hotel.

'Juliet, that's Hamlet into your car park,' said Reece.

'Roger, I have him,' answered Cousins. 'Hamlet is parked up and out and into the hotel. Not appearing to look for surveillance.'

'OK let's keep on our toes,' said Reece.

'I do believe Romeo has just passed me in a red Golf, going a bit fast to be sure, but in your direction,' said Middleton.

A few minutes later a Red Volkswagen Golf slowed and without indicating turned into the car park.

'That's definitely Romeo,' said Ari over the radio network.

'Are you sure?' asked Reece.

'Yes, I've observed him before a few times.'

'Good enough. Juliet that's Romeo into your area,' said Reece.

'Roger. I have him. Romeo out of car and into hotel,' replied Cousins.

'We don't know how long this is going to take but let's keep our current positions,' said Reece.

'Roger that,' came the reply from both Cousins and Middleton.

Reece knew that on occasions such as this conversations were brief in case the operatives carrying out the surveillance were distracted so everyone remained quiet, watching, waiting, ready.

'Delta, do you want me to go in and have a look?' asked Cousins.

'No, Juliet. In there, everyone notices strangers.'

'Roger, understood.'

In the darkness Ari didn't see Reece smile.

For Ari's benefit Reece explained.

'We don't take unnecessary risks in Bandit Country. And the Imperial Hotel has always been a favourite haunt of the Bandits from South Armagh.'

'Now I understand,' said Ari.

'Even if you went in, Ari, there would be questions asked about who you are, and with Mary's life on the line we've to be as careful as we can, so they don't know we're here.'

They returned to the silent watching. An hour later it was Murphy who came out first.

'Delta that's Romeo out and into his car. No sign of Hamlet.' It was Cousins' voice breaking the silence.

Reece answered quickly. 'Roger Juliet, you, and Golf stay with him but don't spook him. We will back you up as much as we can, but we've the meeting at midnight so may have to pull off in thirty minutes at 23.30.'

Both callsigns acknowledged with a 'Roger that.'

'Are we leaving Costello here?' asked Ari.

'By the look of things, he's staying for some reason. We must stick with Murphy. he most likely knows where Mary is, and he's Real IRA whereas Costello isn't. I know it's a risk, but we must go with the most likely target who will lead us there and I think that's Murphy.'

They watched as Murphy's red Golf turned left and headed north up Park Street. A few cars behind was Cousins giving a running commentary over the radio of Romeo's progress. Ari pulled into the light traffic and followed.

'He's not doing any anti-surveillance as far as I can see,' said Cousins.

'He's on his own turf and he'll be more relaxed. If we get onto country roads, we may have to hang back further,' replied Reece.

'That's Romeo on the main north road out of town,' said Cousins.

'Roger that. Golf, get ready to join us. With three of us, we can interchange,' said Reece.

'Roger that, Delta,' replied Middleton.

The three following vehicles spaced themselves out and when Cousins thought he had been behind Murphy too long, he pulled in to let Ari take over with Cousins joining the rear of the convoy.

'That's Romeo left, left, left onto the Kilcurry Road. Golf take point,' said Reece.

Ari pulled in and let Middleton take over point behind the red Volkswagen. Ari then took up the rear of the line of cars behind Cousins as he passed. Now they were on a country road the lack of street lights sharpened the white and red lights given off from the cars. Middleton braked slightly so that his headlights appeared further back. It was at that moment that Murphy accelerated at a bend and when Middleton drove around it, there was no sign of the red taillights of the car that should be in front of him.

'Romeo lost.' Middleton spoke quickly into the radio.

'Lost? What happened?' asked Reece.

'He accelerated just before the last bend and when I came around it, there was no sign of him.'

'Everyone pull in. We just came around the bend and there are two smaller country roads, one on each side. He must have taken one of them. Let's talk,' said Reece.

All three vehicles pulled up at the side of the road. There was very little traffic, so they had a few minutes before losing Murphy for good. Ari had reached into the glove compartment and brought out a map. Using a penlight, he quickly highlighted where they were. Placing it on the bonnet of the Izuzu they could see the two small roads, one that led across country towards Cullaville near Crossmaglen and the north in South Armagh, and the other towards Jonesborough and close to the border in Northern Ireland.

'He must have taken one of these roads and they're both going to South Armagh. There are a lot of farms along each road so we'd have a job checking them all, but we must try,' said Reece. 'Ari and I'll have to leave now to meet with his agent at midnight, so it's down to you both taking a road each.

'You will have to be very careful. The best way would be to park up when you see a farm and if you can approach on foot to try to spot Romeo's car. He may have already driven across the border.

'If that's the case, God knows where he is. That's why I must go with Ari and hope his agent knows exactly where they have Mary. I know it's splitting our resources, but it's the best we can do right now.

'For fuck's sake, don't expose yourself, and get caught. If you must shoot your way out from a bad situation, then do so. Everyone understand?'

'Yes, understood,' replied Middleton, answering for the two men.

Reece looked at his watch.

'It's now eleven thirty. We have half an hour before we meet the agent, so do what you can. We'll catch-up with you after the meeting.'

All three vehicles moved off with Cousins taking the small road towards Jonesborough and Middleton towards Cullaville, while Ari turned around, and headed back towards the main Belfast Road north, heading for the Ravensdale Forest.

CHAPTER 34

THE BARN

Mary heard the car pull into the yard, followed by footsteps, but not to the barn. She could hear loud voices and she knew one of them to be John Jo Murphy's. Then the footsteps were coming closer, and John Jo and Brian McDevitt entered the barn. Kevin stood and moved behind Mary.

'Well, Mary, how are you feeling?' said Murphy, asking a question when he didn't care for an answer. 'Sorry to keep you waiting, but these things happen sometimes when we've to get everything in order before we can start. But it won't be long now before you and I can have that nice little chat we've been promising you.' He grinned.'

McDevitt came right up to where she was sitting, putting his face so close she could smell his bad breath, which reeked of cigarettes and whisky. She also noticed he hadn't cleaned his teeth for some time.

'We're waiting on a very special visitor who you'll know. He wants to see you before we put a bullet through that pretty head of yours. But that doesn't mean we can't start. So here's what's going to happen, Mary, and it's up to you whether the whole process is bad or very bad.'

Mary's stomach was turning, and she felt sick. She watched as he stood and walked around her, talking all the while in voice that she felt was full of menace.

'Our Belfast friends wanted to be here and watch, but I told them there's plenty of time. That Mariad one doesn't like you, does she? She especially wants to do bad things to you. But again, there'll be time for everyone. I wanted you and I to get to know each other a little better first.'

Mary noticed how he had lowered his voice almost to a whisper as he moved behind her. Then he pulled her hand back and, taking hold of the finger with her engagement ring, he continued to talk quietly.

'I see you're engaged. I hope your Special Branch boyfriend got what he needed from you. And I don't just mean information.'

Murphy was smiling. 'I saw the ring, Brendan. It looks expensive. I hope it was worth all the pillow talk.'

Still holding the ring finger, McDevitt squeezed it before pulling it in the opposite direction to dislocate it from its socket. Mary screamed at the sudden pain exploding in her brain, then the bile, and vomit surged into her mouth before she spat it out on the floor.

'You bastard,' she shouted.

McDevitt was standing in front of her once more.

'I've been called that before.' He smiled. 'I can assure you, it's going to get a lot worse. Now, this is how we're going to proceed. First, you'll receive little bouts of pain such as the one you just experienced. That's just to make you feel at home and for us to get some satisfaction before you tell us everything…and take it from me, my dear, you will tell us everything. You want to resist, you want to try to make us believe we've got it all wrong, but we've done this before. We know the process works.'

'Go fuck yourselves,' Mary shouted between the pulses of pain running up her hand and arm.

'Ah, that's my girl. Before we are finished you and I are going to have some fun. For now, this is how it's going to go. John Jo?'

Murphy reached into his jacket pocket and brought out a small cassette recorder, placing it on the ground a few feet from where she was sitting.

'It's not on record yet. That will be just for you a little later when you want to tell us everything, and you will, and there'll be a surprise guest here to hear you confess,' said McDevitt, smiling.

He's enjoying this, thought Mary. The pain was now a constant throbbing and the feeling of wanting to be sick was still in her stomach.

'No matter what I say you won't believe me. You enjoy this too much, so, as I said, go fuck yourselves,' said Mary through clenched teeth.

'Keep your mouth shut. That will only make my job even more enjoyable. Then when you beg for it to stop, we'll tape what you want to say,' replied McDevitt. 'Kevin, light the drums, please.'

Kevin handed the rifle to John Jo. Then going over to the drums below the large water tank he used his lighter to light the logs and kindling in each drum. The flames, high at first, soon settled, the heat slowly warming the water in the tank above.

'You see, Mary, when that water is hot enough, we'll lower you slowly feet first on that block and tackle into the tank. That's when you'll really confess and answer for your sins. I've used it many times before and I can assure you it works every time,' said McDevitt.

'And they say you're a great Republican leader. You're just a butcher of women and children and those who can't fight back,' said Mary, angry at herself for even speaking to this monster.

McDevitt just laughed. 'Well, in the meantime, while your bath warms up I'll leave you with Kevin. He will give you a little taster of what's coming. Kevin, keep those drums burning. John Jo and I'll go and get a cup of tea and bring you one back later. In the meantime, show her what you can do.'

John Jo leant the Armalite against the barn door and both men headed back to the farmhouse. Kevin lifted a couple of logs from a pile next to the water tank and placed them into the drums. Mary watched him as he made sure the fires weren't going out. Kevin walked deliberately towards her then suddenly punched her on the side of her head. The side of her face felt like it was going to explode with the pain, then she blacked out, the last feeling she had was when the chair toppled over.

CHAPTER 35

RAVENSDALE FOREST

At ten minutes to midnight when Ari pulled into the car park it was quiet and dark.

Reece had expected the blackness, the trees drowning out any light from the night sky. He had met agents in forests many times in his Special Branch days and it always scared the hell out of him. Instinctively he took out the Smith and Wesson and held it on his lap.

'Are you worried?' asked Ari, noticing his actions.

'Not worried. I just never take these situations for granted, better to be prepared.'

'I've met this man here once before. He was on time and the meeting went well without problem,' said Ari.

Just then they could see the headlights of a car approaching. Reece flicked the safety catch off, ready for trouble if it came. Reece made sure not to look directly at the headlights, as he knew he'd be temporarily blinded when they were switched off.

'It's him,' said Ari as the car pulled into the space beside them.

The driver turned off the engine and quickly moved to the back of the Izuzu getting into the seat behind Ari. Reece wasn't sure. He had only caught a glimpse of the man in the reflection of the rear window when the interior light came on in the few seconds when he entered the car. Reece had seen his face before. He knew him from somewhere. Then it struck him like a bolt of lightning, the files he had read in his room in the Hilton hotel in Belfast with a photo of the man now sitting in the back seat, the MLA Paul Costello. Reece turned towards him, passing his gun to his left hand so that he could aim squarely at the man's chest across the back seat. Costello remained calm, staring back at Reece.

'Surprised, Mister Reece? That makes two of us and I can assure you I'm not armed, unlike my brother, when you shot him.' The accent was South Armagh, a bit north Irish, and a bit southern, but softer than most that Reece had heard.

'Why didn't you tell me?' Reece asked Ari, without taking his eyes, or his aim off Costello.

'You didn't need to know, as they say. You know our first rule is to protect our sources of information and I didn't tell you in case he didn't show up. His code name is Prefect but of course you will know him as Paul Costello, the Sinn Fein MLA, and brother of the late Sean Costello.'

'Prefect. This is David who I believe you know, anyway. Thank you for coming. David, I think you can lower your gun now. We have some serious business to discuss.'

Reece noticed his own breathing had been shallow, but when he lowered his gun he moved it back into his right hand. He wasn't going to trust the man in the back seat just yet. If Reece knew one thing in life, it was that to keep alive, the only person he truly trusted was himself.

'Nice to meet you at last, David. You're probably wondering why I'm here and what brought me here to be working with Ari's people? Let me give you the quick version.'

'That would be nice, but for now can you keep your hands where I can see them?'

'Understood. To answer the first part. Yes, I was a member of the South Armagh PIRA during the war.'

Reece was pleased to hear Costello call it a war not the political speak of 'The Troubles.'

Costello continued, 'I could see a lot earlier than some that it was a war we couldn't win. Your inroads into our organisation by your intelligence teams were starting to hit us hard. You were killing or imprisoning more of us, and we couldn't afford to lose good men at the rate we were. I'd started to think politically, but I never wanted to work with the British, especially the RUC and Army, or MI5 for that matter. To make matters worse, the new young recruits we were bringing in to replace those we were losing were amateurs and more innocent people were being killed. They didn't care, they were fanatics of the wrong kind. You couldn't talk to them, they wouldn't listen. I was on the run and taking a break in Dublin. The papers were all talking about back-door moves by the British government to try to bring about some sort of peace. It was then I had the idea of approaching the Israeli Embassy. I wasn't sure how it was going to go, but they were very open to my help and willing to pass on my information through diplomatic channels. The rest you probably know through Ari and his friends. I joined the Adams, McGuinness faction of Sinn Fein and worked for the peace process to succeed and to convert the minds of the military mindset in the Republican organisation. Unfortunately, there were those like my brother who wouldn't, or couldn't change. I know you killed my brother, Mister Reece. If you hadn't, someone else would have. Try to understand. I loved my brother, but in the end, I didn't like him. We didn't agree on the way forward and no matter what, I couldn't change his way of thinking. I'd decided that the killing and bloodshed, especially the blood of the Irish people, was not the way to go. I don't know if the current process will ultimately be a success, but to my mind it's a better way than that chosen by my brother and people who think like he did. That's why I'm here now and when Ari contacted me, I decided to help him once more. Don't get me wrong, if the Real IRA kill you or your woman, then that won't help the peace process at all. It's a process that has come through worse and is still on track although those tracks would be wobbly for a while, like the time after the Omagh bombing in 98 that killed twenty-nine innocent civilians. The thing that has made the difference to me this time is that these people are using my brother's and my family's name as an excuse to try to derail the peace and start the killing all over again. These people came to me at my brother's funeral to tell me they intended to do something and weren't asking my permission. That's where we are now.

They have your woman and my agreement with them is that they do not kill her until I hear a confession from her own lips that she was a traitor during the war with the British. I knew Mary McAuley. I'd met her on many occasions at high-ranking meetings during the peace talks.

She was highly regarded, and I had no reason to doubt who she was. My plan is to have them exile her. I'll try to convince them that the current peace is the only way forward. I'll tell them that by their actions they'd proved they still had the resources but that they could demand a place at the table. I know it sounds naïve of me, but until Ari contacted me, it was my only plan. So, that's my plan, Mister Reece, as far as it takes me.'

Costello took a long, deep breath, and sat back further in his seat, keeping his hands on his lap where Reece could see them.

'What evidence do they have that she worked for us? After all, you know her from your own meetings with her. Is this just a fishing expedition or, as you say, a way to try to break the peace and get back to war?' asked Reece.

Costello took a few seconds before responding. 'That's where you come in, Mister Reece. At my brother's funeral, they showed me photos of you and Mary McAuley, and they were able to say that my brother spotted her with you in London during his operation there. Further checks by them showed that she was also in London when that Islamic Jihad terrorist was shot. They also showed me the photo of you with the body of the Arab. They are happy that she's an informer, and they have the evidence. They had hoped to get you as well. That's why they deliberately knocked down her mother, hoping you would both come to Belfast and help make their job easier.'

'You keep saying they! Who are they?' interrupted Reece.

'I'm sorry. I thought that as we've come this far, you knew who they were. After all, the press has said it for days. They are the so-called

Real IRA, and I can assure you they're right. This has nothing to do with the Provisional Republican Movement,' answered Costello.

'So, you mean the likes of Brendan McDevitt and John Jo Murphy?' answered Reece.

Reece could see a look of surprise come across Costello's face. 'So, you've kept your fingers in the pie?'

Reece smiled. 'We're not stupid. If the whole world knows, we know.'

'Yes, Murphy and McDevitt are involved. It was them who approached me at the funeral.'

'I'm sure we all agree we don't want the war back. Where is she? Can we get her out? Is she still alive, then?' Ari's voice broke through the two men's conversation.

Ari had asked the questions that brought them here. Reece waited for Costello to reply.

'She's being held at the McDevitt farm near the border with Jonesborough just inside the southern side. They won't kill her, at least not until I've heard her confession from her mouth. They are expecting me at 2 a.m. so if you're going to do something, you haven't got long.'

'Do you know this farm?' Ari asked Reece.

'Yes, we covered it during the war, but that was some time ago, and we'll be going in the dark at short notice with little time to plan. Anyway, we're putting our faith in Costello here. I'm not sure we can fully trust him.'

The sound of Costello laughing filled the car.

'You don't trust me? Now there's a dilemma because you're asking me to trust you, the man who killed my brother. The man who, no matter what happens, could expose me to the world as working with our sworn enemy. Do me a favour, get with the programme. The peace process is bigger than all of us here and everyone out there, including your own bosses. While we talk here, your woman's life hangs in the balance. If you're serious about her, we need to move soon. Besides, what kind of life would I have if your people and Mossad were hunting me down? A short one, I think.'

Reece knew what he said was true. No matter what he felt about Costello, he had no choice but to take the information he had given them and act on it now.

Ari opened the glove compartment and removed the map he had used in Belfast.

'Perfect. Can you show me on the map where the farm is? Have you been there before?' Ari used the small penlight torch to light up the map.

'It's just here, up a long laneway,' replied Costello, pointing to what looked like a small set of brown buildings that were almost exactly on the line that divided the border.

'Do you have any idea how many people are there?' asked Reece.

'There will be at least a half dozen, including both Murphy and McDevitt. They will want to be there when she confesses and anyway, torture is McDevitt's favourite pastime.'

'It's just coming up to one. How long will it take you to get there?' asked Ari.

'From here, the best way for me to go is back across the border and cross back to the farm from Jonesborough, about thirty minutes. If you do hit the place, make sure I'm not in the line of fire.'

'If we can get in and out without any shooting, I would be happy. But if shooting starts, you get down fast and stay down until it's over,' answered Reece.

'Oh, that really reassures me,' Costello replied sarcastically.

'Just make sure you're still wearing that sweater if you go there. We can't miss it,' said Reece, pointing the barrel of the gun at Costello's chest once more.

'Thank you for your help. We should all move and do whatever 'we have to do,' said Ari.

'Before I go, this little gem is just for you Mister Reece, a sign of good faith let us say,' said Costello.

'Good faith is important,' answered Reece. He still didn't trust Costello, and he didn't like the way he called him Mister.

'During the war and still working with the Real IRA for money is a rogue RUC Chief Inspector called Wilson. His son, Tom, is the top man in the Intelligence Department of the PSNI. So, watch what you tell Tom Wilson because his dad has big ears and deep pockets as far as the Real IRA is concerned.'

Reece felt as if someone had kicked him in the stomach. He knew DCI Paddy Wilson from his days in Newry Special Branch when Paddy Wilson was one of the senior officers in Armagh.

'How am I supposed to believe you?' asked Reece.

'Believe me or don't believe me, it doesn't matter to me. All I can tell you is that he did it for money and plenty of it. He told us when you were expecting us to carry out attacks and by doing so, we were able to identify some of the informers within our communities and deal with them. I tell you this because he has a gambling habit he needs to feed and now he's working with the likes of McDevitt for his pay day. By his actions, I consider him a thorn in the side of the peace process. The main people in Sinn Fein think to expose him wouldn't be believed but would reflect badly on them. I'm telling you this in the hope you can do something from your end.'

Reece and Ari remained silent.

'Well, there you have it. I'll have to go as they'll be expecting me,' said Costello, starting to open the door.

'Wait,' said Reece quietly. 'How many people are at the farm?'

Costello sat back in the seat. 'As I said, I would think at least six.'

'What would be the best way to approach the farm? How many buildings? What's the security like?' Again, Reece was looking for answers, for information.

Costello listened. he knew why Reece was asking these questions. Taking his time, he looked directly at Reece before answering.

'It's been a while since I was there. The family has CCTV, but if the coverage hasn't been changed, it's looking to the north, because that's where they always expected trouble to come from. They had one dog, a sheepdog, not a guard dog. It's friendly and licks everyone's hand. The farmhouse is a large two-storey building with a large yard in front of it. There are two large barns and the one to the south is usually where McDevitt does his dirty work, so my guess is that's where you'll find your woman.'

'Thank you for your help,' said Ari.

'Don't get me wrong. When McDevitt and Murphy first showed me the evidence they had and the photos proving that Mister Reece and Mary McAuley were responsible for my brother's death I wanted them both dead in return. But then, I took the time to think about what could happen if they were killed. How it would affect the peace process and the danger of going back to the bloodshed again? My gut feeling said no, I cannot let that happen. As I already said, my brother was on his own destructive path and sooner or later he was going to end up doing a long prison sentence or dead. That was the choice he made, and the fact it was you, Mister Reece, who fulfilled his destiny. I can understand. Now I really must go.' Without waiting for an answer, Costello was out of the Izuzu and into his own car and away.

Both men silently watched the red taillights of the car disappear into the blackness of the forest.

'What do you think? Do you think it's a trap?' asked Ari, breaking the silence.

'To tell you the truth, I'm not sure. I'm still getting over the shock of who your agent was. But I don't think he'd take the risk of what would happen to him if it was a trap. It would be bad enough if my people were after him, never mind yours. I think he's genuine about keeping the peace. He's more of a politician now than a terrorist, so the peace process is his bread and butter now.'

'Bread and butter?'

'Just an expression we use to indicate what is more important to a person.'

'What now?'

'We meet up with Joe and Geoff and put together a quick plan to hit the farm around 2 a.m. before any decisions are made to kill Mary. Let's drive north and we can meet outside Jonesborough. I'll get onto my boss and get him to lift the police road checks on the Belfast to

Dublin Road. Realistically they're looking at traffic coming from the north but if they're there when any shooting starts, we might have a problem if we want to escape back into the north. Let me have the map. I need to look at something while you drive.'

Reece quickly worked out the map reference number for the McDevitt farm. Then he opened the Google Earth application on his phone and typed in the number. The search brought up an aerial daylight photo of the farm complex and the surrounding fields and roads.

'Got it. Thank you, Google. That will do nicely,' he said out loud.

'What will?' asked Ari.

Reece explained what he had found.

'That will do nicely indeed,' agreed Ari.

Reece hit some buttons on his phone and heard the ringtone before the voice of Jim Broad answered.

'David? It's good to hear from you,' said Broad, but Reece recognised the sardonic tone in Broad's voice.

'We have been kind of busy here, boss, but needed to catch-up with you,' replied Reece.

'I've already had phone calls from Wilson and Bryant, both concerned that my SG9 operators are in the Republic of Ireland's jurisdiction. I could only tell them you'd gone dark, and I didn't know what was happening but that they should keep quiet for now. So I'm glad you called, hopefully to tell me good news and what the hell you're all up to.'

Reece quickly brought his boss up to speed from Belfast to the reason they crossed the border. He told Broad about Ari and the agent, but without mentioning the agent's name, instead just referring to him as Prefect, Costello's code name. He kept the Costello part to himself. Instead, he just told his boss that Prefect was able to provide them with the details of where Mary was being held.

'You believe she's still alive, then?'

'Yes, until 2 a.m. at least, when Prefect has agreed to meet with the abductors at the farm.'

'I take it you have a plan?'

'Formulating one and that's why I called you. We might need your help.'

'I can't give you any more resources if you're in the South of Ireland. I'll be in enough trouble for sending you Cousins and Middleton, which, I might add, my bosses don't know about.'

'I know and I'm truly thankful, but if we are successful, we'll be running for the border, crossing into the north near Jonesborough. If we get that far, a chopper would be greatly appreciated.'

Broad was silent for so long that Reece thought he had lost the connection.

'Hello, are you still there, boss?'

'Yes, I'm still here. I don't know who you think I am or what I can do, but something like getting you a helicopter is no small task. Do you really think you'll need it? Getting one will raise all sorts of questions.'

'I'm not sure. But having one on standby would be helpful, especially if we run into more trouble than we can handle. It will only be needed if we are being chased when we get across the border into the north. We'll be in the Bandit Country of South Armagh, and you know from your own experience how quickly those bastards can call up reserves.'

'Leave it with me. I'll see what I can do, but for God's sake, David, try to be as quiet as you can. This could raise an international stink to say the least. We will need a code name for any help team.'

'Let's go with Extraction Delta. It should do the trick,' Reece answered.

'Sounds about right. What about this ex-IRA source? Can you trust him?'

Reece was aware of Ari trying to follow the conversation as he drove.

'You know me. I don't fully trust anyone. We will be prepared for any problems. I'm sending you a Google Earth shot of the farm with map reference to where it's located along the border. If you get the chopper back-up, let them know and get them to send you a safe location nearby where they can land to pick us up if needed.'

'Leave it with me. I'll work from our operation room here. Another late night.'

'Tell me about it. Will be in touch.' Reece ended the call.

'Thank you for protecting the name of my source,' said Ari.

'He's your source. It's not for me to tell, but I think he gave me the extra titbit about naming the police traitor for a reason. To show good faith and to have the name in my back pocket should I need it in the future.'

As they travelled back across the border, Reece could see many landmarks that brought back memories of his days of service in the same area. There were new houses and now a motorway that started in

Dublin and ended in Belfast. They took the country back roads and before long they were parked up on the outskirts of the village of Jonesborough South Armagh. Reece got on the radio.

'Delta to Golf and Juliet. Pull out from what you're doing and meet us just outside Jonesborough in the north. Take the main roads. We now know where Mike is.'

Both SG9 men replied, 'Roger, Delta.'

'You would know this area pretty well then?' asked Ari.

'Too well. It was in these fields, roads, and hills that some of the most vicious fighting took place. The IRA here was the deadliest unit in the land at the time. Most of their fighters had lived here all their lives and were related. That, more than anything, stopped them from becoming sources of information for us. Most of our intelligence came from army road stops and house searches or when we lifted them in early morning raids. We took them to holding centres for questioning for a maximum of seven days. They had been schooled in anti-interrogation and would just sit there saying nothing. They knew we couldn't hold them any longer and were back out home. Back again to their killing. They controlled the area so well that the security forces could only move around by helicopter. Most roads had landmines and booby traps. The other thing the South Armagh unit was good for was shipping large lorry bombs across to England where they caused devastation in places like Manchester and London. Yes, Ari. I know this area very well and I'd hoped I would never have to come back here.'

CHAPTER 36

JONESBOROUGH

The SG9 team sat in the Izuzu twenty minutes later. At one thirty in the morning, there was no one else about in the village of Jonesborough in South Armagh. There was no light inside the car other than that from a half-moon shining in the sky when the clouds cleared. Cousins and Middleton arrived at almost the same time and, sitting in the rear seats they listened as Reece laid out his plan.

'According to Ari's source we now know where Mary is being held and we've an idea of what we are up against. I've sent everyone the Google Earth pictures of the farm complex and the map reference.

'The farm is only five miles south from here on the road through the small townland of Drumbilla, with a lane about a half mile long leading from the road to the farm. The best plans are simple ones, no need to complicate things. Anyway, we don't have the resources to do anything bigger.

'I propose we work in two teams. Ari will drop us off at the bottom of the lane, then park up. The rest of us will go forward to the complex. We know that there'll be at least six of the opposition there. The farm itself will probably be lit up with security lights. There will probably be some sort of CCTV, so our approach needs to be ultra covert. Mary is most likely being held in the southern barn in the complex. Ari has kindly provided me with a Baretta with a silencer, so I'll move to the southern barn with Geoff backing me up if things get noisy. I'll still have my own weapon for back-up.

'Joe, you'll make your way to the side of the northern barn to cover the yard and farm building for any opposition trying to prevent our progress. Ari's source might be there.

'We've told him if shooting starts to hit the dirt and stay there. He will be wearing a bright green sweater, so you'll recognise him. I just hope no one else is wearing one.

'Both Geoff and Joe will be using the heavy firepower. The enemy should be relaxed. They know the local police won't bother them and they'll feel safe in their own little castle not expecting visitors, especially at two in the morning, and that's when we need to be in there doing the job. Any questions so far?'

'Assuming all goes well, and we get Mary out of there. What's to say we won't encounter more of their friends? I'm sure they could get the word out quickly for reinforcements if they needed to,' asked Cousins.

'No matter what happens the plan includes an escape. After Ari has dropped us off at the bottom of the lane, we'll approach the farm on foot, down this ditch, which runs down the side of the lane.

'When we have Mary inside the barn, Geoff and I'll stay there with her while when I give the go over the radio Ari drives into the yard we all pile in and drive out.'

'Now that sounds simple, if the opposition play along we should be all right,' said Cousins.

'Hopefully, if we've caught them by surprise we'll be in and out before they know what's hit them. We will then drive back across the border where we'll go our separate ways.

'Ari back to Dublin and you and Geoff back to the Hilton in Belfast with Mary and I as passengers. I've asked Jim Broad to get us the use of a helicopter in case we run into trouble where we can't use the cars. But again, we can't depend on that,' answered Reece.

'Well as they always drilled into us in selection training, adapt and overcome,' said Middleton.

'Let's do that if we must. Now any more questions before we move?' asked Reece.

No one replied, with only Cousins nodding his head.

'OK,' said Reece looking at his watch. 'It's now 01.32hrs We get going and if as expected most of our opposition will be in the barn with Mary at 02.00hrs then we hit it at the same time.

'Take no chances, don't think for one minute about how killing one of these bastards will affect the peace process. They don't give a fuck about the peace process, and neither should we. As my trainers always told me Geoff, keep shooting them until they're dead.'

'My trainers told me the same,' replied Middleton.

'And mine,' said Ari.

'All right, let's go and good luck,' said Reece.

Ari put the IZZUZU in gear moving slowly at first towards the border.

The half-moon cleared the clouds lighting up the road ahead.

CHAPTER 37

THE FARM

Mary came round slowly. Her head ached, the pain mostly around her nose. Her head was down and as she opened her eyes a bit at a time, she could see her blood drying on her blouse. The bleeding had stopped but had dried in her nostrils, making it difficult to breathe through her nose. She didn't know if her nose was broken. it felt like it. It reminded her of the punches and slaps she used to get from her husband Brendan and how one night David Reece had saved her from further beatings in a street in Newry when he knocked Brendan out with one punch.

'Where are you now, David? I need you,' she thought. It was painful, but lifting her head she could see Kevin sitting in his chair watching her, smiling, with the Armalite across his knees.

'Don't worry bitch. If I wanted to I would have broken your nose and you wouldn't be awake for a while yet,' said Kevin, grinning.

Mary spat blood from her mouth in Kevin's direction. Her nose was sore and slightly swollen but when she tried to breathe through it she realised she could, just. It wasn't broken.

There was the sound of a car coming into the farmyard. Kevin got to his feet and walked to the barn door. Then she heard the voices. it sounded like everyone was in the farmyard talking over each other. Kevin stood back as the barn door opened. Brian McDevitt entered followed by John Jo Murphy, then a man she recognised both from her days in the movement and the media, Paul Costello. For a moment her body seemed to freeze as she realised here was Sean Costello's brother and she'd been there when her lover David Reece, code name Joseph, had shot Sean dead. Now she began to understand why they waited to get on with it. They were waiting for Paul Costello, brother of the dead Sean, and MLA in the new Stormont Government. The three men stopped at the door in deep conversation which, being too far away Mary couldn't hear, maybe because her ears were still ringing from Kevin's punch. McDevitt looked in Mary's direction as he spoke to Costello, then pointed to the water tank being heated by the burning logs. She didn't need to hear, she knew McDevitt was in his element pointing out Mary's future, and how he was going to progress it. Conversation over, the three men walked over and looked down at Mary.

'I thought you were going to wait until I was here?' said Costello when he saw Mary's bruised and bloodied face.

'We did wait, we just said we wouldn't kill her until you were here to hear her confession. We had a little fun letting her know what to expect and what was coming. I must admit she's stronger than you think, it might take her some time to really understand pain,' answered McDevitt.

'Yes and just for fun the bastard broke my finger as well,' said Mary through clenched teeth.

Costello walked behind the chair to look at her dislocated finger which protruded in the opposite direction to that normally done by a finger.

'I'm sure that's painful. But if you tell us the truth and quickly, then this will be over soon,' said Costello.

'The truth, the truth about what?' replied Mary.

McDevitt started laughing. 'Oh this is going to be fun if you keep that up, bitch.'

'The truth about your working with the Brits and setting my brother up for them to be murdered by your Special Branch boyfriend. You see we know. we've photos of him, and we know the both of you were together in London when Sean was killed and then lately when the Arab was killed. Denying everything means it will just hurt longer. And in the end you'll want to tell us everything.'

'I couldn't have said it better myself.' McDevitt laughed again.

'You're both enjoying this. I don't know what you're talking about. I know you, Paul. I sat in meetings with you when we both worked for peace in this country. I'm no traitor. The cause I worked for is over, there's a new cause, peace, and that's the cause I would work for now. Not the one these fanatics support.'

Costello stood closer, putting his face directly in front of hers.

'Then I'm sorry, Mary. The peace you talk about doesn't mean we can't deal with the things that happened in the past. Especially if those things involve someone who worked with our enemies to destroy the cause we then fought for, and that those people might still be working with the same people who killed my brother. If that means being here with you to deal with a spy, then that's what we must do.'

'No matter how you try to justify this, you know it's wrong,' said Mary.

'I'm sorry you feel that way. I wanted to hear the truth of your deals with the Brits before Brendan and his people get to work on you, to try to understand why you did what you did. But, I guess it will have to be Brendan's way, and as I said, before they execute you for your crime I'll still be here to listen to that confession. I'll go and have a nice cup of tea and when I return you should be a little more helpful. Brendan, can we've a few words outside please?'

'Of course, I'm sure Mary can wait. In the meantime, John Jo, and Kevin can make her a little more comfortable.' When he answered he pointed to the pulley hanging above the water tank. Both John Jo and Kevin knew the signal. they'd been here before when another traitor had to be dealt with. Mary could see from their reaction that this wasn't going to be good. Kevin set the rifle on the chair near the door then walked to stand beside her with John Jo. John Jo produced a long-bladed knife from his belt and quickly cut the restraints from her ankles and hands. Kevin held her arms behind her while he pulled her to her feet. As she stood, the blood in her body rushed into her arms and legs causing her to stumble in pain, but John Jo held her in front. She could smell his stale breath as he smiled through smoke-stained teeth.

'Ah, now, Mary, don't hurt yourself there's a good girl,' he said.

'Let me go, you bastards.' She tried to struggle free, but, from the hours of sitting she felt weak. The grip of the two men holding her felt like a vice squeezing her arms.

John Jo stood slightly back, then slapped her across the face with his open palm.

'Struggle all you like, you're going nowhere,' he said.

Two things struck Mary as they dragged her across the barn towards the heat of the steel drum and the logs burning. Her broken finger ached more than her cheek and nose, and she could hear the raised voices of McDevitt and Costello just outside the door. They were arguing over her, and she was sure she heard Costello say something about amnesty and exile. John Jo and Kevin must have heard it too because they stopped and stood still, holding Mary up between them, just feet from the burning logs, listening.

Then the argument stopped, and McDevitt stormed back into the barn, the door swinging backwards to smash loudly as it crashed against the barn wall.

'Right, you two, what are you waiting for, get her up there!' he shouted at the two men holding Mary.

'What was all that about?' asked John Jo.

'He only wanted to give her an amnesty and exile her from the country. Would you believe it? And her a fucking traitor that set up his own brother. Says it would be good for the peace process. Well fuck the peace process. This bitch is not getting away with what she's done.'

'Maybe you need to listen to him Brendan, there's a lot more at stake here than just torturing and killing me. Think what happens afterwards. You will have no friends anywhere if you damage the peace and that will include here in the south as well as Britain and America,' shouted Mary, still struggling to get free.

'You know what you all can do with the bloody peace process. Remember Ireland will never be at peace if she's not free,' replied Brendan. 'Now get her up there, no more talking.'

The two men dragged Mary closer to the water tank and Kevin swung the pulley away from it to lower it before he helped John Jo hold the struggling Mary to tie her hands with the rope hanging on the large hook at the end of the pulley.

Mary could feel the rope tighten and the strain on her arms as Kevin switched on the electric motor to operate the pulley. Her arms being lifted above her head, John Jo let her go and she started to feel her legs slowly rise above the ground. She stood on tiptoe to try to take the strain off her shoulders. Then her feet left the ground as Kevin pressed the raise button on the handheld control. She felt the pain in her shoulders like they were coming out of the sockets.

'Stop it!' she screamed. Looking down, she could see the bubbling water tank below her. Kevin took his hand off the button and the pulley stopped, with Mary swinging gently above the steaming tank.

'Don't fret, my dear, the water will soon warm you up and when your toes touch it, you will want to talk, but by then I might not care one way or the other. Now tell me the truth and we'll get you down and everything will be over quickly. Were you an informer for RUC Special Branch?' asked the grinning McDevitt.

'Stop this now. I've done nothing,' she answered through gritted teeth, the pain in her shoulders getting worse. She could feel the bile in her stomach rising once more. Her body was shaking uncontrollably. Sweat started to fall down her forehead. She had never felt such terror in her life, and she knew she was losing control of her senses.

'I can see you don't think we'll do it,' answered McDevitt.

Ari had dropped them off at the bottom of the lane. Driving quietly in low gear with his headlights switched off, relying on just the side lights, he drove on for another 500 yards before finding a gateway to a field, where he turned, and parked facing back along the road he had come. He parked up with the engine running. Reece and Middleton had reached the end of the hedge cover by sticking to the trench alongside the lane to the farm. Joe Cousins had done the same on the other side of the lane. Although the whole yard was brightly lit, there was no one about to see Cousins with the AK47 as he swung it right to left as he ran crouching across the yard to take up position at the side of the north barn where it was in dark shadow.

'Juliet in position. I can cover the yard,' said Cousins into the radio.

'Roger, Juliet. We're ready to move,' answered Reece.

Reece could see three vehicles in the yard. John Jo Murphy's red Volkswagen, Costello's car, and a battered Land Rover. There was no dog. Hopefully, he was lying by a fire in the house. The downstairs lights in the farmhouse were on, but from what he could see through the windows, no one was looking out into the yard. Reece felt calm. He had been trained to control his breathing at times like this. He was about to move towards the southern barn, where he hoped they were holding the still-alive Mary, when the barn door opened. He crouched lower where he was, as did Middleton just behind him. He watched as Costello and another man, who he'd identified as Brendan McDevitt, stood outside the barn, seeming to have an argument.

Costello seemed to be making the argument he'd said he would, telling McDevitt that it would be better if he let Mary live. McDevitt was having none of it. Then he stormed off back into the barn. The sound of the raised voices had also brought faces to the farmhouse windows. Reece could see a woman and a man, but not clearly enough to identify who they were. Costello, head down in thought, entered the farmhouse, and the faces disappeared from the windows.

It was then that he could hear Mary's loud voice swearing at her captors. For a moment Reece was glad she was still alive and in fine voice, but then he realised she was really pleading for her life. He knew they didn't have long and now they needed to act fast, no matter what the odds. Again, he worked to control his breathing. The anger inside him had to be controlled and aimed in the right direction. Even though he wanted to charge through the barn doors and shoot every enemy fucker in there, he knew any rushing would only lead to mistakes. The kind of mistakes that could put Mary in even more danger.

'Everyone from Delta. We have identified where Mary is being held. Golf and I are going in. Everyone ready now, go, go, go,' said Reece, taking another deep breath.

Reece ran straight for the barn door while Middleton just behind him swept the front of the farmhouse with the Armalite rifle for any enemy response from there. When they reached the door, both men waited each side of it for a few seconds. They could hear McDevitt give the order to get her up there, then the noise of the pulley, squeaking as she was being raised.

Reece held up three fingers for Middleton to see the countdown.

When the last finger dropped both men moved as one. Middleton pulled open the barn door and Reece entered first with the Baretta pointing straight ahead at the three men standing in front of the water tank. Middleton followed, the Armalite sweeping the barn for any other opposition before settling back on the three men. It was Kevin who moved first. He let go of the pulley control and ran towards the chair where he picked up the rifle but before he could swing it into position Reece had aimed and squeezed the trigger of the Baretta three times, the silenced weapon making hardly any sound: Putt, Putt, Putt. Kevin made no sound as he fell, two holes in his chest and one in his cheek, all torn, and pouring thick red blood. As he fell the rifle fell from his hands. John Jo started to move towards the rifle, but the voice of Middleton cut through the barn. 'No, no, John Jo, unless you want to join your friend here.' John Jo froze when he saw that the man speaking with an English accent was pointing the Armalite rifle straight at him. One thing John Jo knew from all his time of killing people was that you can't outrun a bullet, and this man knew how to send them.

'That's a good boy, now both of you move away from the tank and put your hands behind your head,' said Reece, directing their movements with a wave of the gun in his hand.

Both men did as they were told while Middleton covered them.

'Am I glad to see you. Get me down from here,' said Mary, still swinging gently, her toes only feet from the boiling water.

'I'll as soon as I work out which button is which on this thing,' said Reece grabbing hold of the controls.

'Don't mess around, David,' said Mary.

Reece pressed the button to swing Mary from over the water tank and then lowered her to the ground before untying the rope from around her wrist.

Mary collapsed into his arms. her strength almost gone. He carried her over to the chair she'd been tied to earlier and let her sit to get her breath back.

He could see the damage to her bloodied bruised face, and the dislocated finger. He could feel the anger inside him, and he swung round, the Baretta pointing straight at McDevitt's head.

'Give me one reason why I shouldn't blow your fucking head off,' said Reece quietly, the menace in his voice clear.

'Do you think you'll get out of here alive, Mister Special Branch man?' McDevitt leered.

'That's the plan McDevitt and you and John Jo here are going to help us. We are all going out to the yard where our transport will pick us up. Any stupid move by either of you will be your last. As you've seen, I've no hesitation when it comes to pulling this trigger. Delta ready for pickup,' said Reece into his ear mic.

The response from Ari was immediate. 'Roger on way.'

'That's two men and a woman out of the farmhouse. Both men have AKs and the woman a handgun, walking towards the barn,' came the voice of Joe Cousins over the radio.

'Roger, Juliet. We're ready to move. Can you cover from your side?' asked Reece.

'Yes, but will have to make sure you don't get in my firing line,' replied Cousins.

'Will do. We will break right when we come out the door towards the lane entrance,' answered Reece.

Reece lifted the AK47 and checked there was a full magazine before handing the Baretta to Mary.

'You know how to use this. Use your good hand. The safety's off, you just point, and pull the trigger. Geoff and I'll go out first with these two in front of us. You follow and stick close to me, keep low. OK you two front and centre,' said Reece pointing the rifle at Murphy and McDevitt.

'Fuck you. You will shoot us anyway. Why should we help you?' shouted John Jo.

Reece swung the rifle in one quick movement, the butt of the weapon connecting with John Jo's cheek. He fell to the ground, grunting with pain, holding his face.

'We don't have time to argue. Now get to your feet and move,' said Reece, once more pointing the rifle at both men. This time they both moved slowly, just then he heard Joe Cousins AK47 firing. Geoff Middleton was pleased to note that Joe had the rifle on single – aimed shot mode.

It was Mariad who had seen Reece and Middleton on the CCTV monitor in the farmhouse, as they were crossing the yard and entering the barn. They had quickly grabbed the weapons from the store under the main stairs in the farmhouse. Now as she ran outside with her brother Jimmy and Frank Walsh they came under fire from some other place in the yard. The shots didn't hit them but were close, smashing into the farmhouse wall behind them as all three dived for cover behind the Land Rover.

Jimmy Bailey could see where the fire was coming from and fired on fully automatic, splattering the wall, and windows of the north barn. Joe Cousins lay flat and aiming, fired two quick single shots, hearing the man cry out as one of the rounds hit home.

Jimmy fell behind the Land Rover clutching his right leg. Mariad could see that the rifle round had torn a large gash in her brother's leg just above the knee. The blood was gushing through Jimmy's fingers and his face was white and sickly looking. Right then she was so angry she just wanted to kill someone and if she could see the traitor bitch in her sights that would be a bonus. She pointed the Browning pistol over the bonnet of the Land Rover and fired blindly in the direction of where Cousins was lying. The rounds hit the wall high above him and he returned two more rounds, hitting the windscreen of the Land Rover to keep the enemies head down.

'Go, go, go now!' Joe spoke into his radio mic.

'We are out and moving,' replied Reece. He could see one of the men at the back of the Land Rover break cover slightly and point his rifle in their direction.

'Stop where you are,' shouted Frank Walsh. Where he stood gave him cover, from both Cousins and the people bringing McDevitt and John Jo out of the south barn.

It was then that Ari and the Izuzu screamed into the scene. With a roar of the engine and a screech of brakes he broke the tension as he entered the yard, driving straight between Walsh, and Reece. Walsh couldn't fire anyway in case he hit his people. Instead, he swung the weapon to take aim and fire at the Izuzu and Ari. Middleton fired off three rounds, forcing Walsh to take cover once more.

'Get in,' shouted Ari out of the lowered driver's window.

Reece grabbed Mary and, opening the rear passenger door, he practically threw her onto the back seat.

'Keep your head down,' shouted Reece before turning back to help Middleton cover the two IRA men.

'Get in,' he told Middleton.

'What about these two?' asked Middleton.

'Leave them to me. Juliet, jump in the back of the truck,' he shouted over the radio.

Joe Cousins was already on his way. When he had seen Walsh dive back into cover he didn't need to be told twice, he ran for the Izuzu. Mariad saw him running and fired the pistol at him, but missed before the chamber stayed back, empty. the unaimed shots she'd fired, had quickly emptied the gun.

Reece turned to face McDevitt and John Jo. Both still had their hands behind their heads.

'Get down on your knees,' shouted Reece, aiming the rifle at the men.

Both could see a coldness in his eyes.

'So this is how you kill? In cold blood on unarmed men?' said McDevitt.

'No. That's your way, McDevitt. But don't give me an excuse. Just stay where you are.'

Middleton jumped in beside Ari. 'Come on,' he shouted back at Reece, who turned, and jumped in the back beside Mary just as Cousins jumped into the back of the truck, landing on more guns, and ammunition.

Walsh did not stand and wait. He ran around the Land Rover and seeing the key in the ignition he jumped in and started the engine. Putting it in gear he drove in a wide circle before stopping it parked across the entrance to the yard, blocking any escape. He then took cover behind the bonnet, then aiming the AK47 fired at the Izuzu, which was moving in a circle in the yard. Ari had seen what happened. He revved the engine and taking his foot off the brake he accelerated straight for the Land Rover and Walsh.

'Hold on,' shouted Ari above the noise.

Two of the rounds fired by Walsh hit the windscreen, but it didn't shatter. It was then Middleton realised it was bulletproof. Smiling, he reached out of the passenger window. holding the Armalite he fired three rounds towards where Walsh had taken up position. He didn't need to bother. Walsh could see the large vehicle racing towards the Land Rover and he jumped to one side just as it smashed headlong into his temporary barricade. The bull bars on the front of the Izuzu did their job. With a crashing noise of metal against metal, the Land Rover was pushed out into the side of the lane, leaving just enough room for Ari to reverse a little, then drive past it when he had straightened up. As Walsh got to his feet to take aim once more at the back of the escaping vehicle, he saw the figure of a man kneeling in the back of it taking aim and firing. Walsh dived for cover once more as the bullets from Cousins' rifle burst through the branches and smashed into the small stone wall at the yard gateway. He kept his head down as he heard the noise from the engine of the escaping truck disappear into the distance. Walsh thought the strange thing was that the old Land Rover, although badly dented and sitting almost on its side into the laneway ditch, still had its engine running. He could see the red taillights disappear as the Izuzu turned out of the Laneway onto the main road heading north.

'Are you all right?' It was Mariad standing beside him.

'Yes. We need to get after them,' answered Walsh as he ran to the battered Land Rover and, jumping in, he put it in low gear four-wheel drive and slowly steered it out of the ditch and straightened it up on the lane.

Brendan McDevitt and John Jo came running out of the farmhouse, both now armed with AK47 rifles. Paul Costello, unarmed, came out behind them.

'I can't get involved in this, Brendan. This must be your business from now on. Anything you do now is down to you and the Real IRA,' said Costello.

'Only to be expected from you,' said McDevitt sarcastically. 'The least you can do is take Jimmy and his sister to the local Parish House in the village and leave Jimmy to get a doctor. I need to get on the phone for back-up in Jonesborough.'

'I want to come with you. I want to kill that bitch myself,' said Mariad.

'You will do as you're told. That's an order. Anyway, he's your brother. He's more important to you right now. If we can bring the tout back, we will. If not, we'll kill her and her friends where we find them,' answered McDevitt.

McDevitt jumped into the passenger seat of John Jo's Volkswagen while Walsh drove the Land Rover behind them towards the end of the laneway and north towards Jonesborough.

McDevitt used a number on his mobile speed dial. The call was answered almost immediately. 'Tony. Get the boys out now. I need you to set up a reception for a Izuzu truck heading your way. If they stop, hold them till I get there. If they don't, shoot the fuck out of them.' McDevitt didn't wait for a reply. 'I don't give a fuck what time it is. Just get the boys out, now,' he shouted into the phone before ending the call.

'Do you think we've time?' asked John Jo.

'I hope so. But no matter what happens we'll track them down. Those bastards have killed their last Irishman.'

'What about Kevin, and what if the guards investigate the gunfire at the farm?'

'Don't worry about the guards. I have a senior officer in my back pocket, and I already told him to make sure we weren't disturbed tonight. As for Kevin, he'll get a secret burial on the farm. Let's worry about that later. Get your foot down John Jo, this is a straight road.'

John Jo knew these roads well. he did as he was told. Walsh, travelling behind in the old Land Rover, and didn't know the roads had trouble keeping up. even though he pushed the pedal to the floor he still could only get sixty out of the old engine.

Chapter 38

Irish Border

Reece hit the speed dial number for Jim Broad who, despite the time, answered after the first ring.

'David, what's happening?'

'No time to explain, boss, but we need to bring on Extraction Delta right away. Were you able to get the chopper?'

'I had to pull in a lot of old favours. I have one of the special forces' choppers from 658 Squadron. By luck they were on a training exercise in Northern Ireland. The pilot's one of the elite, a special forces man, so he'll have no problem finding you and picking you up. He had flown from their base at Credenhill outside Hereford earlier today. So you're getting picked up by the best.'

Reece knew of the Squadron and the secrecy surrounding them.

'This better work, David, or both of us could end up in the Tower. I've had Sir Ian on the phone and he's getting it in the ear from Sir Martyn Bryant and the Home Secretary.'

'Or dead at my end,' Reece answered.

'Where do you want it?' Broad asked.

'There's a large car park at the back of the Four Steps pub at the southern end of the village. We will be there in ten minutes. How long will it take for the chopper to reach us?'

Broad looked at the large digital map display on the SG9 operation room wall.

'I can see where you're talking about. The chopper is on standby at Bessbrook Mill so I guess twenty minutes.'

'Get them airborne. Tell them to push it as fast as they can. The car park is big enough for them to land and it will be empty at this time of the morning. I'll keep this line open for direct comms with them. They will only be picking up me, Mary, Joe, and Geoff. Ari will be heading back south.'

'David, remember, try not to have a shooting incident especially north of the border.'

'I'll try,' Reece answered, ending the call.

'Are you all right?' Reece asked Mary.

'Yes, I think so. A bit sore here and there. Thank you for coming for me.'

'What else would I do? I'm only glad you're not badly hurt. It's not over yet. Now we must try to get out of here and back to safety.'

Mary nodded her understanding. Her stomach still hadn't settled down and she felt an overpowering need for sleep.

They had already crossed the border. The road ahead was clear as they came to a crossroad just outside Jonesborough. Ari drove straight into to the car park of the Four Steps, where he parked up. Everyone exited the vehicle, Joe Cousins having a bit of a problem climbing out of the back of the truck. It was then that he felt the trickle of blood running down the side of his right leg.

'Ouch,' said Cousins, sitting down on the ground.

'What is it, Joe?' asked Middleton.

'I think I was hit back there,' he answered, feeling his leg as best he could through his trousers. Everyone gathered round and Ari removed a pair of small scissors from the first-aid kit he had in the glove compartment. He cut into Joe's trousers where the blood seemed to start.

'You're lucky Joe, it's just a flesh wound, no bullet,' said Ari.

He quickly swabbed the wound with gauze and placed a large surgical dressing over the wound.

'You've done that before,' said Joe.

'It's surprising what you learn to do quickly in the Golan Heights.' Ari smiled and patted Cousins on the back.

'Can you stand?' Reece asked.

'Yes, I think so,' replied Cousins, getting to his feet.

'Good man. We will leave the BMW here. The Hire Company can pick it up later. Joe, you go with Ari. We might have to move quickly on foot and the leg might slow you down. Ari you can get out of here now. You've done your bit and if it goes bad here, I don't want an international incident between the British, Irish, and Israeli governments on my hands. Go back to the crossroad and turn left to the south. That road will take you directly to Dundalk and the road to Dublin. They know we went north. They won't expect you to head south. Thanks for everything.'

'OK Joe let's get moving. David, you're welcome. Jacob Lavyan asked me to give this to you and he's looking forward to seeing you and Mary in Malta,' said Ari, handing Reece a sheathed knife. Reece pulled the combat knife out of the sheath. In the street lighting he could just make out what looked like writing on the shiny blade.

'The engraving on the blade in Hebrew is part of the Mossad motto: "By way of Deception." 'Don't worry about Joe, I'll get him to our people in Dublin then home to London on a comfortable flight.'

'Thank Jacob for me. Now get going. I'm sure our friends are not far behind. Good luck Joe. See you in London,' said Reece, pushing the sheathed knife into his trouser pocket.

'You can thank Jacob yourself when you see him. Right, Joe, let's get you up front with me. Oh, I'd leave all the rifles here when you leave. If the authorities get hold of them for examination, they'll find they came from a PROVO weapons dump. That will throw some confusion into things in case you have to use them. As the motto says: "By way of Deception".'

Ari reached into the back of the truck and removed two full magazines, one for the Armalite, and one for the AK47.

'David, you can keep the Baretta. It came from the same hide as the rifles, so if you need to use it and leave it behind that would be no problem.' He then helped Joe into the jeep before leaving with one more wave and a thumbs-up.

Reece watched the lights of the Izuzu disappear into the night. Turning to Mary and Middleton he could see they wished they were going with Ari.

'OK, you two, I know what you're thinking. We could all have jumped into the jeep with Ari but if the word gets out to the southern security forces, they'll be on the alert and it's a long run to Dublin. They will be especially looking for Mary and that would only put Ari at greater risk of being captured and arrested at the least. Another diplomatic headache we don't need. Anyway, I don't trust the Irish security forces. Too many have sympathies with the likes of McDevitt and John Jo. The helicopter will be here shortly, and we'll be in a safe location before Ari gets anywhere near Dublin. His diplomatic immunity will protect him. Let's find some cover. We could have tried to make a run for it in the cars, but I have no doubt McDevitt will be phoning ahead to have his cronies intercept us. We can't take that risk. The nearest safe place for us would be Newry, about fifteen miles away.'

'What about the military car? Do we set it on fire?' Middleton asked.

'We will just have to leave it. They won't be looking for it and it's well parked up. The military can come back for it on a future date.'

Looking around the car park Reece could see it was surrounded by a large stone wall and in one corner there was a small garden including two trees and a few large shrubs. That was as good as anywhere to hide, and it gave some protection against being seen. Anyway, they didn't have time to find somewhere better.

'Let's get into the cover of the trees and garden over there,' said Reece, pointing. He noticed Mary was shivering.

'Mary, you're cold, here put my coat on,' said Reece, putting his Barbour jacket over her shoulders.

'But what about you?' asked Mary.

'You need it more than me and besides, that's what these sweaters are for, to keep me warm.'

'It's heavy,' said Mary feeling the weight on one side of the coat.

'That's my old faithful. If you need to use it don't wait. Remember, if you don't kill them they'll kill you.'

Mary felt the grip of the Smith and Wesson in the pocket and had to admit it gave her a little reassurance. She remembered when she was David's agent inside the Republican movement. He had shown her how to use the gun, saying it was the same for most semi-automatic pistols. How to pull the slide on top to put a round in the chamber. Then how to push the safety catch into fire mode, before holding the gun with a two-hand grip in such a way that she could ensure more accuracy. This time she'd have to depend on a one hand grip. Above all take time and aim for the torso, the biggest target, then pull the trigger twice to make sure.

They ran to the cover of the shrubs and settled down behind them just in time to hear the noise of a car approaching from the south.

'Tony. Where are you?' McDevitt shouted into the phone.

'There's four of us on the northern road out of the village. We've set up a roadblock, but nothing has reached us yet,' replied Tony.

'Stay there. We are in John Jo's Red Volkswagen and will be with you shortly,' answered McDevitt ending the call.

John Jo drove north through the centre of Jonesborough Village for just over a mile when he stopped the car beside Tony. He stood in the middle of the road with a torch in one hand and a semi- automatic pistol in the other. John Jo could see the other three men, all armed with rifles, at the sides of the road. All were dressed in camouflage clothing. Tony walked to the passenger side of the car, where McDevitt had scrolled down the window.

'What's happening?' he asked.

'There's at least four men and a woman, all armed, trying to get north. They are all British enemy forces, and we need to catch them dead or alive. The last we saw them they were in a large Izuzu jeep heading this way,' answered McDevitt.

'We have been here since not long after you called, and nothing has come through. How far were you behind them?'

'Not far, a matter of minutes at the most. They might still be somewhere back in the village. You come with us. Tell the rest of your men to walk back through the village checking every nook and cranny. We will start from the southern crossroads.'

Tony shouted the instructions to the men before getting into the back of the car. John Jo made a quick three-point turn and accelerated back through the village.

They watched from the cover of the bushes as the Volkswagen drove past the car park into the village. Followed about one minute later by the old Land Rover being driven by Walsh. Both vehicles returned a short time later with Walsh parking the Land Rover across the crossroads, blocking access to the village. Walsh got out and standing beside it he was able to stop anyone trying to enter or leave the village. John Jo parked beside the Land Rover and the three men started to walk back into the village, checking laneways and side roads as they moved.

'Extraction Delta, we're five minutes out. Are we OK to pick up?' Reece heard the voice in his earpiece.

'Roger, this is Delta leader. We are ready for pickup. When you land, keep the blades turning. There's opposition in the area, so be aware,' answered Reece.

'Roger that. How many passengers do 'we have?' came the reply.

'Three. Two men and a woman. Do you have any back-up on board?'

'Yes, four Troop people,' the voice replied.

'Great, we'll be ready. The car park is flat and central, a good spot for landing. You'll have to use the street lighting. See you shortly.'

They could hear McDevitt. His voice carrying in the quiet of the night air. Then Reece could see the heads of the three men moving along the wall on the outside of the car park. They would disappear as they checked alleyways and gardens. Then reappear, all three armed with automatic rifles. It was Tony who walked into the car park first. Then crouching low, he swung the AK47 from right to left. The tree area at the bottom corner of the car park was a possible hiding place, so he took his time, aiming the rifle as he moved towards the trees and bushes.

The three fugitives kept very still their breathing shallow. Tony kept moving slowly towards them. Reece and Middleton had both taken up kneeling positions behind a tree while Mary lay face down on the ground behind them. Reece set the rifle on the ground and lifted the Baretta pistol into the two-hand grip he had shown Mary all those years ago. The silencer was still fitted, so that meant he'd have to let the target get close to ensure accuracy and effect when he fired. Middleton had been covering the man approaching since he had entered the car park. If the man looked like firing into their hiding place, he would be dead by the time his second round left his weapon.

Just then, the sound of an approaching helicopter distracted the man's attention. He looked up in the direction he thought the noise was coming from.

'Extraction Delta, I see the landing area. We're about to land. Be ready.' The voice of the pilot was loud in Reece's ear.

'Roger. We have at least four enemies in the area and may need to engage while you land. We are in civilian clothes. The enemy might be in camouflage clothing. One of our party is a woman,' answered Reece.

'Roger. Understood.'

The man being distracted and looking up gave Reece the chance to break cover and he started running to get closer. The man seemed mesmerised by the sight of the helicopter flying in close over the roofs of the village and it was only at the last moment that he realised there was someone running at him. He started to point his rifle to fire at the approaching figure, but too late. The man knelt, and pointing a pistol at him, fired twice in quick succession. The first round hit Tony's solar plexus, the second in the throat, knocking him backwards onto the ground. He tried to shout but realised his voice was drowning in the blood coming out of the hole in his neck. Reece stood above the man who had dropped his rifle and was now using his hands to try to stop the blood spraying from his throat. Reece had hit the man's carotid artery with his second shot. He had aimed the two shots for the biggest target, the man's torso, just as he had been trained, but he now realised the downdraft of the landing helicopter had blown his aim off course. Despite this, the man lying at his feet had given up the struggle to stop the blood, instead, closing his eyes in death. Reece stood above him, slightly out of breath himself.

Now he could see sparks bouncing off the ground around him, the noise of the landing helicopter drowning out the fire coming from McDevitt and John Jo who were standing at the entrance to the car park. The killing of the man up close and personal had left Reece frozen for a few seconds. Then Middleton was beside him, the loud noise of his rifle bringing Reece out of his thoughts. Middleton being the better trained than the two gunmen firing at him and aiming his rounds he brought down one of the men. His firing forced the other to take cover behind the wall on the street side.

McDevitt just made it to the cover of the wall when he heard John Jo cry out in pain as he fell where he stood. Brendan could see the bullet had blown away half of John Jo's face. He lay quite still, and, McDevitt realised, quite dead. He kept his head down as he could hear the smack, smack, smack, of the bullets hitting the concrete and stone protecting him. Then the loud noise as the helicopter began to land in the middle of the car park. The three local men and Frank Walsh came running to crouch down beside him.

'David, get Mary,' shouted Middleton, bringing Reece out of his thoughts.

Reece nodded and ran back to the trees.

'Mary, come on, we need to go now,' he shouted above the noise of the landing chopper, its landing lights lighting up the ground.

'Let's take these bastards on,' yelled McDevitt.

Now that Walsh had joined them the five terrorists, some standing, some kneeling, moved to the car park entrance and started firing in the direction of Middleton and the landing helicopter. Geoff Middleton returned their fire, bringing down another terrorist. The down draft of the helicopter almost knocking him off his feet as the giant machine landed, its three wheels settling on the car park tarmac.

The special forces helicopter was a Dauphin 2, coloured with civilian colours, the dark blue instead of the normal military camouflage which would confuse the enemy on occasion. The colour also made it easier to move to different locations without bringing unnecessary attention from prying eyes. As it touched the ground the four SAS men on board jumped down onto the car park and fanned out in a small circle at the front and side of the machine. With the blades still turning, Reece and Mary ran to the side door where Reece helped Mary into the cabin behind the pilot. Reece could see the sparks as the bullets from the terrorists hit the fuselage of the helicopter. Reece knew that the important parts of the machine, such as the engine, were protected with heavy-duty armour making the bullets bounce off safely.

It was then Reece saw Geoff Middleton spin around and fall backwords. Realising he had been hit, Reece and one of the troopers ran to where he lay. The other three troopers started firing back at the terrorists, forcing them back into cover, the shooting from their end stopping for now. The SAS men were under strict orders to regard the operation as an extraction. If they came under fire, they could return the fire, but only to improve the chances of making the extraction a success. They were not to go on a killing spree but get in and out of danger with the least possible casualties.

Reece knelt beside his friend. He was still conscious but breathing rapidly. Reece could see a wound in Middleton's right shoulder.

'Geoff. Can you hear me?' He had to shout above the noise of the aircraft engine.

All Middleton could do in response was blink his eyes.

'Don't worry we're going to get you home,' shouted Reece.

'Leave his rifle,' Reece instructed the SAS trooper as they pulled Middleton to his feet. Middleton was moaning loudly as he fell in and out of consciousness. Each taking a shoulder, they hoisted him quickly forward and into the back of the helicopter with the help of two more troopers, while the fourth trooper aiming his rifle at the car park entrance gave cover. Reece and the remaining SAS soldiers jumped into the aircraft and, pulling the cabin doors shut, it lifted from the ground. Nose down it made a fast-forward movement towards the rear car park wall. At the last second, the pilot pulled back on the stick and the engine roared as it quickly climbed up and, turning to the left, cleared the village of Jonesborough.

Geoff Middleton lay on the floor of the machine as one of the troopers quickly cut away the clothing around the wound and applied a field dressing. He was pale and sweating.

Reece pulled on a set of headphones so he could talk to the pilot.

'Our man is badly hurt. Can you fly straight to the military wing of Musgrave Park Hospital in Belfast? Tell them you're coming with a gunshot wound to the shoulder and to have a surgical team on standby.'

'Roger, will do. It should take us about twenty-five minutes.'

'Make it as fast as you can. We'll do what we can for him in the meantime.'

Reece looked at the rest of the passengers, including Mary. He could see their concern for the man on the floor of the aircraft. The trooper who had stopped the bleeding for now gave Middleton an injection of morphine for the pain. In every SAS team, for such a mission, Reece knew one of the troopers would be a medic and trained in treating combat injuries. Reece knelt beside his wounded friend.

'Stay awake, Geoff. It won't be long before we are at the hospital. Keep with us.'

'Now, let's have a quick look at you,' said the medic, taking hold of Mary's hand to look at her damaged finger.

'Dislocated. Can you bear a little pain for a couple of seconds?' he asked.

Mary just nodded, gritting her teeth.

The medic massaged the finger and then in one quick movement held the finger tightly with one hand and with the other pulled the finger towards him. There was the noise of a small snap and Mary cried out, the pain bringing the tears down her cheek.

'All done. I'll put a little splint on it.' Taking the small splint sticks out of his medic bag, he strapped the finger. Mary felt a gentle throbbing around the finger, but the strong pain had gone. The medic then reached into the first-aid kit and produced a silver foil strip of tablets.

'These are just paracetamol. You can take two of these now. Then another two in a couple of hours. Should be like new in a couple of weeks. The bruising around your face and lips will heal even quicker.'

'Thank you,' said Mary.

The medic kept checking Middleton's pulse.

For now, Geoff was in the best hands they could provide, thought Reece.

CHAPTER 39

FOUR STEPS

Brendan McDevitt raised his head slowly from behind the wall. He had seen three of his men go down during the firefight with the Brits. Tony and John Jo were dead, and another of Tony's men were badly wounded. With the noise of the gunfire and the landing helicopter, he had no doubt it had wakened the whole village. Someone would surely phone the emergency services who, with the report of gunfire being so close to the border, would contact their counterparts in the Republic. Walsh and one of the other men from the village lifted the wounded man into the back of John Jo's Volkswagen.

'We need to get out of here now,' shouted Walsh to no one in particular.

McDevitt threw his rifle in the back of the car with the wounded man and got into the driving seat as Walsh jumped in beside him. The remaining two village men ran back through the village to get to a safe house, leaving their comrades on the ground where they fell.

Walsh jumped out and drove the Land Rover behind McDevitt back to the family farm across the border. McDevitt made a quick phone call to the local doctor, who was a sympathiser, and had been treating Jimmy Bailey at his house. McDevitt told him he needed him to look at another volunteer with a leg wound. He explained he expected to be raided by the southern security forces and he needed to hide stuff before they came. The doctor agreed to come to the farm and pick up the wounded man. He would drop off Jimmy who was now patched up.

When they got back to the farm there was no sign of Paul Costello or his car. He had obviously cleared out after the shooting, thought McDevitt.

The doctor arrived twenty minutes later and after dropping off Jimmy took the volunteer back to his surgery.

McDevitt and Walsh had been spending the twenty minutes moving weapons and ammunition from the house to a hide that had been dug into the ground about forty yards from the rear of the farmhouse and covered with a heavy sheet of steel with turf on top of that. They poured water over the bloodstains on the ground where Jimmy Bailey had been hit. Then they put out the fire under the water tank in the barn and made it look like a barn again.

Although Jimmy was still in some pain, the doctor had given him some strong painkillers and the address of another doctor who supported the cause who lived in West Belfast. He told Jimmy he'd phone ahead to tell him to expect him at his home early next morning. The Belfast doctor would then take care of Jimmy's ongoing medical needs.

'You should all try to get back to Belfast tonight,' said McDevitt. 'Take John Jo's car. If the police here ask why there are bullet holes in the ancient Land Rover, I'll just tell them the Brits shot at me years ago when I was crossing the border to sell my cattle. But in the meantime, I don't intend to wait around here to answer their questions.'

'What about the men we lost tonight? What about their bodies? Do they get a decent funeral?' questioned Walsh.

'You leave that to me. After tonight we'll all have to keep our heads down for a while, you three included. If we get another chance to pay back that bitch Mary and her boyfriend, we'll take it. No interrogation next time. No holding back because of the Peaceniks. we blow them away on first sight. Now get your stuff together and don't carry anything that will incriminate you. It's John Jo's name on the registration so if you're asked, he loaned it to you, and hope that does the job. If you're pulled in give them the silent treatment. they can only get you for theft. I'll be in touch as soon as I can. Good luck.'

The three got into the Volkswagen, Jimmy able to stretch out in the back. With Walsh driving they turned right out of the laneway back towards Dundalk. Walsh knew the back road to Omeath where he could cross the border into the north, well away from the main Dublin to Belfast Road.

McDevitt made another call this time to arrange for two of his local men to come to the farm help to him clean-up the mess and take Kevin's body and McDevitt to a safe house just outside Crossmaglen.

He needed time to think.

The whole thing had been a complete ball's-up. He had lost important men. And what was worse, his reputation as commander who carried out successful operations against the enemy. Now was time to keep his head low.

CHAPTER 40

BELFAST

When they landed on the helipad at the military wing of Musgrave Park Hospital in Belfast there was a medical crash team waiting with a stretcher. Reece and the troopers helped lift Middleton down from the aircraft. The SAS medic told one of the doctors about the wound and how much morphine he had given. A young-looking doctor in green scrubs told them Geoff would be taken to surgery where their top surgeon, who had been woken at home, was now waiting. The team rushed the stretcher into the hospital, leaving Reece, and Mary to thank the men. The SAS medic told Reece they were heading straight back to Hereford for a complete debrief, and as far as they were concerned, they were never here. Smiling, he shook Reece's hand, and within a minute the chopper was airborne and flying to the east over the city. When they entered the hospital Geoff Middleton had already been moved into surgery. They decided to wait, and Reece got them two coffees from a machine which, he had to admit, the coffee actually tasted like coffee.

'What happens now?' asked Mary.

'We let the rest of the world worry about that for now. Let's just see how Geoff gets on. He didn't look too good in the chopper.'

'I'm nice and warm now. have your coat and what's in the pocket back.' She smiled as she removed the Barbour jacket and handed it to Reece.

He had deliberately left the Baretta on the helicopter. No sense in being caught with a weapon on him that had dispatched a couple of terrorists. He still had the knife in his trouser pocket.

'I'll have to find out about my mother,' said Mary.

Reece took out his mobile phone and found the number of the City Hospital, pressed the ring button, and handed the phone to Mary. 'Ask them to put you through to your mother's ward. If they start to ask you any questions about your abduction, just say you're with the police and you can't say anything for the minute.'

Mary waited and when the hospital switchboard answered she gave them the information to be put through to her mother's ward. She stood and walked around the waiting area while talking. When she'd finished, she came back and sat down, handing the phone back to Reece.

'Well?' he asked.

'They said she had a rough few days but was now doing well and sleeping comfortably. I really need to see her, David.'

'If she's sleeping, we can wait here to see how Geoff is, then we'll go there tomorrow,' said Reece, taking hold of Mary's uninjured hand.

The chairs were surprisingly comfortable, and Mary fell asleep, her head resting on his shoulder. They were the only people in the room apart from medical staff walking through. The noise of the staff talking seemed, to Reece, to be in the distance and it had a calming relaxing effect on him. Reece must have dozed off himself before he was wakened by the young doctor shaking his shoulder. When Reece moved Mary woke as well.

'Hello, are you waiting for news of your friend?'

'Yes, how is he, doctor?' asked Reece.

'He's in a bad way, I'm afraid. He lost a lot of blood, and the surgery went as well as could be expected. He has bone damage which will need more surgery when he's strong enough. But for now, he's on what we'd call the stable list.'

'Can we see him?' asked Mary.

'He's in recovery. The operation was a long one. You can see him, but we've him under deep sedation, so he won't be aware you're there. I'll tell the nurse to let you know when you can go through.'

'Thank you,' said Reece. Looking at his watch, he realised they'd been there just over four hours. He could see the sun through the window starting to lighten the day.

'We must have been more tired than we thought to sleep in these chairs for four hours,' said Reece, sitting back down beside Mary.

'At least he sounded positive,' said Mary trying to smile.

'You still look tired. I'm not surprised with what you've been through. Do you want another coffee? The last one wasn't too bad?' asked Reece.

'Yes, but while you're doing that, I'm finding a toilet with a sink to throw some water over my face.'

Reece was at the vending machine waiting on the second cup of coffee to fill when the phone in his pocket started to vibrate. The screen showed the call was from Jim Broad.

'Good morning boss,' Reece answered.

'That's to be debated. My phone has been red hot since you shot up half of Ireland. I thought I told you to keep things low key.'

'Things went beyond my control, boss. They didn't want to play quiet.'

'Two dead on their side and two wounded on ours. How's Middleton?'

Three dead, thought Reece but telling Broad that now wouldn't help things.

'He's recovering. They say he's stable for now. Bad shoulder wound. I'm going to pop in and see him shortly.'

Reece moved as he was talking to avoid the noise of people walking through the waiting room area.

Broad's voice sounded strained. Reece could only think the boss had been awake for the whole operation and now had the added problem of speaking to his superiors and political masters. Broad continued to speak.

'At least that's good news. Joe Cousins is doing fine and flying back later this afternoon. It seems your Israeli friend is a good friend to have. Anyway, you might have got away with this one. The Northern Ireland SOS, on instructions from the Home Secretary and number ten, will issue a statement later stating that the PSNI believe this was a shoot-out between a dissident Republican paramilitary group and a drug gang. People won't believe it, but if we stick to that story it's the only one they have. This way we can get the media on board, then the Dublin politicians. The SOS is working the phones to the northern politicians as we speak. We think Paul Costello, who represents that area, will come out with a statement condemning those who bring violence to his community. He will say the people support the peace process and they don't want these people anymore.'

Now Reece was starting to feel exasperated.

'I hope it works, boss. Mary and I'll stay here for a while, then head to the hotel to freshen up before we go to the City Hospital to see her mother. We deliberately left weapons behind on the advice of Ari. The weapons came from a PROVO hide so that will put even more pressure on Mister Costello to keep things quiet.'

There seemed to be a few seconds pause before Broad answered.

'That's good news. I must go to Downing Street with Sir Ian later this morning. It was good thinking to bring Geoff to the military hospital. That way we can keep things quiet concerning our involvement. We weren't even there. What are you going to say about Mary being free?'

'I've been thinking about that. We can stick close to the truth and say that she was abducted by, she thinks, a Republican group with drugs links. Maybe she could even say that she got the impression that they kidnapped her because of her previous senior rank within the Republican movement and her support for the peace process to try to disrupt it. The hayshed she was kept in should be empty now, so she can say where they held her, and she escaped when one of her captures was asleep. It's thin, but I think the police will accept it as they'll be following their own enquiries. If the SOS can put pressure on them not to chase things up too much to protect the peace process, then we can hopefully get away with how things really went down.' Suggested Reece.

'That's good thinking and something I can give number ten. They will be looking for a get out of jail free card, so I'm sure they'll be glad to grab your ideas. In the meantime, give my best to Mary and Geoff. Do you need anything else?'

'We had to leave two cars behind. One was my hire car. I can give them a call to pick it up. The other is a military surveillance car, which the military will need to pick up being careful when they do so.'

'The Troopers already told us during their debrief in Hereford and we've arranged for both to be picked up,' replied Broad.

Reece saw an opportunity and thought he'd chance his luck.

'That takes a load off my mind, thanks. Would there be any chance, seeing that you're in a helpful mood, to get me some transport here? I don't want to use taxis. We don't know who we can trust.'

'Leave it with me. I'll get one of the Belfast MI5 team cars for you. Should take about an hour.'

'Thanks, boss. I owe you one.'

'I'll remind you of that,' replied Broad, ending the call.

Mary looked a lot fresher when she returned.

'Ah, you look better. How are you feeling?' Asked Reece.

'I feel better. It's amazing what a little cold water can do,' Mary replied.

Reece told Mary about the call from Jim Broad and the plan to keep things as low key as possible. Mary was happy she could answer the questions when they came.

'If they get too rough, I could always say I don't want to talk about it anymore. It's too stressful, and just keep my mouth shut. Don't forget when the war was on we were always taught to say nothing if we were arrested by the police. I think I could do that.'

'Excuse me.' It was a young nurse interrupting Mary's thoughts.

'You can go through and see the patient now if you would like to follow me?'

Reece took Mary, holding her good hand, having an idea of what to expect when they saw Middleton. The room was bright and quiet apart from the constant beep of one of the machines that the patient was hooked up to. His eyes were closed and his breathing steady although, thought Reece, this was probably because of the tube in his mouth. Another nurse in surgical gowns was just finishing making notes on a laptop on top of a small trolley. When she finished, she left the room, taking the laptop and trolley with her.

'Will he be able to hear us?' Mary asked the nurse who had come for them.

'He's under very deep sedation, so I'm not sure.' The nurse had a strong Belfast accent and spoke quietly. 'They do say that patients can hear sometimes and that you should always be positive when around them. I'll leave you for five minutes. I'm sorry, but that's all the time you have, as we'll be monitoring him regularly.'

They moved closer to the bed. Mary was frightened in case she moved a tube or one of the wires that seemed to cover his body. There was a large piece of surgical cloth covering the area of the wound and it was stained with a little spot of blood that had seeped through.

'Oh, David, he looks so hurt,' said Mary.

'He's in the best place for now. The doctor said he was stable, and that's good news,' said Reece.

The five minutes passed quickly and the young nurse, true to her word, returned with a trolley of fresh medication and the laptop that she entered details into.

'Sorry, folks, but that's it for now. He will be like this for at least twelve hours. You can come back tomorrow, or you can phone the ward and they'll update you,' said the nurse.

Reece nodded, then bent down close to Middleton's ear. 'You need to get well soon old friend. You have a wedding to go to,' he whispered.

The promised driver, a girl who didn't look old enough to have a driving licence, picked them up in a silver Renault Megane. She didn't say much, only that the car was theirs to use for the rest of their stay and could they drop her off in the city centre.

After a shower and some sleep, they grabbed an all-day breakfast in the hotel bistro before heading to the City Hospital. Reece phoned Tom Wilson PSNI and told him the good news that Mary was all right, and he could see her later back at the hotel.

CHAPTER 41

WEST BELFAST

Mariad Bailey was angry. The woman she'd wanted to see suffer and be there when she died had escaped. The brother she loved had been wounded and now he was back in Belfast in the safe house on the Ballymurphy estate. She couldn't stop thinking about what had happened. They didn't hang you for murder these days, so she felt she had nothing to lose. If she succeeded, she'd be a hero. if she failed she'd be either dead or in prison. Both held no fear for her. She didn't tell anyone, not even her brother, about her thoughts, or plans. She knew they would only tell her to do nothing. To keep her head down in the safe house and if by chance she was lifted by the police, say nothing, they need to prove things, it's harder if you don't talk, say nothing. Her brother Jimmy was happy to spend his day with his wounded leg up on the settee. Trolling the TV channels and drinking endless cups of tea. Mariad needed to do something, she thought. A plan started to formulate in her head. A plan she had to do on her own, one she couldn't tell her brother about because he'd try to stop her.

'What was the sense in stopping a war that was hitting the Brit enemy hard then hiding? A soldier doesn't hide, they fight,' she thought.

'I must get some air,' she said.

She stood from the chair and threw the magazine on the table. She had been reading it for half an hour but couldn't remember one word of the articles.

'You can't take the risk. It's daylight out there. At least wait until dark. Now that Brian McNally is dead everyone is lying low until they find out what happened. I don't believe the story that he was killed during a burglary. What fucker in their right mind would burgle the home of the top IRA man in Belfast? He was too well-known. Stay in until after dark, sister, or until we get more news.'

Mariad smiled as she pulled on her parka coat. Pulling the hood up, she stroked her brother's hair.

'Don't worry, brother. I'll keep the hood up and I'm only walking round the block. I'm going stir crazy here and if I don't get out, I'll go mad.'

She bent and kissed him on the forehead. She didn't know if she'd be back, but she loved her brother and of all the people in the world, if things went wrong, she'd miss him the most.

It was one of those grey Belfast days with a slight drizzle of rain but no wind. As she walked with her head down, the plan continued to form in her head. First, she headed to another part of the estate where, in the nearby grassland, she knew there was a small hide where she'd moved a handgun in and out of when it was needed. The weapons hide was hidden from view, protected by a large circle of trees. The hide was placed in such a way for easy access and close to the road and estate for a quick drop off or getaway. Making sure no one was following or watching her, she walked down the pathway from the road, then quickly into the tree circle. There she moved a metal drain cover that was hidden under the turf beside one of the trees. She quickly lifted the cover and removed the.357 Magnum revolver that was covered in waterproof gauze. Checking the pistol was still fully loaded with six rounds she put the gun in the right-hand pocket of the parka. Quickly replacing the hide covering she left the tree cover and, making sure once more that no one was watching, she walked back through the estate. She headed for the main road where she jumped in a black cab and asked to be taken to Roger Casement Park.

During the journey, the talkative driver told her the good news, that the heavy security presence had been lifted and now there was no sign of the police checks. She had seen the driver before. He was one of the regular cab drivers that covered most of West Belfast. She could just smell the smoke from his recently extinguished pipe tobacco that she knew he used.

'Probably because of that bitch being found,' said Mariad.

The driver looked at the woman in the mirror and, raising his eyebrows he thought she looked like someone he knew.

'I heard a short report on Radio Ulster saying she'd escaped. It said something about her being held by dissident republicans connected to drugs,' said the driver.

'Usual Brit propaganda,' said Maraid.

When she was dropped off, she knew she was taking a risk. She walked back to the hay shed where they'd held the bitch when they first lifted her, but she still had to take the risk if her plan was to succeed. The security forces might already be aware of the hay shed. She'd have to make sure as much as possible that it wasn't under any kind of surveillance. She crossed the road back and forth three times and walked down the side streets before coming back onto the main road, passing the hay shed, and walking on about 500 yards before returning. As satisfied as she could be that everything was clear, she entered the barn. She found and quickly changed into the nurse's uniform and pulled on the blonde wig before pulling on the parka coat, then leaving the barn to return to the main road. She flagged down another black cab, this time asking to be dropped off at the City Hospital.

CHAPTER 42

BELFAST CITY HOSPITAL

When she arrived at the hospital, Mariad sat nursing a coffee in the Starbucks just inside the main entrance and corridor. She sat in a chair that allowed her to watch the people coming and going through the hospital entrance. She was on her second cup when she saw Mary McAuley enter followed by Reece. Both were deep in conversation, paying no attention to the people sitting in the café behind the large plate-glass windows that looked out onto the corridor. They walked towards the lifts leading to the hospital wards. Mariad left the table and entered the ladies' toilet. There she found an empty cubicle and after locking herself in she hung the parka jacket on the door hook and removed the Magnum revolver from the pocket, covering it with a scarf from the other pocket.

Leaving the jacket on the hook in the toilet she walked to the lift and, confirming which floor was female surgical, she pressed the button, hoping the woman's mother was still in that ward and that would be where she'd find the bitch and her lover. If only the mother was there, she was happy enough to shoot her as well for bringing the traitor bitch into the world.

Mary was pleased to see her mother sitting up in her bed, propped up by pillows. She was looking much better, and someone had tidied her silver hair. She smiled when she saw Mary and held out her arms to embrace her daughter.

'Oh, Mary, it's lovely to see you. Where have you been? What happened to your face and finger?' Her mother never missed a thing.

'An accident, Mum, but I'm all right. It's good to see you up and about.'

'They insist you get moving as soon as possible. Do you know they've even been getting me to take a few steps along the corridor? Who's this?' she asked, looking at Reece who was standing just behind her daughter.

'Mum, this is David. We are going to be married and we want you to get well and come to Malta for the wedding,' said Mary, holding out her finger to show her the ring still visible below the splints.

'Married.... Malta who.... what?'

'Hello. It's lovely to meet you and I'm glad you're doing well,' said Reece, shaking the woman's hand.

She smiled, then looking at her daughter she asked, 'Wedding in Malta? When did all this happen?'

'It's a long story Mum, but you must get well so that I can tell you everything.'

Mary sat down on the only chair beside the bed. Her mother's bed was the furthest into the ward. The ward was warm but a comfortable warm thought Mary. Reece took off the Barbour jacket and hung it on the chair behind Mary and went to look for another chair.

Mary told her mother how she loved Reece but left out his secret background.

Mariad thought the gun felt heavier than she remembered. Leaving the lift, she walked down the corridor and entered the ward. There was a nurse sitting behind the nurses' station. She did not notice Mariad, the notes on the computer screen having her full attention. Mariad could see the bitch sitting at her mother's bedside, her back to Mariad. Looking around, there was no sign of the man. Removing the scarf, she lifted the gun as she got closer. A woman in another bed could see this strange nurse with the gun in her hand and started to scream. Hearing the scream, Mary started to stand, and turn towards the noise when she heard the loud bang, bang of the gun as Mariad started firing. Mary recognised Mariad. The same nurse who had abducted her from the same hospital, who had promised to kill her. The screaming patient meant that Mary had moved just before Mariad fired. The two shots missed. She started to dive to her left when she saw a strange expression come over the nurse's face. Then, as she watched everything seemed to be in slow motion. The hand holding the gun fell to her side. Blood started to trickle out of her mouth. She fell first to her knees, then slowly forward onto her face, the gun clattering across the floor before she lay still; the knife sticking out in the centre of her back.

Reece had only been away a matter of minutes and, not finding a chair, he was returning when the nurse without the hat in front of him started to raise a gun, aiming it at Mary. For a split-second, he realised his Smith and Wesson was still in the pocket of the Barbour jacket hanging on the back of the chair Mary was sitting on. He was at least ten feet behind the nurse and too far to stop her from pulling the trigger. The scream from the patient gave Mary that split-second warning and time for Reece to pull Jacob's knife from his trouser pocket. He threw it with all his might directly at the nurse's back, but not before she got off two rounds.

When the nurse hit the floor, she didn't move. Reece quickly lifted the revolver and pointing it at her head, moved to her side, and turned her over. Her eyes looked at the ceiling with a blank stare. Mariad Bailey was dead. The patient had stopped screaming but then heard another scream and Reece realised it was Mary, who was holding her mother in her arms.

Reece ran to her side and his heart sunk when he saw the limp body of Mary's mother, the blood spreading across the bed onto the floor.

Mary was crying loudly, her blouse stained with her mother's blood. Reece held her before sitting her back on the chair.

'Mary, sit there. Let me help your mother.'

Reece could see the blood was coming from the centre of her chest. Mary's mother was dead, and he felt angry that this innocent woman had become another victim of the mindless violence he hated. Thoughts ran through his head. What happened? Why did it happen? Did the dead woman with the knife in her back not know these days were supposed to be over? What now? What a bloody waste.

Medical staff came running, but he knew it was too late for two women in the ward.

'I'm sorry, Mary,' was all he could say, holding Mary as she sobbed into his chest. She knew, thought Reece, that her mother was dead before he did.

CHAPTER 43

LONDON

The two weeks after Mary's mother was killed were a blur of police interviews and meetings with senior politicians. The funeral took place three days after the shooting, as was the custom in Northern Ireland. Mary sobbed throughout the service. Reece caught her at times sitting alone and sobbing quietly. The politicians as usual were looking for someone to blame but in the end, with some persuading from Sir Ian Fraser and a threat of his and Jim Broad's resignations, they went with the original statement of Mariad being a rogue terrorist working on her own. The statement in the press stated she had mental issues and had opposed the peace process and her target was someone in favour of it. There was no mention in the press of how she'd died or who the target was. It was felt the less said the more people could use their own imaginations and decide for themselves. Mariad Bailey had a simple family funeral at which her brother Jimmy was the chief mourner. A week was taken up with dealing with Mary's mother's estate. There was a will leaving everything to Mary, which made things easier. Reece was determined to get Mary back to Malta. She needed time and that was what he was prepared to give her. Before leaving for Malta, they'd flown to London where Reece met with Sir Ian and Jim Broad in the MI6 building at Vauxhall Bridge.

'How's Mary?' asked Sir Ian.

They were in his office overlooking the Thames River. The large windows letting in bright sunshine which filled the whole room. Sir Ian sat behind his desk with Broad and Reece in chairs facing him.

'It'll take her some time to get over things. I don't think she'll want to go back to Ireland, which perhaps isn't a bad thing,' answered Reece.

'You'll be pleased to know that Geoff Middleton will make a full recovery. What about you, David? Where are you now in all this?' asked Broad.

Reece took his time in answering, as he knew there was much depending on what he said.

'You remember boss, that before the abduction of Mary I told you I was resigning?'

Broad nodded.

'Well, as far as that goes I'm still resigning. I know you both have put your reputations and careers on the line for me, and without your back-up when I was, as someone said, working outside the shadows, Mary, and maybe me would be dead. But for now, I must think of both our futures and that's why we need to get to Malta, where I hope she'll recover, and we can get married. I don't know how long that will take but I do know from the day I met her and recruited her as an agent I've brought nothing but danger and death into her life. In a way I feel I'm as bad as her Republican masters, using her for my own cause. No, my days of hunting are over. I'm going to retire to my island with the woman I love and live happily ever after.'

Sir Ian nodded to Jim Broad.

'Sir Ian and I both understand how you feel right now, but we want to reassure you we are here for you should you ever need us. You have been one of our best operators and of course we'll be sorry to lose you. When you talk, people listen. You are a leader and that's rare in someone who has come through what you've come through. That's why we put our necks on the line when you needed us, and we were hoping you would agree to remain in some sort of position that we could call on you if we needed your help.'

Reece understood the tactics. Make him realise he owed them and put pressure on him to stay in harness.

'I know how much you put on the line for me. But for now, I'm burnt out. I see no future for me and Mary if I stay in. She's had enough as well. The only way forward for us now is to leave all this behind. But, to show my appreciation for what you've done during my time in Ireland, I picked up some information which should be of concern to you and your political masters. The agent I met with Ari, told us about an ex high-ranking Special Branch Officer from my old RUC days who worked for the Provos during the war and is still working with the Real IRA today. I knew him when I worked in Southern Region. He was one of my bosses. Detective Chief Inspector Paddy Wilson, the father of the current head of the intelligence Branch of the PSNI ACC Tom Wilson.'

Both MI6 men looked at each other and again Fraser nodded to Broad.

'What do you think about this information?' asked Sir Ian.

'If he was right here in front of me, I would kill him,' answered Reece.

'OK, David,' said Broad, 'I'm sorry we can't persuade you, but you must understand because of the secrets you have in your head we may need to contact you now and again. Leave the Paddy Wilson information with us. I'll chase it up and deal with it. In the meantime, I'll keep you on the books from the point of view that you'll need some money to ensure you and Mary have a good start. It would also cover you for carrying your firearm through customs. Now go get Mary and enjoy your future together.'

'And I would like to thank you for everything you've done. You're a brave man, David. I've known a few and you're at the top of the tree,' said Ian Fraser, standing to shake Reece's hand.

Reece then shook Jim Broad's hand.

When he had left the room, Reece felt relieved. He knew that Broad's mention of keeping him on the books was his way of holding on to Reece, but now at least it would only be on Reece's terms. For now, he'd tell Mary he was out and that they would be married. That was the only thing that would get her out of her pain. He had kept in touch with Geoff Middleton, and they visited him in the Belfast Hospital before they transferred him to his local hospital in Hereford. Reece had asked him to be his best man, and he had accepted with a big smile.

CHAPTER 44

MALTA

'In the end we are all alone and no one's coming to save you.'

It was three months before Reece started to see the change in Mary. Despite the sun and fresh air of St Paul's Bay, she still walked with her head down and the smile was gone. Reece made sure he was with her when she wanted him to be, then left her on her own when she wanted that. But nurse time slowly began to work and gradually her head lifted. She started to become aware of the change in seasons and the world around her, but most of all she started to notice Reece by her side. She began to make sense of what happened and how to deal with it within. It was something she could leave to her memory and just get on with life, with living for now, and Reece was the most important part of that life. At first Reece felt she blamed him for her troubles but now he knew she was determined to go forward with him, here in Malta, their home.

They had planned the wedding by the sea with a small group of guests. Geoff Middleton had recovered from his wounds well enough to attend as his best man. Middleton had to leave his beloved SAS regiment, but Jim Broad had taken him on board as his latest recruit to his band of waifs and strays in SG9. Broad was there along with Joe Cousins and from Israel, Jacob Lavyan, and Palo Stressor. Lavyan and Palo had both brought their wives, but really the only woman Mary would have wanted there was her mother.

The ceremony was carried out by a local Roman Catholic priest out of respect for Mary who still associated herself with that religion. The scene for the ceremony was on the beach below their favourite spot beside St Paul's Bay for the end of their walk and morning coffee. When it was over and the licence signed, they had the small reception on the terrace in a nearby fish restaurant overlooking the sea, it was a favourite of Mary and Reece. For the first time in months Reece could see the old Mary he had fallen in love with. Smiling, talking with everyone, and at one time after the vows he could see a small tear slide down her cheek, but he knew it was a happy tear.

When Mary excused herself to go powder her nose as she put it. Both Lavyan and Broad came and sat on either side of him.

'David, I know this is your wedding day,' said Lavyan, 'but we really need your help.'

'We won't discuss it now. But can you meet with both of us in Tel Aviv after your honeymoon?' said Broad.

Reece didn't want this day destroyed by these men and the world they brought to his life. Instead, he just nodded. Whether he would go to Israel or not was a decision for another day.

About the Author

After twenty=six years working in Counter Terrorism, David Costa brings the background knowledge needed to bring the reality of that world to the written page. From recruiting and running agents, to planning operations to stop some of the most dangerous operations that were being planned, his knowledge of how the terrorist thinks and operates earned him special commendations.

Because of that background, David Costa is a pseudonym.

He is married to Helena and now lives peacefully in the Northwest of England.

Outside the Shadows is the third book in the trilogy that follows the Black Ops Team SG9, a unit within MI6. Because of his background the main character David Reece has been head hunted to lead the team in the war on terror. The unit has one remit track down the threats to the United Kingdom and eliminate them.

David says.

'I've been a writer for many years and until now, I've only been writing for my friends and family. Now I bring to the page the hidden work of the security community and the hidden undercover work most people never see going on around them. I hope you read and enjoy, but most of all understand.'

If you like Lee Child, Tom Clancy, and Frederick Forsyth you will enjoy reading the books by David Costa.

Acknowledgements

I would like to thank the following for helping to make this book possible.

Dr Karen Ankers

Andrew Dobell

Emma Mitchell

Kathryn Hayward

Neil Black

KEEP IN TOUCH

If you would like to keep in touch with David.

Facebook: David Costa Writer

Twitter: @David Costa Write

Email: David.Costa.Writer@outlook.com

Web: www.https://DavidCostaAuthor.com

Other books by the author available on Amazon.

Tested By Fire

Light of the Sun

Printed in Great Britain
by Amazon